FIVE NIGHT STAND

RICHARD J. ALLEY

LAKE UNION
PUBLISHING

Text copyright © 2015 Richard J. Alley
All rights reserved.

Published by Lake Union Publishing, Seattle
www.apub.com

Amazon, the Amazon logo, and Lake Union Publishing are trademarks of Amazon.com, Inc., or its affiliates.

ISBN-13: 9781477827741
ISBN-10: 1477827749

Cover design by Jason Ramirez

Library of Congress Control Number: 2014952410

Printed in the United States of America

For Kristy,
There from the very first note.

OPENING NIGHT

1.

Oliver Pleasant doesn't know anybody in the seats, not well enough to say hello to anyway.

And yet, he knows everybody, the music bridging past and present to bring eras together like a family reunion. This is the same audience, more or less, that Oliver has been playing to since 1935 when he was a fourteen-year-old boy onstage at a talent show in Winona, Mississippi. Back then he'd hammered out rags as rough as the planks that made up that schoolhouse stage. Over the years he's taken a saw and rasp to those tunes and smoothed them at the edges, sanded them slowly over time with finer and finer grit paper, and applied a polish to them. The songs are comfortable now. People can take their shoes off to dance without fear of a spike in the foot; they can lie back on that smooth and waxed wood to take a nap in the afternoon or make love all night long. Oliver sees himself as a carpenter, a craftsman putting notes and melodies together, fitting them when they will, stepping back to rest and reconsider when they won't.

He lets himself get caught up in the music, the backbeat and horn solos, and thinks that he can understand all of human nature in the space of one song, in only one of those ascending flights of notes. Fancying himself a poet, he'd caught some shit for it back in the day on the band buses going from one gig to another, some of the lines on those maps little more than old wagon ruts. He felt good about the music back then and he is feeling it again here in the basement bar of the Capasso Hotel in New York City. He's always liked this room, the size of it, the lights, the way his piano sounds when it comes back around to him. That sound of it leaves his fingertips and goes to the bar for a gin and tonic, takes a tour around the place to touch the pretty ladies on their bare backs, tingling their spines right between the shoulder blades before landing softly back on his ear. He sees men and women all up on each other, rubbing and stroking, kissing in the dark when he plays one of his slow numbers, his fingers falling on the keys so you can barely hear the melody. He likes the effect his music has on people and he's glad to know the ability is still with him after so many years. He's grateful this audience is here for him.

Oliver Pleasant is having a wonderful time and so is everyone else in the room as far as he can tell, especially one young girl whom Oliver is thinking might climb right up onstage with him any minute. That girl is into it, and every time Oliver turns to talk to the audience he sees a big grin on her face, her hand swirling a tumbler of good brown booze. But when she sips from the glass, there is something else. Pulled from the music, even in the few seconds it takes to swallow a tear of liquor, he sees something in her face. Pain? Maybe. But perhaps not—the light is low, and a cumulus of blue smoke moves like an ocean between the two, and this girl is too young to know anything about pain.

Oliver has been away from his piano too long and knew it was time to come home again, even if it was only to close the door for good. He needed that door to be closed from the inside, on his own terms. When he decided it was time to retire—that eighty-five years was a round enough number for him to fit his girth through—he called his old friend Ben Greenberg, who'd been asking Oliver to play his club again for years. "Any time you want, Ollie, any time you want, you just send word and I'll clear out the

2

calendar. If Dizzy himself is scheduled, I'll tell him to pack up and come back the week after."

"Shit, Benji, Dizzy dead," Oliver would always reply. "If he's onstage I'm comin to sit my black ass at a table up close to hear him blow. I'll even buy some of them overpriced drinks you sellin."

The men's friendship goes back almost fifty years, back to when Ben Greenberg was a boy making a nuisance of himself among his father's friends—jazz musicians from Harlem and visiting bluesmen from Chicago. Ira Greenberg, Benji's old man, had been a friend to the musicians. An attorney and impresario, he'd booked some gigs and represented a few artists back in the 1940s and '50s as a hobby because he enjoyed the camaraderie and music, and because jazz musicians always had the best dope. Later, it turned into something more lucrative and afforded him a business trip or two a year to the West Coast or Europe.

Ira had met Oliver when he was a young player just beginning to make a name for himself in New York clubs and recording studios. Soon after, Oliver had gone to Amsterdam and Paris for his first solo shows—small club dates—but came back to the States broke. An unscrupulous European agent had refused to pay him for the gigs. Ira, still young and full of piss and steam, made some calls, sent some telegrams, and even caused a ruckus with an ambassador. Oliver was paid in full. With a heightened sense of justice and empathy for the underdog, and always eager to help an up-and-comer, Ira never asked for anything in return.

Since then, Oliver and Ira had been lifelong friends and, by extension, Ben became family as well. He has offered his home to the pianist anytime he wanted, and Oliver thought of no one else— no other club—when it came time for his final shows. He made the call and Ben accepted, then hung up the phone to call his press agent. Ben loves the music, but he is every bit the businessman Ira had been.

When he'd made the decision to retire for good and play his last shows, his final five-night stand, all he'd told Ben was that he needed four musicians who knew how to play. "Don't put me no schoolboys up there, Benji. You make sure they can blow," he'd said.

"Which tunes should I tell them, Oliver?"

"All of 'em."

And Oliver will be goddamned if he's found a one that would stump these boys yet. He's pulling out titles and shouting tunes by Monk, Peterson, Basie, his own compositions, and all the way hell and back to King Oliver. These boys can play—drums and bass, tenor saxophone, trumpet—and Oliver is having a great time. He can't help but talk and play like he's twenty-five again and not eighty-five.

* * * * *

She'd come in late, just before the lights dimmed and the band members took the stage one by one. She sits now at a table to the side of the stage and watches his hands move across the piano keys. A shitty little table, the worst in the club, barely even a seat, jammed as it is into a corner and partially blocking the doorway that leads backstage. Even so, she is grateful for it.

"We're full tonight," the hostess had said without looking up from her fashion magazine.

"Oh." Agnes was caught off guard, having expected to just walk in and hear Oliver Pleasant play. "Could I stand somewhere? In the back? I traveled all day and just came in a taxicab from the airport to get here."

The hostess carefully dog-eared a corner of the page she was on, closed her magazine, and set it aside, then looked the girl over. She smiled as though to an inside joke, and made a noise in her throat that was either sympathy or mild contempt. "Leave your bag

4

and coat at the counter, and I'll see what I can do, sugar." The *sugar* was contempt. "Name?"

"Agnes Cassady." And then, as an afterthought, "Thank you." An offering of gratitude and a reflection on the good southern manners her mother had instilled in her, but that would be the last of such manners. Agnes doesn't suffer fools gladly or for long—also a lesson from her mama—and this woman, Agnes's first face-to-face contact in New York City, had pushed her limits already.

"Mm-hmm." The hostess, in her own condescending way, had taken pity on Agnes Cassady and treated her guest like a lost kitten, the table a saucer of milk.

* * * * *

The music ends with a crash of the cymbal and then silence, and Oliver makes his way to a large booth near the front of the room, where he sits with his ever-present porkpie set squarely atop his head to cover the baldness. The table's stark white cloth, spotlighted with a pendant fixture from above, holds a "Reserved" placard, a bottle of Campari, and one small glass. It is here that Oliver makes his home. This is his backstage, having given up on the cramped dressing rooms, dingy in their fluorescent lighting and filled with the dope smoke he'd long lost a taste for. Those rooms are a younger man's lair, lonely even as they fill with musicians' admirers in low-cut dresses and made-up faces. He prefers the solitude of his booth and the feel of the cool leather through his sweat-soaked vest and starched shirt. He likes to watch the crowd and the pretty girls who walk by and smile. They leave him alone, presuming that genius needs time to rejuvenate, and he appreciates that distance. This is also where he sits on those nights when he feels like hearing live music, seeing what the young bucks might be up to, or when one of his few remaining friends is in town for an engagement. There aren't many of them left, most having succumbed to age or infirmity, gone to see their fathers. He'll be there with them soon enough, he knows. Until then, though, he's happy in his booth, sipping Campari and smoking his Gitanes, vices he'd found with those friends across a time and ocean so far away now.

"Beautiful, my friend, just beautiful," Ben says as he slides into the booth and asks Marcie, the hostess, for an aperitif glass. Ben bends and kisses the back of the pianist's hand as though he were a living saint, his lips just grazing the massive onyx ring there.

Ben looks just like his daddy, sitting across the table. He has the same salt-and-pepper hair as his father and it courses through his thick, woolly beard. But Ira Greenberg would have been in a sharp, shiny suit, while his son wears a loose silk shirt—untucked and open at the collar and then some—linen slacks, and sandals. Oliver is always giving his friend shit about those sandals worn no matter the season. And the silver ring in his earlobe. "Don't you let your daddy see you dressed like that," Oliver often tells his friend. "Liable to kill ol' Ira."

"Ira's gone, Oliver, and times have changed."

"You think he don't see you?" Oliver would shake his head at his friend.

Oliver nods his head now. "It's a good room, Benji. Sounded real nice, tight, coming back up to me. Good crowd, too."

"Here for you. Tomorrow night, too."

"Oh Lord. Been a long time since I had five nights. I got to pace myself." He pushes the Campari away just as Marcie returns with a glass for Ben, who pours himself a drink.

"Are you not feeling well? Don't push yourself, Ollie; you know we don't have a contract. You beg off if you aren't up to it and I'll find a fill-in."

Oliver waves him away. "Now, now, Ben, don't get them sandals of yours all twisted up. I'm just tired, old and tired, and that set there took a hell of a lot out of me. It's not in a bad way, though— but like sex, if I recall right. Makes me want to just roll over and go to sleep." He brings the bottle back to him and refills his glass, but only halfway. "Miss her, too. You know, out there in the crowd watchin me."

"Francesca?"

Oliver nods. "She was my muse, Benji. All them long nights on buses and strange cities. Treated her wrong, too, them lonely nights away."

"Don't beat yourself up, Ollie; it was ages ago. Things were different then."

"Love still love, ain't it? Respect still respect. That changed any?"

"That's still the same, still what makes the world go round and what keeps the music playing. Keeps all these good people coming in to hear you, too." Ben holds his glass up to toast the musician.

"Yeah, well, I don't know why these people should care so much. Most of 'em weren't born when the tunes was written, don't know what it is they're about."

"And what are they about, Ollie?"

"Struggles. Pushin and pullin. Sex. Loneliness. Loss."

"Francesca?"

"Yeah." Oliver lets out a long sigh and stream of smoke, the weariness carried away on curlicues of gray.

"How about something to eat? The kitchen never closes for you."

"Thank you, no. I think I'd just like to go."

"As you wish. I'll call your car."

* * * * *

Oliver's apartment is on the ground floor of an old crumbling row house on West 115th just off Malcolm X Boulevard in south Harlem. The area had been full of good musicians at one time—Fletcher Henderson, Eubie Blake, even W. C. Handy.

He stops at the bottom of the stoop and takes in the buildings on either side before he heads inside his own. The state of Oliver's home stands out in contrast to those surrounding him as younger folk move in with their ideas of coffee shops and sushi restaurants, Asian-infused soul food—whatever that is. Oliver knows the gentrification will take his place over soon as he's packed up his suitcase and is gone. Won't be long before it takes the whole of the second and third floors as well. *Coming along nicely,* he thinks, climbing the steps. *Won't be long before this whole block looks as pretty as the first time Francesca laid eyes on it.*

* * * * *

Once inside, he removes his hat and hangs it on the wall with the others. He loosens his tie and drops onto the sofa, then puts his feet up on the ottoman and takes a cigarette from a box on the end table. Before striking a match, he picks up a framed picture from the same table and looks at it.

It's been almost twenty years since Francesca passed. He looks at the beauty in the picture, the olive skin that had seemed so pale in contrast to his midnight blackness, the thin red lips, green eyes, and jet-black hair.

He had met her at her father's club in Sacramento when he was a young man on tour with Bechet. Her father was an Italian immigrant who'd farmed the land, selling his produce to markets before scrounging enough money to buy his own market. From there he'd bought a nightclub at the urging of his wife, an artist and native Californian who'd become enamored with the bands and musicians passing through town from Southern California, San Francisco, and points east. The last thing her father wanted was for any daughter of his to marry one of those musicians, so Oliver hustled her back to New York and married her right onstage in a little Harlem club long since gone.

The memory of Harlem as it was, as he and Francesca were, briefly lifts him up before the twinge of regret pinches and pops that balloon, deflating him once again. "I wasn't perfect," he says to the photo, "not even close. Not like you, Francesca. My sweet Chesca."

He sees their daughter's face in his wife's and thinks then of who else was missing from the night's audience. He thinks of his daughter and sons, missing them and hurt by their absence, though he knows he has no right to be; he's made his bed. He puts it all aside, not because he doesn't want to think of his children but because he is a superstitious old fool, and conjuring up reasons for them not to come to any of his final shows might jinx the next four nights and make it so. He still has hope they'll come. In all his life, it was the music and that honest-to-God hope that he's counted on.

He smiles and touches his fingertips, still raw from playing all night, to the glass. "Good night, Francesca."

2.

The club is packed, and she could see each patron's face from where she sits if she wanted to, but she's there for him and can't take her eyes away. In order to see him, to be able to watch his hands, she's pulled her chair away from that shitty little table—sticky on top from whatever service it had been in before being dragged from a utility closet for her—and leans far to the right until she nearly tips over the wobbly cane-back chair.

Agnes feels she has been put in her place, both physically and metaphorically, with this table. A moment of apprehension washes over her; she worries that the attitude of the hostess might be the rule in Manhattan. Ultimately, she won't let herself care, but it still makes her feel better when the elderly woman at the next table leans in to say, "Don't let her get you down."

"What's that?" Agnes says, her eyes fixed on the piano.

"Marcie. The hostess."

At this, Agnes turns to find where the hostess is. She can see Marcie across the room ignoring another patron who tries to get her attention.

"We're not all like that," the woman continues, holding up her own glass for a toast. She is elegant looking with steel-gray hair and diamond earrings that lie against her neck.

"Who?"

"New Yorkers. You're not from here, are you?"

"It shows?"

The woman merely smiles, still holding her glass up, tipping it just a bit to hurry the toast along, and Agnes finally takes the hint, clinking her highball glass. "To Oliver Pleasant," the woman says. "Good music to blot out a condescending bitch."

Agnes grins at her new friend—she's always felt more comfortable with people older than her peers—and then turns back to Oliver, watching intently, her own hand absently mimicking his across the table. She watches his frame on the bench like an Easter Island monolith and the way his shoulders dance, his body swaying with the melody. She picks it all up at once, the sight, the sound, the beat of his heart and of those around her. Her new friend at the next table sways as well.

"You play?" Agnes asks.

She shakes her head, still watching Oliver. "No. Well, for about a minute when I was a child. My mother made me take lessons. I hated it. Now, of course, I wish I'd kept up with it. You?"

"I do—my daddy taught me, and old Ms. Gaerig. My daddy always told me, 'Agnes, if you want to do anything well, you got to practice.' And I did, too. Practiced my ass off."

"I'm sure you're very good."

Agnes shrugs.

"Do you play concerts? In clubs like this?"

"Oh, no ma'am." Agnes laughs and gulps from her glass. "I play in small places back home in New Orleans, but nothing like this"—she looks around the room—"no, this is nice. It's almost like a church in here."

She's come to the basement bar of the Capasso Hotel in Midtown Manhattan as though it is a speakeasy and she a skid-row drunk. It's her first time in New York and she brings along only scenes from movies with their syncopated and scattered dialogue as reference, and a fervent love and respect for the music.

The club is well-appointed and elegant, sconces in all the right places to highlight only what needs to be lit—white tablecloths, sepia walls, mahogany bar, and the bandstand—while all the rest is thrown into darkness and shadow. The patterned carpet is soft and she'd sunk into it with each footfall as she was led to her table. Couples sit in booths of oxblood leather, intimate and alone in the crowd, and sink just as comfortably into the darkness.

If she were to admit it, Agnes would say she had expected a bolted door in a dark and grimy alley to greet her; a password spoken through a slot would have opened that heavy door so she could descend a staircase into a world that smelled of cigar smoke and whiskey. There is a staircase in this club, but little else from her black-and-white, James Cagney imagination.

Agnes feels as though she's made her entrance into a film and the sound track ties the scene together. She's come to New York for other reasons entirely, but discovered Oliver Pleasant was playing and needed to be here with him, to be near him the way the devout flock to the Vatican if only to breathe the same air as their pope. As she settles in with her drink and the music, she becomes more at ease and thinks that this is where she belongs, that all of her father's talk of jazz and the holy land of a New York City club has led her to this night, to this room as beautiful to her as any saint's grotto.

If she closes her eyes and allows herself to melt into the air, the room, the very music itself, she will find it isn't the twenty-first century any longer but the simpler, newly awakened days of the early 1900s. She's never been drawn to celebrity, but rather to nostalgia's sleight of hand and its ability to cast a shadow across any situation. As her life changes now from day to day, as the mechanisms within her deteriorate and short out (terms her father would be comfortable with and know how to fix), she finds her thoughts receding to childhood and those nights beside her father, or dancing with her mother across their kitchen linoleum, where the music found them. She's unapologetic for such feelings of nostalgia and, at times, it seems to her that she's numb to the world and that these are the only feelings of which she's capable.

She's never traveled quite so much as she has today to reach the past; the time spent in airports and waiting on tarmacs has left her feeling just as numb on the outside as she does within. Her flight from New Orleans this morning had first stopped in Houston, then taken her through Detroit, where she'd wandered the airport on a three-hour layover, pulling her black bag on wheels behind her like a nylon terrier and poking around souvenir shops. She sat in a Chili's and ate french fries while reading the *New Yorker*, and that's when she saw that Oliver Pleasant would be playing at the Capasso Hotel while she's in town.

These are to be the final live appearances of his career. It will be a five-night stand.

* * * * *

It is something he doesn't see here too often—a young woman, alone, so obviously enjoying the jazz and drinking top-shelf, single-malt scotch. He doesn't see much of her kind and he's certainly never seen her here in his ten months of waiting tables at the club. But then, they do get a lot of tourists, people coming from all over the country, the world, to hear New York–style jazz, swallowing it up like it's a slice of pizza.

She looks pretty if not frail. He is first drawn in by her eyes, large and brown, but it's the graceful lines of her long neck that intrigue him. She reminds him of Audrey Hepburn. He thinks maybe he's seen her someplace else, maybe in the park where he likes to rollerblade on Sundays, though she looks as though she hasn't been outside in a decade of summers; her skin is smooth and clear and nearly as white as the tablecloths.

She sits, staring at the bandstand and steadily swirling her drink, marrying the scotch and splash. She doesn't seem to notice him—he is just her waiter—yet he goes back again and again just for her eyes. But no matter how often he goes back to her table, that table that hadn't even existed in his station until that bitch Marcie had a busboy drag it from a closet, he gets no reaction from Agnes. And he likes to be noticed. He usually is, too, with his thick brown hair and natural blond highlights that the women he dates covet, his high forehead and stony cheekbones. He takes the audience's attention from the act onstage as he moves around the room, making drink orders, pulling out chairs for women or offering lights for their cigarettes. Most of the staff are women—girls, really—whose erupting cleavage and short skirts distract the men, leaving their bored wives and dates to watch him instead of the musicians.

He stands at the service bar and waits on another scotch for his mystery table. He leans over to pour a shot of vodka into a coffee cup, drinking it down without taking his eyes off of Agnes. She grows on him, mainly for her refusal to allow him to grow on her. The vodka burns and makes his head swim momentarily with a new challenge.

"Your scotch."

"Thanks." She doesn't look away from the stage, and cranes her neck as though trying to see the keys themselves.

"From out of town?"

She nods.

"Where?"

She breathes an exaggerated sigh and looks up at him full on for the first time. "Hmm?"

He falls into those eyes. "Um, I was just wondering where you're from?"

"Memphis." She considers this boy, different from any of the boys she knew growing up. The boys back home have dirt under their nails and on their sunburned necks. They wear ball caps and apologize for spitting dip in front of her. This boy is fine; he's fine like a girl with magazine hair, nose thin like a cuttlebone and a fat, silver ring on his thumb.

"Tennessee?" It's all he can think to say, lost for the moment in those eyes.

"That's the one."

"Is there another?"

"You tell me." She is put off by the distraction, yet can't help but wonder what a man like that might offer her, what he might be like in bed. She knows the feel of the hands of a farmworker or mechanic, all rough and gritty with the faint smell of motor oil and Budweiser. She even knows how a musician moves in bed and over her body like a fret board. But what about this boy? He smells vaguely of cologne and has probably never known a day's hard labor with hands as smooth as her ass, she imagines. Still, she considers him, conjures up images of them together. But he has a ring on his thumb and she just can't see her way past that.

* * * * *

After the final number finishes in a crash of the cymbal and Oliver takes numerous ovations, Agnes leaves the club floor with her head swimming in the music and scotch. She hasn't spoken with Oliver Pleasant, though she wants to. She might have talked to him when he passed her on his way to the backstage door; he'd had to brush against her as the rest of the band had, sitting in the doorway the way she was. She'd steeled herself for it all night, thinking of what to say, plying her confidence with more and more alcohol. She wanted to say hello, tell him what the show had meant to her and maybe mention that she plays, too, taught by her daddy who'd shown her how to play Oliver's songs with the love and tenderness they deserve. Or maybe she'd just reach out and touch his hand.

Those massive, poetic hands, she thought, might even have some healing in them.

But she didn't get that chance. He'd left the stage by the front, and not the side where she sat, and was swallowed by the crowd. She considers stopping at the table where he finally ends his journey, if only to say thank you for such a fine performance. As she approaches on her way out, though, that hostess leans over the table to whisper something to him. Her cleavage spills out all over the white tablecloth and her skirt rides up enough so Agnes can see the garters of her thigh-high stockings. Agnes keeps walking.

As she collects her coat and sole piece of luggage from the coatroom, the waiter catches up with her. He wipes his hands on a bar towel. "Hey, I didn't see you leave. Have a good time?"

"Yep, the music was perfect."

"Where are you going now?"

"Manhattan. Is it far?"

He looks confused for a second, cocking his head to the side. "Up the stairs and through that door. Where are you staying?"

"The Algonquin, if they haven't given my room away."

"Can I get you a cab?"

"I'll walk."

"Hey, um, do you want to get a drink? I just need to finish up, probably another half hour. You could wait in the bar or I could come by your hotel."

"I just had some drinks, lots of them. You should know—you charged me for every one. Besides, I don't even know your name."

"Oh. Andrew. Andrew Sexton."

"Oh my, it's right there in your name, isn't it?" she says, affecting her best, and most insincere, Blanche DuBois charms. "I'm Agnes Cassady from Memphis, Tennessee, by way of New Orleans, Louisiana." They shake hands, and she considers him again. Andrew, with the face of a statue and inflated confidence and expectations to match. It's her first night in New York—does she want to be alone? She thinks of the music that still fills her head, and Oliver's radiant face as he moved back and forth with his playing. She isn't alone at all, she realizes. This night is all she wants to take to bed with her. "No, thanks. I've been moving all day. You take care, Sexton." She touches his hand, right there at the silver ring on his thumb.

She walks out into the cold New York night and the lights and sounds—more music than noise to her ears—greet her.

* * * * *

Agnes stands now at the window overlooking what she thinks must be all of Manhattan. She can't imagine there might be more of it out of her sight; that would be just too much concrete and steel for one island. She's already undressed, tired of the feel of the clothes she'd put on so long ago in New Orleans.

Early that morning she'd stood at the open doors of her balcony as the sun greeted the French Quarter and cast its light on the evils and beauty of the streets and sidewalks where late-night revelers still staggered about. She's lived there for three years with her roommate, Terron, an old friend from Memphis, now a graduate student at Tulane whose father has the means to buy the entire top floor of a building for his daughter to live in and complete her studies. Agnes had gone to New Orleans for the music, the connection to Louis Armstrong, King Oliver, Sidney Bechet, Buddy Bolden, and a time past. She's been playing piano in bars and hotels throughout the Quarter, up and down Canal, and the occasional private reception in Garden District homes. Though she'd been recruited by music schools nationwide, these haunts and corners are her graduate program.

"How long will you be there?" he'd asked.

"I don't know."

"Well, what does it say on your ticket?"

"It doesn't. It's one way."

"So you're going to stay in New York."

"For as long as it takes, yes."

She's been seeing Sherman off and on for nearly a year. He's a saxophonist who spends most mornings on café patios playing his baritone for the lovers who have only recently stumbled from bed for beignets and chicory coffee; the low tones of his instrument hit their solar plexuses and remind them of the rumbling from the night before.

Agnes and Sherman drank thick coffee. He had taken the morning off to see her go, though hoping she wouldn't, selfishly wishing she'd change her mind. He lay on the bed, still rumpled and warm from their goodbyes the previous evening and early that morning, and watched her in the open doors of the balcony, the sunlight making her lightweight nightgown transparent.

She was having her moment with the city, a hello to the new day and goodbye for who knew how long, maybe forever. There was a chill in the air that rippled her skin. She held the coffee cup with the fingertips of her right hand, her arm resting against her hip. Her left hand held the door latch, that hand always grasping something in an attempt to hold it steady.

"I'll go with you."

"Don't be silly—you have to work. No work, no pay."

"Just like you."

She didn't say anything.

"So he's paying for it all? Travel. Hotel. Food. It's his doctor, so he's paying that as well?"

She shrugged. "I can't let myself worry too much for that."

"What does he expect from you?"

"Nothing."

"I find that hard to swallow," he mumbled.

"What would you have me do?" She turned to face him and the look on her face was not how he wanted to remember her. She

18

held her left hand up for him to see and he looked away. "What? I'm losing control, Sherman. It's eating my arm, my spine, and what else? My brain? Heart?" She turned back to the sunlight. "It's eating my soul," she whispered to the city below.

"I'll miss you is all," he said, and she didn't answer. Sherman liked to think he was her only one, and she went ahead and let him think that—it was a parting gift. She wasn't sure what would become of her in New York, whether the hospital there could work some miracle, or whether she might disappear into the night, into a river she'd never seen before.

Instead of more conversation, he took up his saxophone from the floor beside the bed and played "Mean to Me," her favorite Lester Young tune, for her and for what he feared would be their last moments together.

But tonight she's on her own in New York and stands naked in front of her hotel window, thinking she can hear a tune brought up from New Orleans. She wonders if anyone can see her here. With so many other lives in a place like this, does anyone notice just one more, whether it's new and full of possibility, or winding down and dying? The window doesn't open, so she imagines the glass isn't there. If she concentrates, she can feel the cold from outside against her thighs, stomach, and chest. If she leans forward, she can picture herself falling, falling through that cold to the sidewalk below. Certainly the fall would cause her to black out; surely it would all end as in her dream, the same dream that has followed her for years. Though it isn't a river far below but concrete and metal and peace. She holds her hand up to the window to feel the nighttime chill, presses her fingertips against the glass to try and stop the tremor there.

3

He's pulled to the curb this evening instead of into the driveway around back for no other reason than to gain a different point of view. He sits in his car, the engine off and ticking in the cool air, and looks up at the house. The trees brushing against the upper windows are bare in the white winter sky; he'll need to cut them back in the spring. The house looks empty. He knows there is no one inside; Karen is still at work and here he is sitting in his car. The second story is never used anyway, save for a small bedroom in the back that he keeps as an office and only rarely visits. Even if he and his wife were inside, he thinks, any passerby on the sidewalk would look up and think the same thing: *empty.*

He's returned home from an interview for a story he's writing for a local business news daily. It's a fluff piece, a profile on a twentysomething attorney who's just signed on with an old-money firm in Memphis. He'd let his imagination wander several times, distracted by a riverboat's wake far below on the Mississippi and a pigeon making a home on the granite ledge just beyond the window glass, as the kid told how he would be bringing fresh eyes—and social media—to the firm. The newspaper's editor has a hard-on for social media stories. This one will pay next to nothing, fifty dollars, and be read by no one other than that attorney and his proud mother.

Such is the life of a freelancer, though, a new title for Frank Severs, having only recently been laid off by the newspaper he'd worked at for nearly seventeen years. The severance will carry him through much of the year if he skimps and stretches it, but the idle time at home is driving him mad, so he's begun taking on work with local publications and editors he's met over the years. Be careful what you wish for, he'd laughed to Karen when the assignment had come through. Work is work, she'd said. He said this qualified as a student internship. But he went anyway, if only to break up a day.

The kitchen is just as quiet as the street had been. Details. Winter seems to be that way, though, doesn't it? Quiet, whether indoors or out. He looks at the trees through the large window in the breakfast nook and thinks of how much colder it feels seeing them without leaves on their limbs, without that blanket of color. Details. As if thinking only of the cold and wanting to warm himself, he turns on a stove top burner, the sweet smell of gas in his nose before the blue flame catches. He puts a pot of water on to boil.

Details. It has been his mantra since college when a journalism professor had told him, "Your job will not be, simply, the who-what-when-and-where, but the details. In time, everyone will consider themselves journalists. Let them glom on to the generalities and speculation; you be there, feet on the ground, and use your senses to let the readers know everything you see, feel, taste, and hear. Details." Old Professor Jordan seemed to know about blogs, social media, and "citizen journalists" before there were such things. Frank still respects that old-guard way of thinking, respected it even as he'd packed up his desk in a cardboard box, handed over his press card, and kissed his sobbing editor on the cheek. He wonders where Jordan is these days, retired half a dozen years or more. "I should look him up," he says to the empty kitchen, and takes a notebook and pen from his pocket to scratch "Jordan" on a page.

He'd forgotten to take sausage out to thaw this morning and does so now, putting it in the microwave, the hum aggravating the quiet of the room like an itch. He rubs his hands together over the stove top and finally relaxes into his house as the chill leaves his bones.

At forty-one, Frank had been a reporter with *The Commercial Appeal* newspaper in Memphis for most of his adult life. He and Karen have been married equally as long. They are a couple complacent in their lives, content with each other; the passion has left. It's a relatively recent development, within the past year or so. The lack of intimacy is punctuated by something else, though, and he's wondered off and on, as he pads around the house in the middle of a workday, if his wife might possibly give him his walking papers as well. Perhaps he will become that tired movie cliché of the middle-aged man who loses everything at once—career and wife—his life laid out to be inhospitably sifted through in dank bars and filthy one-room apartments.

Something has revealed itself within their union and managed to push its fingers into a crag in their foundation. He suspects an affair. Nothing overt to give it away, no men's shoes left under the bed or charges to motels across the city in the bank statement. Little things, though: a faraway look in his wife's eye as he tells her about his day, extra time spent in front of the mirror some mornings, a jumpy close of her e-mail when he enters the room. Perhaps it's all in his mind, his overreacting imagination, that tickle in his veteran reporter's brain in the numbing absence of any real breaking news. But then there is the lack of intimacy, and that's real. And there's the complacency, the soft-around-the-middle contentedness that every marriage seems to grow eventually. Details.

It's spaghetti night. Many dinners are themed, a tradition carried through the years since their first year of marriage, a stab at normalcy amid Frank's ever-changing, unpredictable work schedule. Even now, though, when he might spend the whole day reading a novel or in front of the television wallowing in unemployment, it is spaghetti night. He chops onion and garlic, and hums a tune to himself. He wishes he'd thought to stop by the music store to pick up that CD he's been thinking of since lunch. He laughs to himself, wiping the stickiness of garlic from his fingers with a stained dish towel, and flips his laptop open where it sits on the table. It is all so easy in 2006, to get what one wants with the click of a mouse. He shakes his head at the fact that he hadn't immediately thought of downloading an album. He recalls the human resources administrator who'd done the actual dirty work of laying him off describing Frank—and anyone else who couldn't, or wouldn't, see the industry tide changing—as a dinosaur. The administrator hadn't meant it as an insult—he was making a joke—but Frank had told him to shut the fuck up and then apologized to his own boss, his longtime editor and friend, who had begun to cry silently beside him.

He opens his laptop and searches for "Oliver Pleasant." He blinks back tears, not realizing how the onion has affected him. Moments later, the soft piano, bass, and brass of the Oliver Pleasant Trio fill the kitchen and mingle with the smell of sausage and onion in the air.

He leans on the table, an antique he and Karen had picked up at a flea market when they were first living together and broke. The cold of the tin top pushes against the heat of his palms. Music rises up to his face the way the scent of chopped onion had. That afternoon, the idea of writing about Pleasant had sparked something within him that has been missing for some time. It touched off a flintlock of inspiration that's been soaking so long in apathy he is afraid it has become nonflammable. He can't explain such an instinct; no one can—it's something that comes with being in the business for so long and with having writing in the blood. It's that first scent of gas from a stove top burner, the crackle of a first kiss, a first touch. And just like that he was itching to go to New York and talk to the pianist himself.

Frank first considered Oliver Pleasant a subject earlier that afternoon while sitting at a favorite lunch counter in south Memphis. It's a small, close diner situated on the interstate and frequented by the surrounding blue-collar workers, passing truckers, cops, and the odd lost or adventurous tourist. It has been rumored—as it's been rumored about every dive in the city—that Elvis Presley used to eat there. Tourists are powerless against such a pedigree.

Frank and his friend Hank (the rhyme was endless fun for others in the newsroom) sat at the chipped and stained counter eating barbecue and chili burgers with fries. The room smelled of grilled onions, smoked pork, and boiling greens. The chatter of the patrons shoulder to shoulder at the counter and at scattered tables, along with the clatter of plates and utensils, made it hard to hear your neighbor talk, so they shouted to each other as they ate.

Hank is a photographer for the Associated Press and keeps an office, an old and unused darkroom the size of a dry-goods pantry, at *The Commercial Appeal*. He's frequently called to disasters, murder scenes, and political gatherings throughout the region for the wire service. He felt bad for Frank's layoff and had asked him to lunch. Hank cursed the publisher, the nameless and faceless powers that be, and the decline of their industry up one end of the lunch counter and down the other. Between bites and swearing, he worked and reworked a math equation in his notebook with a felt-tip pen.

Frank finally couldn't stand it any longer. "Let it go, Hank, we're all doomed. I'll be treating you to lunch in a year, you dumb bastard. What are you working on there?"

Hank held up a finger to tell him to wait a minute, finished some multiplication, and then scratched it all out before throwing his pen on the counter in disgust.

"What is it?" Frank wanted to know.

"Plumbing. Trying to figure out what I can afford per foot to run a new sewer line from the house to the street."

"What'd you come up with?"

"About fifty cents a foot. Give or take."

"You better give. Hell of a lot more expensive than that."

"Yeah, thanks."

Hank, twice divorced, has recently bought the duplex he'd rented for five years, finding himself as landlord and home owner all in one day. He's in the process of extensive home renovations and looks to Frank, who spent a year renovating his and Karen's old home, as somewhat of a guru.

"I didn't have to do much in the way of plumbing, but Rachel here helped me find a carpenter and electrician—both cousins of hers. Rachel, you got a plumber?"

The lanky woman behind the counter, arms all bone and sinew and hands like a man's, held her finger up as Hank had while she slid an order slip through the window into the kitchen. A bright white and blue Memphis Grizzlies ball cap sat atop her head, over a hairnet, and listed slightly to the side. "Teddy, my uncle. But he working with Lavelle on a house now over in Harbor Town."

"How is Lavelle?" Frank said, and then to Hank, "Her cousin, my carpenter."

"Good. He adding a room to my girl Freda's house. Her grandma lives with her, and now her grandma's brother coming from New York City to live. Need a room to hold a bed and piano. Bathroom, too."

"Piano?" Frank said.

"Mm-hmm. His name Oliver, plays piano. Been playing damn near forever. Oliver Pleasant, that's his name. Nice name."

"Was he with Stax? Sun?" Hank said.

"No," Frank answered for her. "No, Oliver Pleasant is a jazz pianist. He's still alive? He played with everybody, all the greats. He's from here, Rachel?"

"He's originally from Winona, in Mississippi. Freda said he cut out early for New York, leavin all his people down here."

"And he's living here?"

"Will be my cousin ever get done with that room. Shit, I need him over here, fix that back door. Oliver's takin retirement. That's what I need more than a new back door, I need me some retirement."

Frank scribbled notes in his notebook while Hank consulted his math. "Can I get dibs on your uncle? What's his number, Rachel? I need a plumber. I need a damn sewer line."

"I'd help you out, buddy, but somebody has to go interview this infant lawyer," Frank said. "Call me later and I'll see if I can get by there."

* * * * *

When they first bought the home fifteen years earlier, Frank and Karen's house was nearly a hundred years old and in need of upgrades and care. The foundation, however, was as rock solid as anything else built in the late nineteenth century. Frank, with the direction of Rachel's cousins, plastered and painted the upstairs bedrooms, put in new light fixtures, and sanded and stained the wood floors. Those rooms were furnished and decorated with an eye toward hosting visiting friends and family, but Frank and Karen both knew which room would one day become the nursery. Van Morrison called from the stereo, and they each, separately and to themselves, imagined those rooms full of children, the sound of little feet running through the hallways and up and down the stairs. They worked together for weeks with paint and spackle, laughing at each other's splattered faces and passing mental shopping lists for furniture, lamps, and wall hangings back and forth. Workdays ended as the sunlight faded, casting long parallelograms of light across the walls, and they would make love there on the paint tarp surrounded by cans and brushes and ladders.

After Karen lost that first pregnancy, Frank put the crib they'd picked out, still unassembled, in the attic before Karen returned from the hospital. After the second and third miscarriages, the second floor was ostensibly sealed off, if not physically, then in Karen's mind. Frank eventually put new hardware on the bathroom cabinets and a new faucet in the sink, but it was without the camaraderie and talk of the future that had gone into the rest of the redecorating. Karen maintained hope and still does, though it's waning, but does not dare to decorate that nursery for fear of tempting a fate she's already danced with three times.

Frank keeps an office in a spare room next to the nursery. It's an office rarely visited, where an unfinished novel manuscript sits neatly stacked in the center of a neglected desk. He's been thinking again of the novel since being laid off, but isn't that part of the progression? Denial, anger, sadness, revisiting old hopes and dreams . . . It's there, waiting for him whenever he's ready. He's stopped at the bottom of the stairs on more than one morning since his "sabbatical," as he's come to joke about it with Karen, to look up and strain to feel the pull of what he'd written so long ago, to perceive that need to write in his bones. It's there, he knows, waiting and incomplete the way the whole top half of the house feels incomplete, like a life still waiting to be conceived.

Only a matter of days after the conversation in their kitchen, Frank is thinking of the house as the plane leaves the runway and banks left over the darkened canopy of Midtown, where streetlights and the glow of storefronts and porch lights give him his bearings. He imagines he can see his house, a speck of light in so much darkness, and then leans back in his seat and closes his eyes. He's still haunted by the quiet of his home and thinks of it now with only Karen in it, walking from the living room to the kitchen for another glass of wine and back into the living room and her favorite chair. He wonders if she thinks of the house as quiet and whether or not she misses him yet. He wonders if her sister will visit while he's gone or if Karen will have a change of heart and catch a plane to New York to spend time with him holed up in a hotel room eating food brought to them and making love in clean white sheets. Or maybe she has plans for a visitor that he doesn't know about.

He's running these scenarios through his head as he drifts into sleep somewhere ten thousand feet above his house and his life below, while in New York, Oliver Pleasant is putting his career to bed and Agnes Cassady is considering an act far more permanent.

(INTERLUDE NO. 1)

BEGINNINGS

.

as told to Frank Severs by Oliver Pleasant
Junior's Diner
East 103rd, New York, New York

I was six years old, what they might call a prodigy these days. Back
then, though, in 1927, they just said I was "in the way." I was always
in the way, up under my mama's skirts, runnin through the legs of
my aunties and uncles, wantin to see just what everybody was up
to. Guess I was a curious sort, but then, ain't all kids? Should be,
anyway. I was always tryin to help my daddy out with whatever
it was he was doin—choppin firewood, skinnin a raccoon, guttin
fish.

My family ran a home-cookin restaurant just off the Panama
Limited line in Winona, Mississippi, where the railroad men
would come in and eat. Some of them travelers would come in,
too, dressed fine from cities all up and down the line. That is, if
they thought to ask the porters where to get the best meal in three
counties. My mama, she cooked up the best goddamn groceries
you ever put in your mouth. My whole family, all of us—my mama
and daddy, aunts and uncles, my granmama, little cousins—was
fed and clothed from whatever little revenue that lunch counter
brought in feedin white folks.

The man who held the lease on the building—Mr. Sheffield—wouldn't allow coloreds to eat in the main room, so my mama fed them out the back door and didn't charge them nothin for it. Mr. Sheffield, he owned that whole block, damn near the whole town and, in addition to payin that motherfucker collectin rent and demandin my daddy buy his dry goods from Sheffield Wholesale, he got a percentage of the take, too.

Now, I'm only talkin 'bout the take that son of a bitch knew about. The other take, the one he didn't know about, happened late at night when Daddy would roll an upright piano from the pantry and my uncles would move the tables to the far side of that big room, stack the chairs up and out the way, and Mama would take money at the door. Colored money.

At night, the field hands, the house girls, the janitors, and ditchdiggers, every Negro in the county—all black and beautiful as night—paid a quarter each to dance on that white man's floor. You could feel the evening comin alive as clouds parted to show us the moon, and inky figures would come out from behind houses and trees to line up at the door. Those nights were raucous, boy, with song and sweatin bodies gyratin across the floor and in the sawdust Daddy had put down there. They shimmied and shuffled, all fueled by pent-up energy and my granmama Hillbillie's mash she made out behind the shack where we lived with her—me, my folks, and my nine brothers and sisters.

You know, I don't know why they called her Hillbillie except maybe that she grew up in the foothills of the Ozarks in Arkansas, where it was she'd learned to make that liquor, and that her given name was Billie. I never met another woman named Billie until the night I met Miss Billie Holiday at a house party up in Harlem. I told her about my granmama and we toasted that old woman all night long. Lady Day was such a sweet woman, to me anyway. I was young when I met her, wasn't but twenty or so, and she took me under her wing, watched after me and told me to stay the fuck out of trouble. That's what she said: "Ollie, baby, you stay the fuck out of trouble tonight"—and then she'd laugh and drink some more. Sweet lady. Hillbillie, though, she was mean as a snake. She's the trouble everybody shoulda been warned about.

The dancin at my mama and daddy's restaurant lasted all night, them makin a little extra scratch to live on with the quarter at the door and a ten-cent pour. The money helped, made my folks feel like they was gettin ahead, I know. But I think they also liked takin that money out from under old Mr. Sheffield's nose.

Me and my siblings, my cousins, we'd steal away some nights down the dirt road, movin in and out of shadows made by a full moon and them trees covered in kudzu, to the restaurant and we'd look through the grimy, dust-covered windows at the action inside. We giggled and nudged each other, not knowin exactly what we was lookin at then—least I didn't, I suppose my older brothers did—as them men and women in their Sunday best moved the way we ain't never seen them move in church. The men thrust at their partners, all up on their legs, and the women hiked up their skirts so the smooth suede-brown of their thighs showed.

We watched it all. Well, they watched it all. You want to know what I was watchin? I was watchin the man at the piano. He was young and dressed sharp, boy, not like any church clothes I ever seen before. He wore a brown suit with vest, watch chain, green tie all shiny, and two-toned shoes. Had a beautiful brown bowler, not a speck of dust on it, on the back of his head and held a thin cigar in the whitest teeth I ever seen. I saw them teeth so clear, I remember them like I was lookin at my own in the mirror, because of the way that man smiled. That's what stood out more than anything, his smile. A room full of poor Negroes goin nowhere, spinnin their wheels for the white man, and every one of them had to sneak in there at night just so they could laugh and talk and move like human beings. But here this man was sittin up on that bench

31

and grinnin from ear to ear as his long black hands pounded out a tune.

And them tunes sounded like magic to me, son. I was young and naïve enough back then to think it was only that magical music that made all them people forget their lives for a time. I didn't know shit about sex or what it was Hillbillie was scoopin out of that pan, so I thought all that smiling and laughter and thrustin, all them thighs and sweaty faces, was because of the man at the piano. Hell, maybe I still do. I played in Harlem and the Village, in Kansas City, Chicago, Memphis, and New Orleans; I been to three different continents with my piano and I see the same movin, the same grins, and the same sexin goin on in everyplace. Saw it last night. Ain't no difference in that crowd so long ago and the one last night, except last night the blacks and whites sat together, knee-to-thigh. But there was that same hidden magic, the same simmerin sex and tension that only comes when you got the music around. That ain't changed in jazz in over a hundred years. So maybe it is the music, the fuck do I know? I'm just a old man bein made to retire.

Anyway, before first light, as the last of them good revelers stumbled out for their walk home, Sunday shoes covered in mud from dusty streets and dew, or to work, my daddy and his brothers would put the place back in shape, sweep out the floor, arrange tables, and push that piano—so alive as though to buzz with electricity—back into storage so it could sleep and rest for the day.

By the time old Mr. Sheffield came over from the next county for his coffee and grits, and to collect the previous day's take, it looked like nothin had happened. Wasn't no sign that colored men and women had been grindin to piano rags only hours before and so close to where he sat his fat ass with righteous indignation in his heart and a Bible verse in his head, havin a side of hypocrisy with them grits.

I never did see that piano player during the daytime. I looked for him on my walk to school with my cousins, in the faces of the men who came to the back door for a meal and from nearby farms when they hauled in sweet corn, tomato, okra, and peppers for sale from their bosses. But he only showed up at night, like my uncles had packed him away with the piano early in the morning. Maybe that old boy was the night itself. I wished I could've found him, asked him to teach me how to play, asked him what his secrets were of the magic he knew.

I'd watch him playin and I'd feel my own hand movin like I wasn't in control of it, like maybe some spirit had overtaken it come from the night or from inside that piano. At night, lyin in bed with three brothers, I'd hear them tunes playin back over and over in my head and feel my fingers itch. I didn't have a name for them then, but the notes just seemed to make sense the way they fit together, like the way our family fit together or those men and women on the dance floor. I don't know—I don't know that I can explain it right outside my head, but them notes was just a right place for me to be. Be years till I saw them written, pictures on paper, but even then they wouldn't make no more sense to me than they did as a boy outside that window. I just knew I could make them same tunes back, note for note, come the next morning if only that man would show me where to put my hands and how to move them like a magician.

Like I said, never did find him, not in the daylight anyway. So, eventually, when the want in me became too much, I made my way to the back of that pantry between closin time for the food and openin time for the dancin. I lifted the heavy quilts that covered the piano up over the keys and moved my little fingers the way I'd seen the man do. Mama and Daddy paid me no mind—I was out from under foot, and the piano sounds sunk deep into the quilts and the sacks of flour and cornmeal lining the pantry walls.

Nobody could hear but the rats and me. But boy, it sounded real to me; it was natural like what I was supposed to be doin. And I liked playin. Hell, I loved it, and I was good at it. I played there in that food cave every afternoon and into the evenin, givin a voice to the songs I'd worked over and over in my mind while lyin in bed or sittin bored in school. Sometimes I played even before school when the memory was fresh, if I could find a spare minute or two.

And eventually I took over from that piano player. He split and I never did find out what happened to him, never ran across him again nor heard of him in all my travels. Just know that one night I was in his place, my mama havin kept up with my progress without my knowin. She knew when I was good and ready; it was her let me know. So there I was, twelve years old and surrounded every night by Granmama Hillbillie's handmade liquor, dancin, and sex. It was something inside me I'd never known. Pride, I guess I'd say it was now, but back then all I knew was that I was makin people dance, I was makin them smile, just like that man I'd watched before. It was a feelin I didn't get anywhere else, not in school, not in playin stickball, nothin.

Wasn't but a couple years later I won a talent show at school. I won it playin some Joplin and not even knowin there was a man from the riverboat in the audience that night. That old man needed a piano player, his last one lost somewhere down in New Orleans again. "I'm too damn tired to go lookin for him, neither," the riverboat man told my daddy. He'd keep an eye on me, he promised my mama. His own wife was travelin with him and would look after my meals and even make me read a book or two. There was money in it, sure, and the man assured my daddy it could be sent back home to Winona.

So that was that, and on the day before I turned fifteen I boarded a boat big as any house I'd seen at that time, wasn't sure how it stayed floatin. We pushed out onto the Mississippi River and I left Winona for good.

NIGHT TWO

1.

Ben arrives early in the morning. No matter when the club closes, he always waits for the final patrons to leave, then is back again at the same time every morning to unlock the door and turn on the overhead lights. He inspects every inch of the room—the tables without their cloths, looking for nicks and gouges, the padded seats for wear and tear, the carpet for traffic patterns and stains. He walks behind the bar for an inventory of needed liquor. The inspection is intimate; it's his communion with the past, whether it be the night before or half a lifetime ago when his father told him to always pay attention to the details, to accept nothing less than perfection.

He will even step up onto the bandstand and wipe down the Steinway grand with a lambskin hand towel, marveling at the way white light skids over its black surface. Standing on the stage, he looks out over his club, his house, and imagines a crowd, fantasizes, sometimes, that it is there for him. He will also picture his father there, leaning against the bar in a dark suit, crisp shirt, and smoking a cigarette, looking so proud to see his son up on that stage. The mornings are ritual; the fantasy is beyond his control.

Reality finds Ben sitting at a table with an oversized checkbook and bills scattered about haphazardly; he immerses himself in the ugly side of the business. He couldn't become a musician as his father had hoped—tone-deaf, his teachers said—but has found himself a niche, a bridge from the creative world his father had tried to nurture in him with the help of his musician and artist friends and the business world in which he has been so successful.

Once the checks are signed, invoices filed, and that ugliness put to rest, he turns the lights down low and has Antonio, always the first in the kitchen, prepare two eggs Benedict, toast, and a carafe of coffee. Ben eats slowly, beginning his day as impresario while his staff prepares the tables all around him for guests.

* * * * *

Agnes is awakened by the quiet. She's used to the clatter of heels on pavement and the squealing brakes of delivery trucks below the second-floor balcony of her French Quarter apartment. The din of the day coming alive in New Orleans has always moved through her subconscious to let her know she is still alive and adds a sound track to the final act of the morning's dream.

The air-conditioning of her New York hotel room has been running nonstop and its white noise creates a deafening silence. This unnerves her, panics her at first, until she can recall where she is. The bed is soft and warm within the frigid air of the room. Yet still she turns over to find a cool spot on the pillow, a habit from childhood. Her bed back in New Orleans is a single mattress on an iron frame. The springs and loosened bolts creak and groan with every move she, Sherman, or whoever might make. This bed is so unbelievably comfortable that she laughs at the luxury of it.

As she has done every morning for six years, as soon as she wakes, she pulls her left hand from the covers and holds it out in front of her face. The tremor is still there, of course, but she knew it would be. It has been with her every morning, slowly getting worse. So slowly, in fact, that she thinks perhaps this will be the end and the progression will stop. It is mostly constant, though it can be stymied for a bit when she plays piano, like the stutterer who is able to sing perfectly. So she will sit and play for hours at a time, until her mind and body swoon with fatigue and rage against the upright position and perpetual movement. Still she plays on. It's how she's improved so quickly and why tourists and locals alike in the Quarter have come to know her by name. She plays until she is carried offstage, until the last patron leaves and the delivery trucks start their rounds for the day.

But not even the playing is controlling it every time now, and that scares her. Agnes isn't scared of much, but the thought of not being able to play anymore outweighs every other fear—even the fear of death. The piano has become as much a part of her as her memories, and as it fades, she's afraid her childhood and any adulthood she has left may go with it.

She rises and showers, standing under the spray to wash away the previous day's travel. She thinks of Sherman and of Andrew Sexton, the waiter, and finds herself lonely. Agnes likes to be immersed in people, to sit in a café and watch faces and bodies pass by. New York is a big city with lots and lots of bodies, and there is no reason for her to be alone.

Her appointment isn't until the afternoon, so she finds an honest-to-God 1950s diner for a breakfast of eggs and bacon, and to read the *Times* from front to back. She is still a newspaper reader, another habit picked up from her father. "Newspaper reading takes as much time and patience to learn as piano playing. They're both a dying art," he'd say.

She looks through the entertainment section for anything about Oliver Pleasant's show the night before, for anything at all on his retirement, but there is nothing and this pisses her off. There is half a page, above the fold, on a long-haired band out of Seattle that they say began the grunge sound twenty years before. There had been a tribute concert for them and grunge music the night before in Madison Square Garden. Just the name—*grunge*—like a guttural belch passed and lost on the wind, sounds dull to Agnes. Oliver is a national treasure, as much as any other composer or entertainer who's worked for more than half a century—as much of a national treasure as breakfast diners, yet there is not a whisper of him on the pages.

"Gonna be another cold one," the waitress says as she refills Agnes's coffee cup. Waiters and waitresses, no matter their place on the map, are some of the friendliest people Agnes has ever known.

"Warm in here."

"You stay as long as you like, hon."

Agnes wishes she could stay here in this booth all day long and work the crossword (again, her father's pastime). It is warm and comfortable, the people just as much so, and the coffee is good. Those passing outside look harried and miserable, and she has no desire to join their ranks and be carried along on that current to a place she doesn't even care to be. She's had her fill of hospitals and doctors and nurses poking and prodding her body. The sterility of hospitals, even in a place like New Orleans, the dirtiest place she can imagine, is always blinding. She finds it hard to breathe in such places, and she isn't at all looking forward to this day's visit despite the promises it holds. She wishes she could put her body in a cab and send it to Mount Sinai while her mind and soul stay in this vinyl booth to polish off another plate of home fries and a whole pot of coffee, as she watches the city walk by through the plate-glass window beside her.

"Excuse me, ma'am?" she asks the waitress, who buses the next table up from Agnes. "Do you know what grunge is?"

"It's that shit the sink drain won't even take." The waitress looks tired, but Agnes admires the red scarf holding her hair in place.

Agnes smiles at the validation. "Okay, thanks."

* * * * *

Oliver leaves his apartment when the last purple of night is giving itself over to blue skies crisp with winter and a promise of snowfall. He pulls the collar of his coat tighter around his neck against this chill and is surprised to see Winky sitting on the stoop at such an hour and in such a temperature. There's no reason it should surprise him—the kid is always there. "You ever go inside, boy?"

"Hey, Licoricehead. I like it out here; it's quiet."

Just then a garbage truck rumbles by in front of them, steel and rubber leaving a dent in the still morning air.

"Quieter'n what?" Oliver says.

The boy Oliver calls Winky—a ten-year-old dark-headed boy with almond-colored skin—just points behind him with his thumb and Oliver knows he's talking about the apartment where he lives with his mother and her boyfriend. Oliver has heard the adults arguing nightly through the floor above him. Heard things breaking on occasion, too.

"You play last night?" Winky says.

"How you know that?"

"Seen you leaving. Late."

"Maybe I was going to see a movie, or out on a date."

"You wasn't seeing no movie, and you're too ugly to date."

"True."

"Sound good?"

"'Course it sounded good, boy; I practiced."

"Heard that. When you gonna teach me? Teach me how to play like you, Licorice."

"Shit, boy, I'm tired. I ain't got the patience to teach no kid how to tame that monster."

"You going to eat?"

"Might. Might just walk. You know how to do that, or you need an old man to teach you?"

"Shut up, I can walk."

"Come on, Winky."

The two walk south in silence toward the park along streets lined with trees bare in the season. People aren't headed out to work yet, only a few dedicated runners in skintight Lycra like colorful superhero costumes jog past them on their way to the park. None of the runners look their way; not even an old black man and waifish boy walking together can get New Yorkers to turn their heads. Oliver moves with his rolling step like a ship at sea—not a lost ship, but one with a crew so tired it doesn't seem to care which way the wind blows it. Winky runs ahead, kicking a chunk of concrete that has come loose from the sidewalk. Once he gets too far ahead, though, he stops and waits on Oliver, toeing the rubble with the front of his worn Adidas sneaker. They stall at the light traffic before crossing streets, and Oliver comments on what shops and restaurants aren't around anymore.

"Yeah, you've told me. Hurry up, Licoricehead. Why're you so slow?"

"Cold gets into my hip, makes it hurt. Slows me down."

"What happened to it?"

Oliver hasn't talked about the accident as a boy in years. In fact, when he thinks back, Francesca may have been the last person he told, other than his doctor who only talks about degenerative discs and all those years on buses with no padded seats and no shock absorption, of spending so many years on hard and unforgiving piano benches, the toll it takes on muscle and bone to work the foot pedals for hours on end. Oliver just tells people it's from too much fucking. "Makes my hips so damn tired," he says, and cackles in the way that is an old man's right.

Now he turns to Winky. "I was a little boy, 'bout half your age, down in Winona, Mississippi. You heard of Winona?"

"No."

"Well, it's there. Or was. Anyway, it was a summer day and me and my brothers and cousins was out playin in the dirt in front of my mama and daddy's restaurant when a mule broke away from its master and hauled ass down the road, ran up on us quick as wind, boy, and damn near took my leg with it. Rolled right up on me, broke my hip and my thick bone above the knee."

Winky looks up in horror at the story, unable to imagine such pain, unwilling to imagine his friend hurting. "They take you to a hospital? My mom works in a hospital."

"No, there weren't no hospital, son. It was a full day later before a doctor from the next county showed up. My leg grew blacker and bluer; I got me a fever, and my mama was fit to be tied. I believe my daddy would've killed that doctor if my uncles hadn't held him back. That fool come up explainin himself from the yard to my family lined up three deep on the porch that he'd been tendin to the birth of the mayor's first grandchild. You believe that? Shit, lucky I can walk good as I do."

"You don't walk so good, Licorice."

"Yeah, well, that old white son of a bitch almost never walked from that yard the way he took off his straw boater and wiped his brow like he was waitin to be thanked for the work he done between that white woman's legs all the day before. If he hadn't been the only one could fix me, my daddy sure woulda killed that man.

"Anyway, spent half a damn year growin into a plaster cast he set in about ten minutes, and it never did heal up right. Left leg's been an inch shorter all my life since then."

"Can they fix it now? We've got hospitals here."

"Too damn expensive. I ain't got as much money as you. Musicians, we ain't in it for the money, son. No sir."

A surgery might take some of the pressure off those discs, his doctor had said, but a surgery costs money and that's something that's been fading faster than Oliver's memory these days. A musician's income was always hit and miss, feast and famine, so that any saving was almost unheard of. There are those he's known to put away cash in a mattress or wall, then maybe fall asleep with a cigarette and all that good money goes up in flame. A musician doesn't get paid unless he plays, and Oliver's been gone a good long time. Friends have helped out here and there but they've been disappearing as quick as his memory, too, and quicker than his money. His wife's schoolteacher pension (God rest her soul) barely pays for food and get-around. A surgery just to help his comfort is out of the question. So Oliver tries to forget about it, lies down a lot, and self-medicates with a little booze now and again.

"These walks help me," he says, though Winky has run up ahead. "Yep," he continues to no one, "they help me just fine."

They don't go deep into the park but sit on a bench just inside the entrance where they can watch people pass and listen to the city come awake.

"Folks fightin?"

"He ain't my folk."

"Where you from, Winky? You ain't never said."

"You ain't never asked."

"I'm askin now." Oliver has seen this boy almost daily, yet their conversations never go much past the playful barbs they throw at each other. Oliver has found himself grateful for the familiar face in the absence of his own children, or any family at all. Even if it's just to say hello, he likes being able to have someone there to hear it.

"Here," Winky says.

"But you're dark. Not like me, 'course, but darker than most. Mexico?"

"My daddy was from Chile. Mom's from Detroit."

"What brought 'em here?"

Winky just shrugs, bored already with the conversation the way boys get bored with anything that stands still for too long. He squints up at the trees and movement catches his eye. He goes to explore.

Everything looks new to Oliver in the morning, like it's not just the people waking up but the whole damn world—plants, buildings, taxicabs with their bleating horns. He likes it. In his younger days, this was the hour that his world would go to bed. He'd play a club all night, going way past what the club owner had wanted or expected if the music felt right. After the gig, he and his boys, maybe some of the audience, too, would sit around drinking, talking shit, and critiquing the music. They wouldn't stop there, though, but they'd stumble out of the place, pushed by the owner who just wanted to go home to his wife, and stagger a few blocks to a friend's flat or a shut-down club whose owner had no wife, no life of his own other than his bar and the liquor there. They'd play some more, drink some more, smoke some more. Those days were always about *more*, a time when Oliver felt he couldn't get enough music, booze, sex, and friends. They'd pull chairs out in the middle of the floor, sit in the round, and blow their horns, trying to best each other. "Cutting," they called it, while off to the side Oliver gave them the tune on the club's piano. He'd give up his seat if Count or Tatum came by; he was always happy to listen to someone else play and to learn what he might take for himself.

The energy in that room on those nights was something else. It was almost otherworldly, like nights as a boy watching what happened beyond the dusty windows of his parents' lunch counter. They weren't the same tunes played for their audiences, but something new. It was the beginnings of bebop, when new theories and voices were being expressed. It was music they weren't sure the audiences would understand because they weren't sure they understood it themselves, not yet. But they also weren't sure if they cared what the public might think. Maybe this was a language just for musicians, fueled by booze and dope and a fervor to play. Maybe they'd keep it to themselves, play it only for each other and only behind closed and locked doors, the guard of the late-night hour keeping watch over them all.

But things get around. Musicians talk same as anybody, maybe more. They want to show off—it is show business, after all. Midway through a set of standards some night, the saxophonist takes a solo and the crowd is stunned by what it hears; the frenetic wailing sounds like the night itself. It puts a sound track to the age and gives the kids and suburbanites in the audience a taste of the heroin that courses through that horn player's veins. It's a hint of the danger there.

Surprisingly, the audience likes it. They love it, and they can't get enough of it. Like a fever, it permeates the clubs, the street, the whole top half of the island. The jazz writer Jackson LeDuc hears about it and then hears it himself one late night at Minton's, and he pounds away on his typewriter the way Oliver does on his keys. He tells other places—Chicago, Kansas City, Memphis, New Orleans—about what he hears and from there it's an epidemic, a plague from the piano as contagious as any verve and virus.

Those were good nights, late nights. Afterward, after the playing and cutting and clowning, Oliver and his friend Hamlet would go down to a diner in Midtown. Sometimes others would join them, but sometimes not. Most of those cats were eager by then to get home to wives or girlfriends or take one of the women who hung around those clubs home for a taste, where they could gaze at the curves and bare skin in the new light of morning coming through the windows. They imagined then that what they were seeing before them, atop them, was the very music they'd spent the past hours playing.

"You hungry?" Oliver had disappeared into his own world and nearly forgotten the boy sitting next to him, shivering in the cold. The world is awake now. "Let's eat."

The diner is bright, as though the hours of the day sped up and the colors of morning have become all white and chrome in a noon sun. Oliver likes this diner and has breakfast here most mornings after his walk to the park. It reminds him of the one he and Hamlet visited so long ago to sit and talk and drink coffee, eating mounds of bacon and putting their world to bed. He looks across the table at the skinny boy there and misses his old friend the trombonist.

"You want to call your mama? Tell her where you at? There's a telephone over there."

"Nah."

"Mornin, Oliver. Who's this, your son?" The waitress—"Lucy," as her name tag reads—is tall, all legs, with mussed brown hair tied up in a bright red scarf and a smile almost as bright. It's the welcoming smile that makes her customers overlook her tired eyes.

"Mornin, sugar. Naw, hell no this ain't my son. This Winky— he my neighbor."

"Name's not Winky," the boy mutters.

"Tell the lady hello, son."

"Hello."

"And what can I get you gentlemen this morning?"

"I'll have my usual. Get Winky here some flapjacks—short stack—home fries, and sausage links. Juice?"

The boy nods.

"And some OJ, honey. Coffee for me."

"Doctor said anything to you about your usual, Oliver?"

"I ain't asked him about it."

"Your call, I'm not your mama."

"Ain't my doctor, neither, far as I can see. He ain't near as pretty."

Lucy walks off shaking her head, the red scarf just touching the top of her shoulder.

"You think she's pretty?" Winky says, swiveling around in the booth to watch her go.

"Haven't met a lady yet that ain't."

Winky watches Lucy, who has stopped to talk to a customer at the long white counter, and nods to himself.

"Why you want to learn the piano?"

45

Winky shrugs. "I like the way it sounds from your apartment. Sounds better than the other noise."

Oliver nods. Seems like everybody has a reason for what they do, whether it's to cook a meal, write a book, fuck, or take up an instrument. He thinks back, trying to recall what it was that made him first sit down at the piano.

He thinks of Francesca and the kids, and the living he made, of course, but it goes back deeper than that. It flows backward in time down the Mississippi all the way to New Orleans and the soul of that city, then back up the Delta to Mississippi and the man dressed in brown who played his piano so that black people could feel free. That's it. When he thinks back to the start, to the first time his fingers touched the keys and the music touched his ears, there's the smell of his mama's cooking in his nose, the taste of cheap whiskey stolen by the sip on his lips. He played it first for his folks and siblings to see if they liked it any. They did. He played it best he could to make it sound like that man in the bowler hat with the two-cent cigar did. *I still ain't sure I do,* he thinks. But he's sure that this has been his aim for all these many years, to make it sound like that man's playing and to make people feel like the people felt who listened to him: free.

Oliver is grateful for the talent. It rescued him from a hard life of plowing fields or digging ditches in the relentless Mississippi sun and sent him on a journey up the river, over state lines, and across oceans. With that piano he began a life that has carried him to this diner, where he sits across from a wild-haired boy who eats his sausage with a fork.

"Pick that up, boy, and eat it with your fingers."

"Gets me greasy."

"That's for after," Oliver says, and sucks the ends of his own thick fingers.

* * * * *

Frank walks through the bookstore to kill time. He's been to New York only once before; he and Karen had come here a few years after they were first married. They were both wide-eyed to life and to the city back then, and he wonders if it will be a different experience alone this time.

He's an unapologetic tourist enamored by the Empire State Building and the Chrysler Building. He'll be sure to see the Guggenheim and maybe a room or two at the Met. He'll spend a quiet moment at Ground Zero and stroll through Central Park.

But for now he's just a man wandering the streets and it's an overwhelming sense of freedom to be far from home and lost among so many people. He's found his way from his hotel in Chelsea to Bleecker and walked aimlessly with his chin tucked into his coat against the crowds and brisk winds that cut down the narrow canyons to find his neck like a garrote. He can't believe how much colder it is here than it was in Memphis when he'd left.

"Cab's here," he'd said back in Memphis before his trip began.

"This is just so silly, Frank, and so expensive. There's no way the pay from selling this story can make up for the expense of New York." Karen was continuing a days-long debate the two had been having.

He knew that her emotions were genuine, if not her reasoning. She didn't want him to go, that was clear, but she knew he'd been given a fair severance package and that he knew enough people in the industry to sell the story with a phone call. Her persistent arguing was, in some ways, appreciated; he would be missed—he hadn't expected that from her.

"Lots of stories here," she'd said. "Closer to home. Closer to me."

"It isn't about us, Karen. This is a good story, maybe a great one. It just happens to be in New York."

"Happens to be."

He had looked past her and out the window with its sagging, leaded glass. The cab was at the curb, exhaust pouring into the cold air. He wondered if his thin coat would be warm enough for where he was going. He wondered if the cab driver got the same sense of emptiness from the house as he had only days earlier.

"Why don't you meet me there this weekend?" The suggestion felt forced, an automatic gesture as part of their goodbye, yet as necessary as their kissing goodnight had become or the "love you" at the end of a phone call.

She didn't say anything, only sat hugging her mug of coffee with both hands. "Your cab is waiting."

After his tourist stroll through the city, he'll go to the club and meet with Oliver Pleasant. He's spoken to the club's owner on the phone and asked if he could come early to speak with him as well. "I'll be here," Ben Greenberg had said. "I'm always here. Where else would I be?"

For now, though, Frank walks with his hands in his pockets through this bookstore crowded to overflowing within its narrow aisles. Paperbacks and vintage magazines are piled in his way, so he has to sidestep them just as he had the people on the sidewalks outside. He's in fiction, the section where he always finds himself—in any bookstore in any city—with his own unfinished novel back home tugging at him like a phantom umbilical cord. The ember within him that can be so covered and cold on a day like this glows red again as he peruses the names on the shelves. A copy of Jane Austen takes him back again to Memphis, back to the little kitchen where he'd been cooking spaghetti. He'd had every intention of waiting until after dinner, once their bellies were full and a glass of wine or two had been consumed, to tell her about New York. But she'd been first to bring it up.

"Who's this?" she'd asked, referring to the music coming from his computer.

"Oliver Pleasant. It's the Oliver Pleasant Trio."

"I don't think I've ever heard of him." She spoke distractedly while unburdening herself from work, emptying the kitschy, retro lunch box she carried that Frank thought too cute for a woman her age; stowing her briefcase beside the china hutch; going through the day's mail—all actions that were second nature, tasks performed in the same manner and at the same time every evening. The only scenery change over the years seemed to be in the way the sun fell through the windows, the way the seasons caught them there together.

He held out a wooden spoon of sauce for her to taste, his hand cupped underneath to catch any drips. So close to each other, he could see that she looked tired, another stressful day marked in lines around her mouth and eyes. Her hair, worn now in a bob, was still more strawberry than gray, yet was slowly giving up that fight. Even so, he found her attractive, the sort of beauty that comes from familiarity and so much of a life shared.

"He's from around here, a place called Winona, Mississippi."

"Well, I've heard of Winona." She tasted and nodded her approval.

"He's one of the last of his generation still alive. He was young, but he played with them all—Louis Armstrong, Miles Davis, Ella Fitzgerald, Count Basie." He was calling to her now as she changed out of her work clothes in their bedroom. "Anyway, he's retiring and moving to Memphis; I heard about it all at Rachel's today with Hank."

There was no reaction from Karen, no acknowledgment that she was hearing anything he'd said. He could hear only the Pleasant Trio and feel the muffled opening and closing of drawers and a closet in the next room through vibrations in the floor.

"So guess who's going up to New York for his last shows and to interview him for a story?"

He hadn't heard her come back to the kitchen. Padding in on sock feet, she stood behind him in the doorway. "Who?"

"Oh Jesus, you scared me. I am."

She looked at him without speaking. The music came to an end.

Recalling that night and the look on Karen's face, he pulls the Austen off the shelf. She's Karen's favorite and this edition of *Mansfield Park* is beautifully appointed and sparingly illustrated with an antique hand. He opens it and brings the crease to his face to breathe in its aroma and age. He'll buy it for her. She already has the novel, has read it half a dozen times, but she'll appreciate this edition. He reaches up and takes down Paul Auster's *The New York Trilogy* for himself. He thinks maybe he'll have time this week to visit Brooklyn, to walk around and see if he might run into Auster. Like the Empire State Building, Statue of Liberty, and Central Park, perhaps the living icons are also out in the open, leaning against lampposts just around the corner to be happened upon and photographed.

But this trip isn't a vacation; it's work. He'd explained as much to Karen as he ate spaghetti that night and watched her push her food around the plate and sip wine. He told her he'd sell it to somebody, that not every story in Memphis had to do with crime, infant mortality, and felonious politicians. There was still art and culture, and plenty of editors thought these just as important as the others. "Can't you sell it first?" she'd asked.

"Sure, easy, I'll make some calls tomorrow." But he hadn't. Although he was confident in his abilities and skills, both to write a story and to know when a story was a good one, he didn't want to hear no just in case. He wanted to go. He needed a brief respite from home and Memphis and Karen. Of course he couldn't tell her that, he would never damage her feelings that way, but the truth was there and he would heed the urge.

Money is an issue and he thinks about it as he pulls thirty dollars from his pocket to hand to the bespectacled bookseller. He and Karen have both made a decent living—his in sheer number of years spent at the newspaper and hers as a rising financial wealth manager with a long list of clients—but every spare cent seems to have been spoken for over the past two years as doctor bill after doctor bill came in from trying to discover why she wasn't yet pregnant, and then working to get her pregnant. It has been a tense experience with hopeful phrases in the beginning, angry exchanges later, and, lately, mere silence on the subject. It is always there, though, felt in the quiet nights and the unused upstairs rooms of the house.

"When are you leaving?" Karen had asked.

"Early next week."

"I start a new round of hormone shots Monday."

"How long this time?" The "this time" was like a gunshot in the otherwise silent kitchen, Karen having closed the laptop and shut off the music from the Pleasant Trio. Frank wished immediately that he hadn't said it, but she pretended not to notice.

"Two weeks."

"You could fly up and meet me. We could spend the weekend in New York." He didn't push the idea because he knew she wouldn't. He wasn't even sure he really wanted her to.

"Maybe I'll call Helen, see if she wants to come up and stay awhile."

"That's a good idea."

The expense of the trip will make the situation even more tense if Frank doesn't manage to find work soon. He has little hope left that she will become pregnant, though he'd never suggest she stop trying. Just as he spared her from his needing time away, he could never visit the finality of failure upon her.

"Vacation?" the shop owner now asks as he makes change for the books.

Frank is startled from his thoughts. "Hmm?"

"You have the furrowed brow of the tourist. I've always found it funny that the creases tend to follow the patterns of the subway system."

"Aha. No, here for work."

"Where're you from?"

"Memphis."

"He comes in here, you know."

"Sorry?"

"Auster. He stops in from time to time."

"What's he like?"

"Tall. He's very tall."

2

Agnes has been in and out of hospitals since her late teens. They all look the same to her; the first one had had the same color scheme and sterile smell as the one she sits in now. The touch of a stethoscope and the darkness of an MRI were to her rites of passage as common as a driver's license or the first taste of beer to other teenagers. She'd had her first taste of beer around then, too, in a parked car on the banks of the Hatchie River. When the tremor started, in fact, she thought it might be due to the one beer she'd had, and she confided as much to the nurse at Methodist North, who told her to forget all that thinking. A no-nonsense woman in her fifties with close-cropped bleached hair, the nurse told her that she'd be drinking a whole lot more beer in her lifetime and her mama and daddy were worried enough already without thinking their daughter might turn to alcohol.

After that trip to Methodist, and the inconclusive scans and blood work, her daddy took her to the West Tennessee Children's Hospital. He marched her right in the front door and up to reception, where Agnes stood nervously watching a little bald-headed boy—he was off to one side in the lobby, tethered to a tank of oxygen as he played with Legos. They didn't have an appointment but that hadn't stopped her daddy, dressed in his coveralls for work, stripes of grease and paint across the belly and a slight yellowing under the arms. He just wanted one of them doctors to look at his little girl, he explained, just to know what it was, and then maybe they could fix it from there—her daddy, always the handyman, everything fixable with the right tools and know-how.

The receptionist made a call and had a nice woman in a smart suit with identification badges around her neck come and take Agnes and her father into a small meeting room. The woman, Jean was her name, gave him some coffee and Agnes some juice, both in WTCH coffee mugs, and explained to him that his little girl just wasn't little enough, that the West Tennessee Children's Hospital was just that, a place for children. Jean had a soothing voice and even patted his arm as she told them there were capable neurologists everywhere for adults, especially in Memphis, and said that she'd give him a list of recommendations.

He thanked her when it was over, and told her he understood. Looking at his boots, caked with mud that flaked in specks of brown on the white tiled floor as he shuffled them back and forth, he explained he "needed to try, at least, because he'd heard this hospital was the best there was and, you know, free." She understood that, too, she said, and let Agnes and her daddy keep those coffee mugs.

Back out at reception Jean said something to the receptionist, who went back to her computer and started typing. The little boy was still there, playing with the Legos and not distracted in the least by his bald head or the mask covering his nose and mouth, or by his mother, who sat a few feet away with a magazine open in her lap, though keeping her eyes on her son. The woman looked tired.

Agnes wonders now what is in store for her and whether she will ever become as comfortable with whatever is happening inside her body as that boy was with his own sick little self, and she wonders at the fact that Jean had called her an adult that day. It was the first time that Agnes, all of sixteen at the time, had ever thought of herself as such. It was how she would think of herself from then on.

The receptionist had taken a sheet of paper from her printer and handed it to Agnes's daddy, who shook Jean's hand and thanked her. Jean squeezed Agnes's arm, told her to take care, and gave her a look that an adult might give a sick child.

Now at Mount Sinai, when the doctor comes in, Agnes is wearing a hospital gown and only her underwear. "You can strip down to your bra and underwear and put this gown on, please," the nurse had told her.

"I don't wear a bra," Agnes had said. "My titties are too small."

The nurse left the room laughing.

The doctor is a large man with a dark complexion and heavy black beard, wearing a white turban that matches his doctor's coat. In all of Landon's talk about his doctor in New York City, he never mentioned a turban. It doesn't bother Agnes; she just thinks a turban is the sort of thing a person ought to have mentioned. Dr. Mundra rolls a steel stool from the corner until he's sitting at Agnes's knees, having to look up at her to speak. He puts his clipboard and Agnes's file—that file is as thick as the Tipton County phone book—down on the sink counter and takes her trembling left hand in his right.

"Agnes, please tell me what is wrong," he says in a thick Indian accent. The man's eyes, as he looks up at Agnes, are full of kindness.

And then, for reasons Agnes doesn't understand, she starts crying. It is something she hasn't done, hasn't allowed herself, since that day she and her daddy visited the children's hospital back home. After they'd left and were sitting in the cab of the pickup truck driving down North Parkway, she'd thought of that boy who didn't care about anything but his Lego tower; Agnes thought about his mother sitting so close by and not caring about anything in the world but her little boy. She knew her daddy, in the seat beside her, didn't care about anything right then but her, and she realized how scared he must be. More scared, even, than she was. And as she cried that day, her daddy, staring straight ahead at the road they were on, took her left hand in his right, just as this doctor does now.

Dr. Mundra waits and watches her.

"It's all in that file there," she manages between sobs.

"I know, but I want you to tell me. When you're ready, Agnes; we have time."

* * * * *

Time is something Oliver thinks a lot about these days as another year winds down. Winter has always been a contemplative time for him and is even more so this year as he brings his career and his life in New York to a formal end.

The apartment he's lived in for more than forty years is a time capsule; the walls long ago ceased caring about whatever year it might be outside. Outside started changing years ago, too, with the petty crime and poverty creeping into his neighborhood like mold, like the kudzu he knew as a child. Francesca had been so proud of this place she'd chosen to raise her family, of the neighbors and the Pleasants' station in life. He could hear it in her voice when she gave their address to someone over the telephone, the way she would hold for a beat right at the end before saying, "Harlem." It had been like punctuation at the end of a sentence.

Coming back around these days, though. Make Francesca proud to see young couples walking around, pushing baby strollers, sitting outside at cafés. This is the neighborhood she'd known once again, and Oliver is sorry to have to miss it all.

Oliver pads around, looking at the same photos, the same knickknacks, and sitting on the same furniture his wife picked out so long before. It's cluttered and could use a good cleaning. After his morning walks, though, once he's stopped to pick up the papers or some magazines from a stand at the West 116th Street subway stop, he's too tired to straighten up. He reads, naps, and saves the piles of paper, full ashtrays, and dirty teacups for another time. But the sitting room is a comfortable place and he moves around it with the same ease he moves around in his clothes or inside his own mind. He should be packing up all of these lamps and candy dishes and ashtrays, he thinks, or throwing much of it out. He should have begun that weeks ago. He's meant to, just as he means to now, but instead he ends up looking in awe at the shelves full of books that Francesca amassed over the years. It's daunting to look up at so many stories unread by him. He always said he would read them to know what Francesca saw in them, to know the same characters like friends, as she had. But he hasn't. One more thing he hasn't done in a long life of familial regrets whitewashed with professional success and acclaim.

With its random gaps, the bookcase looks like a child's mouth grinning for the camera; volumes are missing, loosened teeth in the canon of Francesca's literature. Charlene took crates of books out of the house when her mother died, the very day she died, if Oliver remembers correctly. "She wants something of her mother close to her," he'd told himself as he tried to sleep on the sofa that first night. He'd tossed and turned, the missing books enforcing his sense of loss. Charlene must have known they'd go unread, he'd told himself. He wouldn't have minded her taking them all in due time, and he'd suggested it to her, happy to know that they'd have a home and be enjoyed as much as Francesca had enjoyed them. But she'd been selective and now he has to contend with those left behind. He'll have to ask her if she wants them now, or he'll have them boxed up and carted off. Maybe the school where Francesca taught for so many years will want them, or Oliver can find the old bookstore she used to shop in and see if they'll take them off his hands.

A giveaway calendar from the American Federation of Musicians hangs on a nail beside the bookcase among plaques and framed photos. The calendar is still turned to July 31, 1952, the day his oldest daughter was due. She would arrive two days later.

Where have the years gone? Oliver wonders for not the first time today.

It is the time away from Francesca that he wishes he could get back. Maybe he'd do things differently, he thinks. Maybe not—he really can't know. He was trying to make a career then, support himself and Francesca and, eventually, three children. But it wasn't all about sending money back home. It was also about the road and the records and the audiences as much as it was any family responsibility. It was about playing a little bit better than he did the night before and a whole lot better than anybody else out there trying to make a dollar doing the same thing. There was the fear of the future and the unknown—the kid in his mama's pantry right then, or onstage at a school talent show down south who, though he didn't even know it yet, was after Oliver's job. These were the reasons Oliver took to the road, sometimes ten or eleven months out of the year: fear, a fear for his very life. These are the reasons he couldn't explain in letters home, written on quiet nights in a train car moving through California or from a dingy hotel room in Berlin.

He sent money so Francesca could buy this apartment she'd chosen without him and a wall of books to read during nights alone on this furniture she chose. He sent gifts to his family, too, and took more pleasure from that—the latest Paris fashions, hand-carved dolls from Italy for his daughter, pocket trumpets found in a pawnshop in New Orleans for his boys. He was the doting father from a thousand miles away. And once home, he lavished souvenirs on Francesca and the kids, and woke early to cook eggs and flapjacks, flipping them high in the air to squeals of delight from the children.

His first day back was always a holiday for the family. No matter what they had going on at school or work, they took the day off and Oliver would take them to the park; to the Met, where he'd search out paintings of places he'd just visited; and out for ice-cream sundaes for lunch. They called those Ollie's Days, and the kids, worn numb by an afternoon of activity and movement, would fall fast asleep in the evenings, leaving time for Oliver and Francesca to reunite, to explore each other the way Oliver had just explored half the world and Francesca book after book.

He believed then that those hours made up for the weeks and months away. Yet it was only a matter of days until Oliver was back to work, only instead of hopping a steamer for Europe, he was on the Lexington Local to the Village. There, he'd spend nights playing clubs, at late-night recording sessions, or in strange women's beds.

"New York is where it is, baby; I got to keep my chops in my own city," he'd say.

"I thought Los Angeles is where it's at, or Kansas City, or Madrid," Francesca would counter. "Where's it going to be next week, Ollie? Near or far, or does it even matter?"

And then he'd leave, first kissing the tops of the kids' heads while they still sat eating their supper.

These days, he walks around his quiet apartment that Francesca always kept so tidy, looking at family pictures and Francesca's great wall of books. He realizes that even if he had that time back in his pocket, he doesn't know what he'd change, even with the advantage of hindsight. The music and emotions of being onstage had coursed through his veins, and it was a force that was not easily tamed. We all make our beds, he'd often said, and then we're told to lie down on them.

Oliver goes back to the bedroom he'd shared with Francesca, though not for many years now, and lies down on his side of it for a nap before his second night of shows.

When Agnes leaves Mount Sinai, all she can think of is a shower. As sterile as the rooms she'd just left were, all she wants to do now is wash. Instead of her hotel shower, though, she finds herself walking south along the park, allowing the rushing, swirling air from passing traffic and bodies to brush against her and scour away the past hours. At the bottom of Central Park, she descends underground for the Lexington Local to Greenwich Village. Standing on the platform, she's amazed there are no barriers between the waiting crowd and the gully where the tracks lie. She fantasizes about stepping off, considers an end to the pain and the tremors—dreams of an end to the unknown, just as she had while leaning against the glass of her hotel window the night before. How satisfying it would be to know, to be absolutely certain of when and how her life might end. She longs to meet that train head-on. The fantasy tugs at her and she steps toward an onrush of air as a horn blasts and light appears around the tiled curve to her left. She closes her eyes, brings her hand to her face, and feels the numbed fingers tremble against her cheek.

Emerging from below, going from the gleaming glass of Midtown Manhattan to the low brick and crooked valley of the Village, is like traveling into the past. Though the handbills are only weeks old, the sense of time and place, she imagines, is half a century earlier. She listens to the voices around her, the languages of the city and of cities throughout the world. She has the sudden urge to travel and see all of those cities before it is too late. The realization of time escaping leaves her breathless for a moment and she stops to lean against a lamppost. The picture windows nearby offer food, furniture from decades before, and clothing and eyeglasses at the height of fashion. A tobacco store shows off boxes of highly polished wood and gleaming lacquer, and through the windows of a barbershop she watches a black man having a pattern shaved into the hair over his ear. A café spills its mismatched tables and chairs out onto the sidewalk, where several patrons huddle together against the cold and blow steam from oversized mugs. She closes her eyes for just a moment as she had in the subway and listens. The electricity in the air is thrumming and she can feel it against her and all around her. The city is alive and will be this way long after she is gone.

The bookshop, tucked in between a Laundromat and a store devoted to chess sets, is deep and narrow with a high ceiling and shelves that strain to reach it. Before she even realizes she's stepped in out of the brisk air, she is standing in fiction and inhaling the musty scent of old leather and yellowing pages. She thinks the bookstore might be a more beneficial environment than the hospitals she's spent so much time in.

She walks around the store beneath towering shelves and peruses titles. She isn't looking for anything, but likes the familiarity she finds in any bookshop anywhere.

The man behind this counter in New York is old and white haired and reminds Agnes of the piano tuner her father used to hire to tend to the family's antique upright. The bookseller had greeted her when she entered with little more than a nod and a look in his eyes—over his small, rimless glasses—that said, "Let me know if I can help you with anything." Other customers come in, the bell over the door announcing each arrival, and the old man calls many by name. Some pick up prepackaged parcels at the counter while others browse as Agnes is doing. Agnes has always heard terrible stories about brusque and rude northerners, but she is finding just the opposite to be true.

She wanders through a section on architecture and picks her way among oversized coffee-table books with beautiful photos of buildings found around the world. Her hand lands on a small volume with a brown paper jacket and line drawing of the Manhattan Bridge. It's a book of architectural drawings, elevations, and blueprints of well-known structures in New York. Agnes thinks of her mother, an artist, though not in any professional sense—she simply loves to create. From as early as Agnes can recall, she has kept a series of sketchbooks close at hand, filling them with landscapes and people, capturing a moment on paper the way some might with a camera. When she fills one, she puts it on a shelf with the others, a small library of her memories as seen through her eyes and rendered in her own hand. She always has a pencil or two with her, stuck in the crease of a novel, in a Moleskine notebook, or in the knot of hair rolled onto the back of her head.

When Agnes was a little girl, she loved to watch her mother lose herself in her drawings. Back then, they just seemed to capture minor details of her life, mundane subjects such as the family cat lounging on the arm of a couch, the eaves of their house covered in snow, or Agnes sitting and watching television. The simplicity and narrow focus of the individual drawings, though, take on a grander scope when she thinks of entire books filled with those views, and whole shelves filled with books. Drawings of family reunions or her father's back as he sat at his piano were the stuff of family albums, everyday moments of life, though without the glare of a lens or the harshness of a camera's flash. Each sketch became a foundation of a book, of a year, of a decade.

Agnes looks again through the architectural drawings, marveling at the simplicity of buildings and bridges and at how easy it must be to maintain and repair them with such detailed instructions. She wishes there were such a simple book of blueprints for neurons and synapses, for thousands of miles of nerves and concentrations of spinal fluid that might point out just where a defect might appear. An image as plain as an air shaft or stair so that Dr. Mundra could unfasten bolts and tweeze out the inferior parts to be replaced by something an instruction tells him will fit.

She decides to buy the book for her mother, who doesn't know Agnes is in New York. Agnes hasn't told her because she's gotten her mother's hopes up too many times already and she can't bear to hear that catch in her mother's voice if these tests tell her nothing. Besides, she doesn't know quite how to explain Landon's generosity. She'll give the book to her with good news, or with no news at all. "It was just a visit," Agnes will say, "to hear some jazz, eat some good food." Her mother will love the book and appreciate the beauty in the straight, vertical lines; she'll lose herself in the geometry and soul of the artist.

The man at the counter grins at her, the skin around his blue eyes disappearing in fields of wrinkles and time, and asks if she has found everything she needs.

"Yes sir. I'm getting this for my mama."

He opens the book carefully and scans several pages as though for the first time. "Elegant . . . Wonderful . . . Beautiful," he says, almost to himself as he takes in page after page. "Is your mother an architect?"

"No, she's an artist." It is the first time Agnes has ever referred to her in that way; she's a receptionist at a psychiatrist's office by trade.

"She'll love this, then. Most people miss the artwork in a building."

"She'll see it."

"Here," he says, turning the book to face Agnes and holding a page. He'd been looking for something specific all along. "The Capasso Hotel, one of my favorite buildings in all of Manhattan."

How could he have known she was there only last night? Agnes suddenly has an odd feeling, dizzying, and she steadies herself on the counter while he rings up her purchase. His eyes are so kind. A coincidence, she tells herself.

"Yeah, I'm familiar with it."

3

Just before opening, Ben sits at the bar looking over some last-minute items on a checklist. A half glass of wine rests next to a smoldering Nat Sherman Blue in its crystal ashtray, both being ignored. He's waiting on a newspaper reporter from Memphis who is late, and Ben feels behind schedule. He is set in his ways and takes comfort in his medley of opening routines.

Andrew Sexton comes in carrying an apron and leans over the bar to talk to the bartender, a beautiful Nigerian woman with over-sized hoop earrings hanging from somewhere within an oversized afro. "Coffee? Please?"

"Late night last night?" Ben says, not looking up from his task.

"Not as late as it should have been."

"Which one was it? The youngish woman with the ancient millionaire? The tranny with the unsuspecting Japanese business-man?" He glances over his half-moon reading glasses at the front door. "Marcie? Again?"

"None of the above, Benjamin. I just stopped by Tommy's for a few drinks. Well, more than a few."

"A strikeout?" Ben removes his glasses and puts his papers down. He picks up his cigarette, which by now has extinguished itself, then takes another from the pack and lights it with a gold

Dunhill lighter. "Drowning your lonely sorrows with Tommy at his shitty swill bar? Who was she, Sexton? Do tell."

"A tourist."

"We're all tourists."

"The girl sitting at number . . . hell, her table didn't even have a number. Marcie sat her just offstage."

"Oh, right. I saw her. Very pretty. And very into Oliver's music. I don't think she took her eyes off the band all night. Maybe that's the problem; maybe you should learn an instrument in the next hour or so."

"She saw me. We talked out by coats."

"You spoke to her—face-to-face—and still nothing?"

"Yeah."

"Shit, Sexton, that's not even a strikeout. You weren't on the roster."

"Felt like I took a pitch to the side of the head."

"Oh my. You aren't in love, are you? Not Andrew Sexton of the Park Avenue Sextons. Not with a simple beer drinker."

"It was scotch, single malt, and would you shut the fuck up with all that Park Avenue talk?"

"Well, I think it's nice. And if it was meant to be, then you'll see her again, you'll get your second chance."

"Yeah, well, first thing I'll do is make sure she doesn't get sat in the damn toilet again."

"Chivalry is not dead," Ben says, holding up his glass and swallowing the rest of his wine.

* * * * *

The club is as full as it had been the night before, the crowd humming before the band even takes the stage. Agnes arrives early enough to be given a proper table, though the hostess, Marcie, still manages to look down her long, aquiline nose at her. She's told to follow and Agnes wonders how a woman walks in heels so high, if it's the heels that make her hips move like that; not even Agnes can take her eyes off the hostess's ass as she follows it across the room. They stop at a table off to one side, though more central than the previous night's location.

As she sits, she watches people mingling about her, shaking hands and kissing the air near each other's faces. She can smell their perfumes and liquor. She watches the waitresses carrying plates of steaming food and glasses clinking with ice. Her senses seem heightened here in this club and she's sure she can sense the start of the music even before it begins.

"Scotch?" It's Andrew, the same waiter from the night before, and Agnes suspects being sat in his section is more than a coincidence.

"And water."

"Of course. How has your visit to New York been?"

"Too early to tell, but stick around." She doesn't remember him being so handsome and is at a loss to explain that oversight—she is an admirer of beauty. She thinks perhaps she's beginning to feel at home in this city, or in this club.

"I think Manhattan has to grow on a person, like an appreciation for good scotch, or jazz."

She watches him walk away, watches the way the women at tables he passes look away from their dates to admire him.

A voice comes from her other side. "The artist's daughter." It's the old shopkeeper from the bookstore.

"Oh, hey . . ." She's caught off guard, that same unease that one can feel in a strange city. Her feeling of comfort suddenly and jarringly disappears, and her mind goes blank.

He picks up on this pause and quickly takes the slack. "I'm sorry to surprise you. Your purchase made me think of this fine hotel and I came around after I closed for the day to have a look at her. I only live around the corner. I saw that Oliver Pleasant was playing and thought I might come back to catch the show. I hurried home to change and barely made it—it looks as though he's commanded quite a crowd. The snooty hostess told me there were no seats and I believe she wanted to tackle me when I told her I only wanted to say hello to a friend, to you."

He is much shorter than Agnes thought earlier and she thinks he must have been standing on something behind his counter. He's wearing a green-tinted tweed coat and vest, and with his neatly trimmed white beard he looks as though he may have been a resident of the Capasso since the 1920s. She is sure if she were to reach into his pocket she'd find a watch at the end of a chain with a slight patina, possibly engraved with something heartfelt dictated by a long-departed love.

"She's a bitch." Agnes offers her own thoughts on the hostess. "Sit down."

"Oh, no, no, no. I'm afraid I couldn't impose on your evening. Your date is coming?"

"I'm alone," she says. "Sit and maybe we can twist that hostess's panties into a bigger wad."

He laughs at her coarseness.

"I'm only kidding," Agnes continues, leaning in now to talk. "She hasn't got any on. But sit down so people will stop staring at the loneliest girl in all of New York City."

He takes a seat and says, "These people will only look on now in wonder as to why such a pretty girl is out with her grandfather."

"Handsomest man in the room."

He blushes red through his beard. "Did your mother like the book?"

"Haven't given it to her yet; she's back home in Memphis."

"Ah, so you are a tourist. You carry yourself like a New Yorker, yet the lilt off your tongue made me think of the South."

Though the show hasn't started, and people are still milling about close by, their voices raised in conversation, Agnes feels the shopkeeper's attention focused solely on her. She feels her cheeks flush just as his had. "Daddy taught me not to take shit from anybody, and not to try and talk like anybody else, either."

"Smart man. Memphis, you say? Huh."

"Been there?"

"No, it's just that you're the second Memphian I've come across today." He fiddles with the buttons on his jacket cuff—a habit of his, fiddling.

"Is that unusual?"

"Must be my lucky day. Are you here for business or pleasure?"

She considers her choices. "Something in between."

The bass player steps up onstage in a pale green suit and takes up his instrument, lifting the massive bass to his equally massive frame as though it were merely a violin, and sets it right. He puts his arm around its body, cradling it like a woman with whom he plans to tango. His fingers, thick like hot dogs, land on the neck lightly, only the tips, while the other hand finds that woman's backbone to tap out a beat. The sound is soft yet commanding, like pillows on a tom-tom, and the chatter in the room falls away but does not disappear. It's the sound to set a tone, to make sure the people, the lights, the air are ready for what comes next.

"Oh, hello." Andrew sets Agnes's drink down and is surprised to find a guest with her.

"Andrew Sexton, this is . . . Sorry, I didn't get your name."

"Martin Lucchesi."

"I'm Agnes Cassady."

"From Memphis, Tennessee?"

"The very one."

Andrew doesn't know what this exchange, this game, is and feels as though he's come in late and uninvited.

"What can I get you to drink, Mr. Lucchesi?" He has to speak up now over the bass and bends over for Lucchesi's soft-spoken reply, then nods and leaves.

"You a fan of Oliver Pleasant's?"

"Oh my, yes, from way back. I used to go hear him in Harlem with Parker, Cannonball, Max Roach, everyone. I sold books to his wife, Francesca, for years. She was a voracious reader, so lovely." He has a faraway look in his eyes as though he can see the music in the air.

The drummer takes the stage then—no suit jacket, but a brown suit vest over a crisp white shirt. He falls in with the bassist, a third and fourth on the dance floor now to cut in on their tango, and they build a beat together. The bass player looks back and grins at his partner, whose eyes are closed. He is deep in meditation.

Agnes watches Lucchesi and how he nods along with the music, his fingers, thin and papery, keeping time on the white cloth and nearly blending in with it. She is taken with him, and jealous of his past, his association with this music while it was in its infancy as well as his personal connection to Pleasant.

Once the rhythm is set, the trumpeter arrives, gray fedora cocked to the side, and he blows a sad and steady tune. It's a melody that misses at all the right places, a heartbeat of whispered salutation filling in the spaces.

Andrew returns and places a small glass in front of Lucchesi, asking if they would like anything else. They wouldn't.

"What's that?" Agnes asks Lucchesi over the horn's wailing. In his small glass is a bright green liquid.

"Pernod. Yet another detail from a time long past."

Agnes is envious of this, too. Green with envy and melancholy over being born in a time too late.

The saxophonist comes on board and doesn't waste any time, launching into a dizzying solo that shoots up out of the ground like the Capasso Hotel itself, leaving the sidewalk and streets in a crater of rubble and the crowd looking on in wonder. He is all brash and polish with his collar opened and gold rings and cuff links catching whatever spotlight his horn doesn't take for itself.

As fiery as the saxophone sounds, Agnes looks around for a star even brighter and catches sight of Oliver just past the entrance to the room. He is helped out of his overcoat by the coat-check girl, but waves her away and pats her shoulder as she offers to take his hat. He rolls into the room, unnoticed by the hostess squinting at herself in a nearby mirror, and speaks to two men at the booth where he'd sat after the show the night before. The three men chat and shake hands, and then Oliver begins his slow, limping stroll to the stage. Passing by tables, he accepts their greetings and offers his own. He is like a ship—an old, four-masted sailing ship—passing newer though less seaworthy vessels in the harbor on his way to the dock. He passes behind Agnes, absently placing his hand against her shoulder, to let her know he is there and to steady himself, and she feels her skin ripple with his touch. At the stand, he stops to watch the band, or catch his breath, and the saxophonist nods to him and backs away, both musically and physically, falling in with the rest of the band as Oliver takes the stage and his bench.

And then they stop altogether.

Silence.

Oliver picks out some notes with his right hand, seems to be tinkering with something, almost as though he wonders what those specific keys might sound like when pressed beneath his fingers, when the felt hammer hits the string and vibrates itself to life. It grows organically into a melody, and his left hand joins in and it all builds up until Oliver is flying across the keyboard with the energy and passion of a man sixty years younger. Even the band looks on, their instruments silent, and they grin and shake their heads, remembering why it was they got into this business anyway, why it was they took up an instrument in the first place, and exactly why it is that Oliver Pleasant's name is on the marquee out front.

The crowd sits silent, knowing, each of them, that what they are seeing and hearing is nothing they could ever even come close to doing themselves—like flying an airplane or hitting a ninety-five-mile-an-hour fastball. Oliver takes them along on the flight, but the technique keeps them at a distance. He winds it back down, quiets himself, and the bass falls in with him. He stops altogether and takes a white cloth from his pocket to mop his brow beneath his hatband, and the crowd erupts with applause. Wiping sweat is something even they could do. The drummer has taken up again with the bass and, as Oliver puts that cloth away, the whole band becomes one and lays out a Duke Ellington tune for the people.

* * * * *

He sees her there again, the young woman with a tremble in her body, sitting now with an older, white-haired man. Her grandfather? He saw her when he came up for air, mopping the sweat pooling in the band of his porkpie. He'd only meant to warm up but got carried away, full of pent-up energy from his afternoon nap and memories of Francesca and the kids. He notices, too, that the large table he'd asked Ben to reserve for his family is empty again, its stark white tablecloth illuminated by an overhead spotlight like a deserted island in the middle of a sea of swaying heads and smiles.

And then he notices the boy. At least "boy" is the first thought to jump into Oliver's head. The second is familiarity. He *knows* that boy standing near the front of the club, just inside the doorway. In fact, Oliver thinks he saw him slip inside when the hostess turned to check for lipstick on her teeth in the mirror.

The quintet finishes the first set the way they'd begun, with each player leaving the stage in turn, this time to applause, the audience having seen what they could do. Oliver is even more impressed with this band on the second night. He's worried over the years about this new breed of jazz musician with their computerized tones and desire for instant gratification. Where are they coming from? The band has been good, made him sound better; he knows just how many beats he missed and isn't afraid to admit it. Even so, he isn't sure what the next generation will do, isn't even sure there is a generation coming up behind these cats that are onstage with him. The schools are putting out some decent enough musicians, sure, teaching them about scales and theory. "But you can't learn this shit in no classroom," Oliver would say. "This ain't no textbook music, ain't even for the radio no more. Hell, I heard of a damn jazz show in an art museum last week. A museum!"

He had been brought up alongside the architects, the greats, and is old enough to have learned the craft down in the swamps, inside the swaying of train cars and on riverboats. Up through Kansas City, Memphis, Chicago, and New York, he'd traveled to find a sound, his voice. The kids coming from Juilliard and this conservatory or that, what do they know of life and love and heartbreak? Hearts of glass beat within their chests and shatter like crystal at the slightest touch of pain. Their hearts aren't malleable, won't bend to bridge that gap between life and loss. It's on that bridge, over a rushing current of uncertainty and inevitable anguish, that the best tunes are written, the ones that touch the people in that same hidden place that holds all their love, fear, and hate.

People drawn to making music are instruments themselves with strings of sinew, but these kids today are taut and rigid with technology. They're unable to be tuned like a piano with its wood soaked through in gin and tears. That piano of old has been played for years in late-night, smoke-filled dungeons of lost hopes and dreams. Those are the places Oliver moved through—not even as a second home, having practically abandoned his first for the road, for strangers and their pieces of silver. Have these kids coming up today and looking to take his place on the bench, Dizzy's on horn, and Roach's on drums given anything up? Anything at all other than the safety of an office to work in with their daddy's name on the door?

Oliver's kids had been the victims of his work ethic, drive, and passion, and it is he who pays for it now as he stares down at that empty table. He'd left them all word that he was retiring, and Charlene, living just across the water in Brooklyn with her own family, knows he'll be moving away. He's asked her to help him, to come to his rescue, but gets only stony silence and empty chairs in reply. His eyes sting with the hurt but are distracted by the kid who keeps moving as though he doesn't want to get caught too long in any one spot—long enough to be asked if he needs something, where his seat is, or how old he is. This boy who watches him with his own daughter's eyes and from a face with Francesca's light complexion. Yes, he knows this boy.

Once Oliver's seated in his booth, he motions the boy over, pointing at the seat across the table from him. The boy slides in, his pressed suit cartoonishly big by one size. He looks down at the table while Oliver pours himself a Campari, taking his time to speak.

"Cedric? That you buried in that suit?"

"Hey, Pops."

"Look at me, boy. Grown up into a handsome one, ain't you? How old are you now? Fifteen? Sixteen?"

"I'm seventeen." He looks up at Oliver and thrusts out his chin, proud of his age.

"Seventeen? Shit, still too young to be in here. What you doin here?"

The boy shrugs, a movement barely detectable coming from inside the jacket. "Came to see you."

"How'd you know I was playin?"

"Mama."

"Your mama? Charlene here?" Oliver looks around the room, hoping he's missed sight of her.

"No, just me, Pops."

"Pops. Who told you to call me Pops?"

"You ain't like it?"

"'Pops' what we call our elders out of respect, those who come before us and show us the way. Pops Armstrong. Pops Blakey. Pops Bechet. You know them names?"

Again Cedric shrugs, more with his mouth this time than his shoulders.

"I don't expect nobody younger than that band onstage there thinks to call me Pops. Maybe not that drummer, though, he don't look no older than you. Where you hear Pops?"

"Mama."

"Mama? She say Pops?"

Cedric nods sheepishly.

"She comin?"

Cedric shakes his head.

Oliver sighs. "Why you here?"

"See you, Pops, like I said. I got a band now, calling it Storyville. I want you to come see us."

"You? You a bandleader now? What kind of band is that? Rock and roll?"

"Hip-hop." Again, the same pride he'd shown with his age, the same jut of his chin.

"Oh shit. Ha! Hip-hop?" Oliver has to take a moment to compose himself and uses the time to light a cigarette. "Hip-hop. Oh Lord, son, that ain't music."

"It's good. Me and my boys, we're good, just come hear us."

Oliver shakes his head, blows smoke from his nostrils, and watches it pool blue around the light over the table.

"It's like bebop; it's our music," Cedric continues.

"What you know about bebop, boy? What you heard about Storyville? You know much about bop as you do Pops."

"Just come hear us, Pops."

"Who is this?" Ben slides in next to Oliver, smiling.

"This my grandson, Cedric. He was just leavin."

"Charlene's boy?"

Cedric nods.

"I see the resemblance. A little Francesca, too."

Oliver beams at this despite himself. "Say hello to Mr. Greenberg, Cedric."

"I didn't think Charlene would have a son old enough to be in a nightclub."

"Like I said, he was just leaving. Came to see his pops play some hip-hop. Boy don't know his hip-hop from his bebop. Run on now, Cedric, before the man come in here and take Ben's sandals away from him."

Cedric stands to go. "Come see us. Please? Around on Third all week, any night after your show." And then, to Ben, "Nice to meet you, sir."

"Cedric."

They both watch him go.

"Your suit he's wearing?"

"Shit, I ain't got one that nice no more."

"Seems like a good kid, came to see his grandpa play. Broke the law to see his grandpa play, even invited you to hear his own band."

"Yeah. Yeah, he did. Shit, Benji, I'm the openin act for a boy's hip-hop show."

The men sit and watch the room. Oliver takes another few sips of Campari.

"Crowd's getting restless. You better get up there and give them what they came for."

Oliver stands with a groan. "I'll see if I got any more in me."

* * * * *

Frank grew up as part of a middle-class family in east Memphis within walking distance of his Catholic elementary school and church. It was a pragmatic upbringing based on the theory that hard work deserves a dollar. It was the 1970s and Frank's father regularly held forth over pot roast and potatoes about the gas shortages and interest rates. The dollar Frank was told he would one day earn was to be expected and he was expected to earn it through smarts and sweat. "There is no simple way," his father would say.

His father was an engineer, his mother the school's office manager. Little, if no, thought was given to the idea of inspiration; art as a vocation never even occurred to him. Not in elementary school, anyway, with its brick foundations laid out in syllables, prime numbers, dates, facts, and parts of speech. Not during those dinners when his father would speak of sums and overtime, and how a mortgage might be reduced. And not in the first few years of the all-boys Catholic high school that his father and uncles had also attended. It was an institution preparing boys to become the pliable material that would eventually be turned into men. The Jesuit order of Brothers ruled with a firm hand that would pull a boy up from his lazy, idyllic, hormone-laden ways by a haphazardly tied Windsor knot and march him along a path that led to finance, leadership, business, and loyalty. Responsibility! Catholicism was the faith, but pragmatism was the religion.

Frank first saw her sitting under a tree and reading Vonnegut. *Bluebeard*. She was dressed in the plaid skirt and white uniform shirt of her own private school; her black-and-white saddle oxfords were marred with a blue ink pen in an attempt to make the uniform her own. Her fingernails were painted black, and tiny, silver hoops ran the length of one entire earlobe, visible below a closely shaved strip of hair. This girl did not give a shit, not about that school, not about the nuns or their rules, not about her classmates, and not about Frank—not yet. She didn't say anything to him that day; it was simply the look on her face that told him she was uninterested in her surroundings, with the compass point of her nose in that unassigned book. Frank only came to know her later—she was the friend of a friend's girlfriend. He was correct about her disdain, yet wrong about the order of such a list. At the top was not the nuns or school itself. The list began with athletes. Jocks. White-bread boys who spent more time concerned with defensive plays and stats and scores than with what she called "the poetry of the world." (The very fact that she spoke that way made Frank dizzy.) Literature, art, social equality, and beautiful men and women were where she cast her youthful, inexperienced lot. Frank was intrigued. He considered himself popular, well liked and sought out by girls and boys both for companionship and for his opinions, filtered as they were from his father's. Her lack of interest was the most interesting thing he'd come across and he began to seek *her* out, this shadow, this pixie, this ripple in the calm tidal pool of high school.

Her name isn't important. It's been kept closed up for decades in a worn copy of *Bluebeard*, along with her virginity, and placed on Frank's shelf of favorite books. What lingers is his love of literature and art and beauty, his senses awakened in public parks, libraries, his parents' living room, and the bedrooms of friends whose parents had left town for the weekend. For this awakening, he is eternally grateful to that nymph under the tree.

Frank began reading—a lot—for pleasure. He couldn't get enough of the authors, their stories and characters. He couldn't get his fill of the ensuing discussions with her after school, over the phone late into the night and half naked in bed, delirious with a youthful familiarity. They listened to cassettes, flipping them over and over until the magnetic tape became faded and slack. Her music—the Cure, REM, U2, the Violent Femmes, Elvis Costello—were new sounds to him and with lyrics like poetry. It became his music; it became the sound track to young love and his awakening. It is her voice in his ear even now when he reads poetry and wonders, when a new and eagerly awaited novel is released, what she thinks of it, wherever she might be.

He neglected learning defensive plays and working with his teams. The coaches noticed. His father noticed as well, and those dinnertime lectures turned from national politics to very local threats and consequences. His grades, however, soared—she found intelligence deliciously arousing—so his parents were torn on discipline. His longtime friends fell off one by one, disinterested in alternative music, magical realism, or the legacy of Andy Warhol. *Fag*, they called him behind his back. *Pussy whipped*, he was declared. So Frank absorbed her friends, scant as they were, and a new persona of his own. In the style of the eighties, he grew his hair long on one side only, pierced an ear over the summer so it had time to heal before the Jesuit Brothers could get hold of it the next fall. He wore bangles on his wrist and shuffled his feet with caustic emotion in worn canvas shoes. Once, at her urging, he let her paint his lids with heavy, black eyeliner.

And he began writing.

It was an urge as primal as eating or sex for him, and one he couldn't explain. But it burned with a warmth in his chest, an ember he could only liken to the feeling of the first time he'd seen her beneath that tree on the campus of her school and, oddly, the sense he had on Sunday mornings when the priest would hold the Eucharist high overhead. There were tongues of fire, yellow halos, black fingernails, sex, literature, hymns, poetry, guitar riffs, creativity, gospels, and inspiration. Isn't it all the same? He speculated on this; he woke up with it at midnight and wrote it down within stanzas of bad poetry and worse prose. He was unaware that what he wrote then was poor, only the feeling he had when the words were pouring from him. It was the sense of something being built, something created.

It would turn out to be the foundation of a passion and a career. The writing continued throughout college, becoming honed and focused—favorite authors, a style developed, a voice, and career aspirations. He made new friends at college, sitting for hours on the brown and green grass of the lawn stretching out before the University Center of Memphis State University, or spending late nights in an off-campus bar that backed up to the railroad tracks. In these familiar places he would talk about writing. It was there in the wood-paneled bar, the sound of billiard balls clicking drowned out by the occasional train whistle, that he came the closest to giving his life over to passion, to creativity. It was on those nights in the bar that his blood boiled, the beer flowed, and Frank and his friends, packed into narrow booths, rubbed shoulders and thighs up against the confidence to live life on their own terms.

It's a frightening thing to say the words "I want to be a _____." You can fill in that blank with "writer," "musician," "poet," "artist" and none of it may come true. It's akin to telling a woman you love her, with all its implications, promises, and inevitable doomed failure. In the believing it, and in the announcement of it, one is opening his chest up and allowing anyone, everyone, to crawl in and see what's there. It's inviting the public to see what it is that makes a person tick and come alive, to see the cogs and all their eternally moving parts glistening in blood and oil and the seminal fluids of art. Frank found that the words and sentences and paragraphs led him along a path to the door of journalism school. In journalism he found a home and a way to make a living at what he loved doing.

Frank stares now at the black-and-white cardboard cover of a composition book the kid sitting across from him is holding in the lounge of the Capasso Hotel. He wrote in one just like it all through college, filling book after book with stories and verse, and placing them on a shelf, never even looking back. The young man facing him in the club, Frank believes, lives life on his own terms just as he and his college friends had planned. Dressed in a black peacoat over a red T-shirt with a houndstooth porkpie and smoking a slim panatela cigar, the kid is about twenty-five, Frank would say. He figures the appearance to be an affectation, a costume kept filed under "Jazz Club" in a plastic wardrobe shoved into one corner of a too-small Brooklyn apartment. There must be similar outfits labeled "Salsa Club," "Grunge Show," "Microbrewery," and "Sushi Bar." Perhaps a kimono for the last one. The kid (an unkind habit Frank has developed since turning forty is to refer to anyone under thirty as "kid") is writing. He's a writer. Frank feels self-conscious enough with his own notebook and pencil, but with someone else at the table taking notes as well, he feels as though he's on a school field trip, a continuing-education seminar on the postwar jazz scene in Manhattan.

The only thing Frank feels he can do is to introduce himself to the kid. "Frank Severs," he says over the music, holding his hand out over the table.

"Davis McComber."

Lost in his writing, he barely looks up from his book, his hand like a cold fish, limp and scaly. Frank instantly recognizes the name. Davis McComber is the byline on many of the contemporary articles on jazz in general, and Oliver Pleasant in particular, that Frank had Googled and printed to read on the plane. Frank had lost himself, not only in the stories of Pleasant and his colleagues, on the state of modern-day jazz and the future of the medium, but in the writing itself. Davis keeps a blog, as well as freelancing for music magazines, that is read by a staggering number of people—davismccomber.com has become the go-to site for what is and what was jazz.

McComber is the antithesis to Frank's dying industry, the very poison, some would say, that is being fed to today's readers. Yet Frank couldn't help being fascinated by what he'd read. The prose read like jazz, scatting and bebopping with flourishes and, when necessary, blank space. It was like poetry; it had a voice and a rhythm and maybe a little bit of trombone in it. There is no way the rigid style of the newspaper would allow such writing; newspapers refuse to bend, which is why they're breaking. The kid is good and Frank feels himself, older by nearly two decades (a bio tagged onto one recent article in *DownBeat* magazine noted McComber's age as twenty-three), shrinking from talent.

On the first page of his own notebook is written "Jordan," and Frank says to himself, "Details." He conjures a history for this character across from him, one with musician parents and late-night adventures while still in high school into Greenwich Village to hear live music; family vacations to Paris to commiserate with musicians and writers; encouragement, at a young age, from family friends such as John Updike and Salman Rushdie before the inevitable acceptance of a short story by the *New Yorker* at the prodigious age of seventeen. Offers of assignments would hound this young man through his undergraduate studies at NYU, where he would decline offers of dates to fraternity parties and homecoming formals to, instead, fly to LA to interview the next big personality for *Esquire* or *GQ* or *Playboy*. Frank's mind is fertile with images of Davis McComber in Iowa among Cheever, Smiley, and Roth.

He's finally caught staring at the composition book and looks into McComber's smiling, eager face. Once the kid's laser-like attention has been turned from his notes, Frank sees that it's a boyish face full of life and the possibilities ahead of him. To Frank, it is as though the elegantly appointed table spans seventeen years, and he's looking at his own twenty-three-year-old self.

"I said, where are you from?"

"Hmm? Oh, Memphis. Tennessee."

"Sun. Stax. Hi. Ardent."

"Rendezvous. Neely's. Corky's. Tops."

"Pardon?"

"Barbecue joints."

"Ah. I'm vegan."

"Of course."

Frank sips his gin and tonic and laments, briefly, even coming to New York, the most expensive city in the country, to ostensibly work for free. The drinks in this place are more than he'd like to pay. More than Karen would like him to pay as well, and he wishes he'd taken more cash from the ATM instead of using his debit card here with its traceable records of spending to be placed in the ledger of bad decisions that Karen keeps. But maybe these drinks are free, he thinks, since Ben sat him here with Davis McComber, who is freelancing for *DownBeat* tonight and said, "Be my guest." His guest? Is everything complimentary?

"Come here often?" Frank says.

"With what Greenberg charges for a drink? Christ. I only make it when I'm working, or when there's somebody I really, really want to see."

"Jazz fan?" Frank can play it cool when he needs to.

McComber nods, taking a sip of his beer. "Comes with the job. Actually, the job came with the habit."

"Habit?"

"Buying up old albums became a habit, became a borderline obsession. So did writing letters to *DownBeat* and then the occasional review until they asked me to cover a show or two, profile musicians, that kind of thing. Weaseled that into music writing for some local papers and AP stuff."

"Backed yourself into journalism, huh?"

"Yeah. What about you?"

"J-school. Shortest distance between A and B. I'm a traditionalist."

"I heard that's one way to do it."

They sit and listen to Pleasant and his quintet, both nodding and sketching out notes from time to time. McComber finishes his beer and waves to the waitress for another and one for Frank. Frank holds his glass up in acknowledgment and in a silent toast to a fellow writer, to one who keeps the fire of inspiration—whatever that is—burning.

The second set is as tight and spot-on as the first and gives way for McComber to sit later at an all-night diner six blocks away, drinking shitty coffee, smoking, and beginning his review in long-hand with a pencil in his composition book this way:

Oliver Pleasant hasn't been seen or heard from much in the past twenty years, ever since the passing of his wife, Francesca. It is unfortunate because, in a time when a musician's sense of history doesn't seem to go back much farther than the birth of MTV, Pleasant's goes back to the birth of cool and beyond. He is one of our last living icons from an age when the blues was heard through brass and bass, and that story of the blues had heaped upon it the sadness of slavery and emancipation, segregation, integration, and a couple of world wars. Jazz, simply, is the sound track to our modern-day history, and tonight one of our favorite and remaining historians took the stage at the Capasso Hotel in Midtown Manhattan for his final performances before retiring for good. It was night two of a five-night stand. . . .

* * * * *

Agnes doesn't have the talent of language to say or write just what it is she feels while watching Oliver play. His music is something that takes her back to her childhood, to before she was sick, to a time so long ago that she can't have known what it might be like to have been healthy. The music tells her what is inside of her better than Dr. Mundra's scanners ever could. She likes to know that others love it as well and watches Lucchesi as he listens, the same wrinkles spreading around his eyes as he'd had while looking through the book of drawings that afternoon. Even Andrew stopped to listen to Oliver Pleasant off and on, his New York jadedness fading away with each note.

"Well?" Andrew says once the music stops and Oliver has rolled his weight through the crowd, again brushing past Agnes, to his booth in the front of the club.

"Good shit, again," Agnes says. "Every note, from beginning to end, was perfect. Lucchesi?"

"Delightful," he says. "Yet I must take my leave. If you'll permit me, Miss Cassady." He takes a bill from his wallet and hands it to Andrew.

"Oh, I couldn't . . . ," she begins.

"Tut-tut. I wouldn't have even known Pleasant was playing if it weren't for you, my dear. And then you shared your table in an otherwise packed room. It's the least I can do. You take care and enjoy your time in New York."

"Thank you." She watches him go. He stops by Oliver's booth and shakes the man's hand, speaks a few words, and a smile spreads across Oliver's face. They nod a few more times and appear to exchange more pleasantries. Before Lucchesi leaves, he takes a pen and small notebook from his inside jacket pocket and makes a note of something Oliver tells him. Agnes had noticed it back home between farmers and merchants, or on Sundays when she and her parents would have supper at the Cracker Barrel down the road, the way older people, people who might not have anything more in common with each other than their number of years on this earth, could strike up a conversation and, within only minutes, connect and construe all that a generation of living has taught them.

Just before Lucchesi left, he'd cocked his head backward a touch and Oliver had glanced her way. She felt her face flush hot.

"Well?" Andrew repeats, growing impatient as he stands before Agnes.

"You said that already."

"How about us? Will you let me show you Manhattan tonight? At least, the parts I can afford."

She laughs at this despite herself, and because Andrew Sexton looks as though somewhere on the helix of his DNA there sits a chromosome in the distinct shape of a dollar sign. Something is coming over her and she is hard-pressed to give it a name. She tries to lay blame on the alcohol that warms her stomach and spreads through her body, or on the brief touch and glance from Oliver Pleasant as he'd made his way through the room earlier. She's just spent her first full day in New York City, the place of film and fame, and picked her way along its streets with a southerner's sense of grace, keeping her awe to herself, though now it is gushing out in a geyser of music and familiarity, and she finds she wants every sensation of that city for herself.

* * * * *

Oliver pokes around his apartment. He remembers when this was the time of night he'd come alive, when he and his boys would be anxious to finish a gig and go on to the next thing, the next tear that might take them across town or across the country. Now he's sluggish and tired, fuzzy-headed from work and drink. He caught himself nodding off earlier while talking to that reporter from Memphis. Oliver had rambled, the words coming to him through smoke and guesswork. He can't be sure, as he slumps on the piano bench in his living room with a cup of hot tea, whether or not he conveyed the importance of that man's city to his past and his future.

"Memphis was the first place I played professionally, on land anyways. There was New Orleans before, but that wasn't for pay, that was just for me to get my nut. And since you came up here all the way from Memphis, we'll talk about that."

"Yes sir. That'd be great, Mr. Pleasant."

"Here, you want a drink? Sit down. Benji, can we get the boy a drink? He been travelin since Memphis."

"Certainly, Oliver. Gin and tonic, Frank?"

"Please." When Ben left, Frank thanked Oliver again.

"Let's do away with the formalities and all that mister talk. Call me Oliver. Gin, huh? Whoo! I been off that shit for forty years. 'Course, it's probably better now than what we was drinkin back then. You born in Memphis?"

"Born and raised."

"Married?"

"Karen. Seventeen years."

"That's nice. Yeah, that's nice. Kids?"

"Well, no. No kids." Frank hesitated, wondering if he should sink into the trying, the losses, the doctors and tests and medications. He decided against it and, in that brief stutter and stop, felt a flash of disloyalty to Karen and what she was going through, her inability to simply skip over the difficult parts.

"Maybe not yet," Oliver laughed. "You still a young man; they'll come."

Frank took those optimistic words with as much weight as those of the doctors he and Karen had seen.

Frank listened to Oliver talk about Memphis just as he'd listened to him play the piano. It was with reverential awe and a slight disconnect in comprehension. Frank loves jazz with the mental capacity of a child. He doesn't understand how it all fits together like so many wooden blocks or puzzle pieces. He grasps that it's technical, that the men onstage so caught up in the tones and solos are also extremely intelligent and that the whole scene, as cool as it is, is closely related to working a mathematical formula. Three-fourths . . . two-fourths . . . four-fourths . . . Frank works in words and grammar, and the numbers only make his head swim.

It was with this same hazy recognition that Frank listened to tales of old Memphis. Talking after a show is like an extension of piano playing for Oliver, and he'd ramble for a burst of time as though taking a solo from his band. Frank tried to keep up. He knew the geographic locations of which Oliver spoke, but they've all changed in some way. They've been disinfected to within an inch of their lives or abandoned altogether to be torn down and rebuilt. It was like he was reading a road map of dirt roads being washed away as soon as he traveled them.

"Now, the first time I stepped foot in your city it was on them cobblestones at the river. Y'all still got them cobblestones?" Oliver said.

"Yes sir, they're a national historic landmark now."

"That right? I'll be. Hell, I guess I'm what you call a historic landmark, too." He laughed and poured a few more sips of Campari into the delicate cut glass in front of him.

Ben brought Frank's drink to him and picked up a lighter from the table to light Oliver's cigarette.

"When are you coming back?"

Oliver shrugged. "Next week, supposed to be. I ain't ready." He was lost in his thoughts and exhaled a tired lariat of smoke.

"Why can't you just stay here? Isn't New York your home now?"

"Shit, I been here for, what, seventy years? If this ain't my home, then I don't know what is. Unless it's New Orleans, or Paris. Maybe even Winona, Mississippi. All comes down to money, Frank, it's all money. Back then, back in the forties, fifties, we thought it was all about the music. We was young and dumb and full of come. And we thought as long as we was playin, we was livin. But, like all the other times in history, it was somebody else thinkin about the money. White man always thinkin 'bout money, Frank. So now he holdin it all and I'm only thinkin 'bout it."

"But you get royalties, right? All those songs and compositions and recordings? Hell, I bought one of your albums on iTunes just last week."

"The hell is that? Royalties, all that shit, that's been gone for years. It's been hell and gone. Now I got a small pension from Francesca's years of teaching in the public schools and an even smaller pension from the musicianers union. That's about it unless I play, which I ain't, until now. Benji takes care of me time to time."

"What about your daughter? I read somewhere that she lives in Brooklyn."

"Charlene. Yeah, she's over the river. She don't have too much to do with me, though."

"Can I ask why?"

"You can ask, son. I ain't gonna tell, though. I reached out to her about maybe stayin with her, maybe gettin a little help, financially, you know. It's a hell of a thing, askin a child for money like I was on allowance, like I want to go to a show or buy me some candy down at the corner store. I done my chores, I spent months and years away from home to play and pay for them kids, and I wasn't perfect, I'll say that, but times was different. I was a different man. But I was a man all the same and I did the best I could."

"Your sons?"

"Hell, they travel more than I did. They ain't got a home, from one end of the country to the next. Charlene, though, she's right there. It's like I can feel her right here with me, but she don't want nothin to do with me."

"So you're moving to Memphis."

"Yeah. My sister down there, lived there for fifty years workin as domestic help for some big-time rich family own half the damn city. Her daughter works for Federal Express now, not in a airplane but in the offices. Anyway, she got a room, told me to come stay down there. I imagine she been talkin to her cousin Charlene, maybe. Maybe not."

"It's changed a lot since that first time you were there. I hope, anyway. Was there any trouble that night you played? It was still so segregated back then."

"Naw. Not that night, if I recall. We took the service elevator at the hotel, of course, and it was all black in them houses and on that street where we stayed. Whites, the law, left us alone mostly. I ain't sayin there was never trouble there—I imagine whites got a head full of liquor and come lookin for trouble any night of the week, but not that night. It was same as when I was a boy in Winona and at the saloons in New Orleans. And it was the same party, too, I think, as all them other towns. Same lettin loose whether it's Mississippi, Tennessee, Chicago, or New York. People blowin off steam. We all got steam—blacks and whites. You got steam, Frank?"

"Yeah. Yeah, I do."

"Hell yeah you do. You don't let that out sometime, explosions happen. White law knew that. You lettin steam out in New York, son?"

"No, no steam, Oliver."

Another bark erupted from the old man.

"Were the parties in Memphis and New Orleans the same as in Paris?"

"You done your homework, boy, I'll give you that. You a fine reporter but we just talkin shit here, right? No, Paris was a whole different animal. Wasn't no white and black, just men and women." Whispering: "Sometimes wasn't even that."

"Can you tell me about Paris?"

Oliver looked at his watch and downed the last of his drink. "Another time, son."

"New Orleans?"

"Tenacious. I like that. Tell you what, I'm tired as shit right now, but you meet me at a diner called Junior's up on 103rd tomorrow morning, I'll tell you about New Orleans and feed you, too. You eat, Frank Severs, or just drink gin?"

"No, no, I'll eat. See you then, and thanks again for talking with me."

"My pleasure. You bring your paper and pen tomorrow, I got more stories."

As if anticipating his thoughts and movement, Ben had appeared by Oliver's side with his overcoat.

* * * * *

Oliver's on his feet again and standing in front of Francesca's wall of books. So many words, so many stories in that wall, in all of these walls. He briefly thinks of the little man with the white beard and touches the spine of a book. Lucky he met that man tonight, the man who sold Francesca all these books. What are the odds? He shrugs, shaking his head at the magic in old Mr. Lucchesi coming to hear his show and then offering to take all these books off his hands, tote them back down to the Village. *Some things I can't figure,* Oliver thinks as he pads in sock feet to the sofa, then lowers himself slowly onto it.

The reporter had taken Oliver back to Memphis, to even more stories. Oliver was in Memphis in 1968 on the night of April 4, playing at the Club Tropicana in those faltering days of jazz when the crowd wanted more Otis, more Isaac. That trip will probably make a good tale for Frank Severs's newspaper readers, Oliver thinks. His eyes fall on the photo of Francesca and the old, black rotary telephone sitting next to it—probably the last of its kind in New York City.

The phone rang that night in Memphis in Oliver's motel room and brought him up out of a deep sleep, pulled him up away from the woman snoring softly beside him. Those motel phones rang loudly—louder than a house phone, Oliver thinks—and it wasn't until he'd fumbled with the receiver to make it stop that he realized he heard the same clangorous noise from the next room over (his road manager's) and the room next to that (his drummer's). Those rooms were coming alive like they were their own switchboards. It was a cheap motel with thin walls—"Coloreds Only," the sign read—just north of downtown Memphis near the river, but close enough to the Firestone tire plant that the smell of rubber was a fixture in the air, the carpet, and the cheap, stained bedspread.

"Hello?" Oliver said, years of smoke and booze already on his throat, mixed in with the sleep.

"Oliver? Ollie, baby, you okay?" It was Francesca in a panic, which worried Oliver.

He looked over to the woman in his bed, still snoring, still asleep, big brown tits lolling off her chest onto the graying sheet. She'd had enough gin to drink that no amount of motel phone ringing could wake her.

"What is it, baby? Francesca, you crying? The kids all right?"

Through sobs, Francesca choked out the words: "Dr. King."

It took Francesca, a thousand miles away, to tell Oliver what had happened across town from him, and it wasn't until she choked out the word "murdered" that Oliver heard the police sirens in the distance and then they were all he could hear. Like a war zone, there were sirens and the screeching of tires up and down the street. He heard shouting and other voices outside his door, commiserating and consoling, angry voices and sad. Oliver assured Francesca he was safe and out of harm's way. He reached over and covered the chest of the woman beside him with a sheet and told Francesca, "I love you, too, baby," before placing the phone back in its cradle.

The next day, some locals eating breakfast at a nearby diner considered it too dangerous to travel and suggested to the band that they not try to leave. "Bus breaks down in the country, as riled up as them white folks are, no telling what might happen. Might be like we in season out there now. I wouldn't do it, not me. I'd stay my black ass in one place."

Money on the road was tight, though, so their waitress made a phone call and had Oliver's whole crew put up in a relation's house. Oliver slept that night head to toe in a single bed with his saxophonist. Before that, though, they'd sat up watching a small black-and-white television enraged with static and news reports coming from just down the street. The lady of the house, in a housecoat and slippers and her thin, oiled hair in a net, cooked away her grief and anger in the tiny kitchen, handing dishes of greens, sweet potatoes, ham casserole, and chitlins to her young sons, who climbed over backyard fences to deliver to the houses of cousins, uncles, and grandparents. The blacks of the city were too frightened to leave the front doors of their own homes. She cooked as though it were a funeral, and the house smelled like a holiday as Oliver played a sad dirge between newsbreaks.

It was the same neighborhood he'd stayed in on his first trip to Memphis, though without the revelry and good times. A pall had fallen over the city, wound around that neighborhood like a lace veil. He played his piano for the city that night, but it was barely heard over the soft sobs of the people.

That was Oliver's last time in Memphis, and now he's about to move there with his youngest sister and his niece and her family. He's been told his niece has a big house right downtown on the river, that she flies around the country in small planes telling people what to do. Black woman in the same town Oliver had run from when they felt the coast was clear forty years before. Times have changed, he supposes, smiling at the photo.

"Leastwise, I hope they have," he says to that picture. "Good night, Francesca, my love."

(INTERLUDE NO. 2)

MEMPHIS, 1937

as told to Frank Severs by Oliver Pleasant
The Capasso Hotel, 1:00 a.m.
New York, New York

Memphis was the first place I played professionally, on land anyways. There was New Orleans before, but that wasn't for pay, that
was just for me to get my nut. And since you came up here all the
way from Memphis, we'll talk about that.

The first time I stepped foot in your city it was on them cobblestones at the river. Y'all still got them cobblestones? Yeah? Shit,
them stones seen slaves and cotton, freedmen and soldiers comin
from and goin off to war. So here I come, down that gangplank all
wide-eyed and starin up top them bluffs there where the city rests,
lookin for all the world like I belong there. Like I got as much right
steppin foot on them stones as any slave or soldier just because I
play some music and got some tail five hundred miles downriver.

I was put in my damn place, though, 'cause when I stepped
on land with the shakiness in my legs from bein on water since
New Orleans, and the slickness there under my feet, I fell backward. And it wasn't to the sound of no orchestra or cheerin for
Mister Nobody Oliver Pleasant, neither. It was to the laughter of

the riverboat men, the dockworkers, passengers, and my own boys from the band. That's how I first entered Memphis, on my ass.

Suppose that's how I'll go back to it now, too.

Anyways, it was my first time in the city and the boys took me all around from Beale Street, down Main, lookin in all the windows to them fine department stores. There was movie houses, too, with their marquees shinin and barkers out front callin for folks to come in and watch a picture show. "It's air-conditioned!" they'd shout.

It was full of people, Memphis was. Like New Orleans, only there seemed to be more purpose, I guess. There was bales of cotton bein sold and shipped right there on Cotton Row and pretty ladies dressed to the nines shoppin or goin for lunch, businessmen everywhere with folded-up newspapers under their arms and sharp-lookin lids to keep the sun off. There was a music to Memphis, the same as New Orleans, but it was different somehow and I'm hard-pressed now to say just how. It was the blues, be sure, shufflin through the town the way I suppose a sharecroppin Negro might have when he come in town for the day to shop or visit kin. Kind of wary, you know? New Orleans was brass and brash and in your face, and our people could be anywhere there, go anyplace we damn well pleased. But there seemed to be a little taste of the unknown in Memphis, like somebody might not like the tunes and have a mind to do somethin about it. Oh, but the sound was there. It was everywhere; you can't stop the music.

We had a night's stay over and some of the boys was known to the manager of the Gayoso Hotel, who wanted some new blood on his bandstand and hired 'em to play up on the rooftop. They needed a piano and asked me did I want to sit in. Cash under the table, all the booze you could drink, and white tail from here and gone? Shit, I'd of been a fool not to sit in on that. We had a hell of a time playin up there in the breeze and with a different crowd than we'd been playin to on that boat. Memphis, the river view, it was a good scene up there on that rooftop. Stars even seemed that much closer in the night sky.

After the show, we was scurried off that rooftop to the basement, where the colored staff and waiters was passing around a bottle taken from the hotel's bar and some smoke I was told was taken from a guest's room. Some a them staff was goin over to a block party not far away and took us along. It was in the black part of town, of course, past Beale and down to where them row houses get smaller and closer in. Had a scare on the way when a couple of cops, white cops of course, stopped us to ask where it was we thought we was headin. Home. Drinkin? Naw suh. Askin us where we was comin from and what's in the case there and was we sassin them? I wasn't but seventeen or so and it scared me a little, put me in mind of old Mr. Sheffield sittin up at my mama's lunch counter and tellin her to bring him the pepper sauce. Tryin to tell her she burnt his pork chop tough. Motherfuckers. But they let us go. No harm no foul, I guess, just the white man's idea of a good time.

Our idea of a good time was over in our people's neighborhood. It was raucous and loud over there, boy. It was a fine time and all that party needed was some more musicianers from downriver. The girls liked havin somethin new to look at and touch like we was exotic animals from some far-off place. And we was, too!

There was parties all up and down that narrow street with dice set up in the front room of one of them shotgun houses, a bar set up in the house next door, and then music callin from the third. Amen, brother. But that music could be heard all up and down the street and, I imagine, all the way to the river and back. Them houses were packed so tight together you could pass a bottle from porch to porch, or peel the paint right off a neighbor's clapboard. That was a good time, Memphis was. Somebody had a old upright pulled out on a porch so it blocked the front door and folks had to climb in and out of the windows to come and go. I played there all night long and my boy Hamlet blew his trombone from the sidewalk. Felt like we was celebratin somethin, but I don't know what, just that free feelin and bein in the South, I suppose. That was thirty-seven back then. It was friendly, like bein among family, you know?

I'd like to get that feelin back when I move down there, but I reckon it's done left with the current and the time. Hopefully them cops left, too—that ain't good for nobody. But it'll be nice to see my sis and baby niece. Get some more of that southern cookin, too, boy. And the music? It's good everywhere, but with somethin just a little sweeter tastin down closer to where it was birthed, and in the face of them who weren't so damn happy about it all bein born in the first place.

NIGHT THREE

1.

The parties of the Garden District are lavish affairs. "Balls," Agnes had called them, giggling with her roommate, Terron, as she dressed. Galas. There were those during Mardi Gras, of course, that would hardly raise an eyebrow anymore and dozens of others similar in taste and a profound lack of it occurring throughout the District, plus hundreds more less opulent parish-wide. The others, though—parties in midsummer with a beach theme, Halloween with its built-in penchant for costumes and decadence, or Christmas holidays and throwing their bacchanalian ways in the face of the Christ child's birth—those were the real treats, the pearls among oysters of New Orleans social circles.

Agnes was invited to some of these parties to provide entertainment. She was discovered in a local dive or passed by on a street corner and noticed, as much for her long neck and the sleepy tilt of her head while she played as for her talent or her light touch on the keyboard. Agnes's thinness, the two barely discernible bumps at the front of a black evening gown cut low in the back and draped along her visible rib cage, added a splash of femininity to the androgynous cocktail of the house staff—the bare-chested boys circulating their wares and the hors d'oeuvres of the dykish caterer in the kitchen. The hosts always preferred a bit of muscle behind the curtain with all the flash and form on the main floor.

And on the main stage, they appreciated the lithe, young Agnes Cassady.

One of the more anticipated and attended of these parties was thrown by Landon Throckmorton. Landon is a collector. Spread throughout his home are collections of antique furniture, first editions of classic novels and scientific journals, nickel-plated handguns, Tiffany lamps, and Civil War–era daguerreotypes. These are nice things to walk among and gaze at where they rest on side tables and mantels. But he also collects people. Upon his shelves are gathered senators and chefs, authors and impresarios, models and the moneyed. He is accustomed to the finer things, having grown up among wealth. Despite his ease with wealth, or perhaps because of it, it's the layer beneath such finery that he seeks. Landon finds predictability dull and likes to mix and mingle prostitutes with the bourgeoisie, the hustlers with high society. He gets a thrill from the friction and spark of recognition where there should be none at all.

The street, as he thinks of those from the underbelly of New Orleans, comes to him in various ways. In general, though, they are attracted to the scent of wealth the way a shark is to chum. Agnes, a busker he'd first encountered in the Quarter, is from the street. But there is something different about her—he'd noticed it the first time she'd entered his home. She hadn't needed to be scrubbed the way others had; her eyes didn't dart from side to side, sizing up the room to learn what might be stolen quickly and easily. She'd carried herself with confidence, but there was something else—she was damaged. Landon was drawn to her just as he was to the pair of hand-painted porcelain teacups kept in the dining room hutch, preferring the one with the chip in the rim. *How did it get there?* he wondered. Who in its provenance chipped such a fragile object? The flaw is where the interest is for him. He looks for the same flaws in his politicians and in his corner boys, though they're difficult to detect, if not impossible—one so guarded, the other so phony.

Hired to play parties, she was drawn to the warmth of the room, the timbre of his instrument. She never really gave Landon a thought then; he was simply the means to an end. In fact, she may have been the first guest in his house not to give him a thought. Agnes came to him through her music and her playing was beautiful. Yet, when he watched her from across the room, it was the hand she would clench into a fist over and over again, as though trying to regain feeling there, that held his attention.

Because of this tiny flaw, this damaged piece of porcelain, he was protective of her from the start, keeping the leeches in tuxedos and ball gowns from her. He wanted to lock her away like that teacup, and suggested as much to her, offering her a bedroom, comfort, and all the luxuries she might imagine. She wouldn't hear of it. Agnes Cassady is not anyone's to keep, not for the short amount of time she has left. So she comes and goes as she pleases, welcome to sit at his piano anytime the mood strikes her, and her music has become the favorite part of these gatherings for her host.

This party was to celebrate the autumnal equinox with its equal part day and night. Guests were expected to wear white and then, halfway through the party when Agnes was told to strike up Cole Porter's "Night and Day," they would change to evening black. The melody would send the more modest scurrying for bedrooms and bathrooms, linen closets and pantries; the less modest would find a shadowy recess or seventeenth-century Oriental screen behind which to disrobe; and the immodest would simply undress where they stood and sometimes, though not always, go in search of their change of clothes. Still playing, Agnes would stand up from the bench, and as a note held in the smoky, humid air, she would step out of a glittering silver dress and into the black gown she'd kept draped across the Baldwin piano, her alabaster skin barely having time to register the air, the furtive glances, or the appreciation in Landon's smile.

It was at such a party, as Agnes was concluding a rendition of "Six and Four," that she saw Terron coming through the crowd toward her as though pulled to the sound of the piano. The look on her face, drawn and pale, told Agnes something wasn't right.

These parties were meant to be private, with formal invitations inscribed with the blackest calligraphy on the thinnest of parchment hand-delivered to only a select circle of acquaintances and hopefuls. Agnes had told Terron where she'd be, because in New Orleans you didn't go to an unknown location without a safety system in place. In the butler's pantry just off the kitchen, Agnes struggled to catch her breath and shook her head as though she couldn't hear what Terron was saying.

Terron repeated herself: "It's your father. A heart attack, Agnes. You should call your mother."

Heart attack. The words left a bad taste in Agnes's mouth as she repeated them back to her friend, words as bitter as whatever it was those waiters carried as they flitted back and forth past young women.

"What happened to the music? Who's this?" It was Landon. Ever the host, he worried for his guests' lack of entertainment.

"This is my friend Terron. She just came to tell me my father had a heart attack." The words sounded foreign and had an unnatural feel on her tongue. She realized then that Terron hadn't said whether he was still alive, and Agnes hadn't thought to ask. "Is he dead, Terron?"

Terron had been sneaking glances at the bare-chested waiters but now looked back to her friend, her eyes brimming with tears, and nodded.

"Oh dear," Landon said. "You must go, Agnes. We'll find another pianist."

Agnes held Terron, sadness filling her every pore, before disengaging herself and wiping her face with the palms of her hands. "No. No, I'll play."

"Agnes," Terron said.

"Darling . . . ," Landon started.

"I'll play," she assured them. "For Daddy. He taught me how, and I'll think of him there on the bench beside me like when I was little. I'll play for him tonight and go home tomorrow." She took a black mask with white highlights and feathers from the china hutch and placed it over her eyes.

For the rest of the evening she played the melancholy songs that were her father's favorites. She played rousing rags when the room was blurred through tears. She kept the mask on, wishing she could be someone else, wishing her father could truly be there beside her. Landon would stop his tour through the rooms periodically to watch her and raise his eyebrows in question. "You okay?" And Agnes would nod along with the music. The music that night, guests would recall for months afterward, had sounded sweeter and sadder than any they'd ever heard.

A car arrived for her at six the next morning to take her to the train station for her departure on the City of New Orleans line to Memphis. She hadn't slept, the party ending around 4:00 a.m. when the last of the guests had either left or retired in twos and threes to bedrooms and basement. Agnes had played for six straight hours, sipping scotch supplied by boys and, for much of the time, with a single stream of tears falling from behind the mask. Terron had refused to leave her friend and was found on Landon's sleeping porch curled up asleep on a cruel iron settee.

"What time is it?" Terron asked, rubbing her eyes.

"Morning," Agnes answered, and the two walked home arm in arm with their grief.

Landon told Agnes he'd arranged for a train ticket and for his driver to escort her to the station. When? He never appeared to stop circulating; Landon is society's Gulf Stream, constantly moving to carry his warmth from room to room. When and how had he made a reservation? A computer? A phone call? Not Landon.

Now that Agnes thinks about it, she doesn't even remember ever seeing a telephone in his house.

Regardless of how it came to be—Landon has a way with making things come to be—Agnes found herself being let out of a white Lincoln Town Car and led by an enormous black man in an equally black suit who called her Miss Agnes and carried her suitcase as though it were a child's lunch box. He guided her into the Amtrak station with its brassy Dixieland jazz and iconic murals on the steel-gray walls. The man presented a ticket to the clerk, handed off her bag, and turned and bowed slightly to Agnes before leaving more briskly than she would have thought such a thunderhead could move.

She was handed off to a porter, a withered black man in a red cap who walked her to the train and took her hand as she stepped into the car as though it were 1904 instead of 2004. A conductor escorted her from the door, up a narrow staircase, and down a dark passageway. She was a relay baton, a fire brigade bucket, though drained of any lifesaving liquid. This man opened a door to a sleeper compartment, a boxy room with a bunk, a closet, a sink, and a sitting chair that held, unexpectedly, Landon Throckmorton.

Landon closed the book he'd been reading and stood to accept Agnes's luggage from the conductor. "Thank you, Roland," he said. Roland, just like Landon's driver, bowed and left.

Agnes wanted to ask him what he was doing there, whether he intended to travel to Memphis, how he had reserved the accommodations on such short notice, and why. But she was exhausted. She was just too tired, too heartbroken, and too empty to form the sentences or put a coherent thought together. Instead, she lay down on the bunk with only the vaguest sense of her shoes being removed and a coarse, Amtrak-issued blanket being pulled over her shoulders.

"Thank you." It was all she could muster and, at such a whisper, Landon missed it altogether.

He'd accompanied her more as a comfort to himself. He felt he needed to make sure his prize wouldn't become chipped any more than she already was, and he stood watching her drift into sleep as they left the station and cleared the city's limits.

Agnes dreamed, not of her father but of his piano, and it made her heart swell even in her sleep. The slow, rhythmic rocking of the train car gave her the sense of her father sitting at his bench, the way the music would touch him and take him with it. She dreamed that his soul was carried up on the music of his piano and her sleep was full of the tones that had sounded so good bouncing off of wood floors and plaster ceilings in the rambling farmhouse built by her grandfather, sinking into randomly laid rugs, worn sofas, and chairs. The age of the home helped to round the edges of the music.

Her daddy had spent money they didn't have to have the piano tuned once a year. An elderly man with long gray hair and narrow glasses whom her daddy called "Professor" would come out to the house each fall like clockwork to crouch behind the console with felt hammers, delicate pliers, and calipers. He'd practically climbed into the open top with tuning forks and his own ears, the most precise instruments of all, turning his head this way and that to listen. Agnes would sit on the floor, handing him tools out of his canvas bag, so she could see inside the piano, learn something of its heart and brain and spleen.

That old piano had made a soothing, comfortable music that made Agnes think of home, and her father, no matter how far away she traveled.

She woke up just outside of Winona, Mississippi, about two hours from Memphis. There had been a delay, a freight train slow to switch tracks as they'd left Louisiana, and the light outside was waning. Landon was still there, stick-straight in the chair and reading a Victorian-era novel. It was as though he hadn't stirred in all those hours. She had idle time to lie there and watch him, something she'd never really done before with his skittering through crowds and her own focus on the piano. With the reading light illuminating the side of his face, he reminded her of an old picture she'd seen of William S. Burroughs. His face was long and lean, the pallid skin sagging and mottled with age. She may have seen that photo framed in Landon's house, she recalled.

The train ticket was a gift that she'd been too drained to reject; she was too tired for any fights just then. She was grateful for the ticket and comforted by his presence. The trip to New York and visit to his doctor would be something else. It was a last resort, perhaps her very last hope. She maintained her dignity and wasn't a kept woman; she was damaged, and she only wanted to be whole.

As the train car swayed gently like a boat, she thought he looked calm, more human than when he played the host or favored guest. She wasn't sure which was the real Landon Throckmorton, but something told her that he was relieved to be sitting in a train, quietly reading in half-light instead of on society's stage. She wanted him to go on reading, to envelope himself in the silence and solitude and rhythmic movement, but he'd looked up from his book and caught her eye. He dropped the book to his lap and smiled and she was sure then that this was the real Landon.

There was a car waiting for them (of course there was) at Central Station in Memphis. It dropped Landon at the Peabody Hotel, where all doors were opened for him by tall, lanky black men in top hats and tails. The driver continued down Highway 51, past the hospital where Agnes's daddy had taken her only three years before and poured his heart out to a woman he didn't know, something that must have been hard for such a proud man to have done. But it was for his daughter, and she knew he would have taken that hospital apart brick by brick and put it back together again if they could have helped her. The bright lights of the hospital and low streetlights of uptown gave way to a scab of a city with boarded-up factories and shops, rusted cars, and men and women wandering from corner to corner as though help, or an answer, could be found the next block over. When they crossed the I-40 turnoff into Frayser, then Millington, and passed fields of soybean and cotton, Agnes breathed easier. She was home, the smell of fresh mowing and wood fires heralded her arrival and she felt her heart speed up. The anticipation, the excitement of home-coming, though, was emptied from her when the driver pulled into the long, rutted drive and up to the gravel, parking in front of her childhood home. She sat in the backseat and looked up at the house through the car window. It was massively white and wooden and looked, for all the lights on inside and the shine of a full moon across its eaves, lonely.

Agnes awakes in the apartment of Andrew Sexton. It is amazing for its closeness; she's never seen anything like it. The room is only slightly wider than the queen mattress she lies on, yet the ceiling is so far from where she rests that it makes her head spin. Though perhaps that's the scotch. She pulls her hand from under the covers to remind herself of its slight tremor. With her other hand—her good hand, as she's come to think of it—she reaches for a pack of Nat Sherman Reds on the cinder block next to the bed and lights one with a brass Zippo lying nearby. Sitting back against the wall, cold against her bare shoulder blades, she blows a stream of smoke the same color as the sheets she's tangled in. She belches and feels better.

There is no clock as she looks around the room and blinks the night back into focus. There was a shitty little bar after the sophistication of the jazz club and an exuberant Irishman named Tommy serving shot after shot of whiskey, whether asked for or not. She was introduced to people, so many she could never hope to remember their names. And then there was dancing. Christ, that music was awful, the throb of it coming back to her temples and making the room swim even more—such awful music. They had walked for what felt like miles through the night, a cold night along city streets still alive with clatter even at what must have been a late hour. The light from cafés and all-night bodegas spot-lighted individuals and groups of people as though she were meant to take notice of them, though she knew she'd never be able to recall their faces. Like the ornately framed and spotlighted paint-ings, centuries old and thick with oil, that she'd stared at on the walls of the Brooks Museum of Art in Overton Park as a child in Memphis while on school field trips. Her classmates ran around her, ignoring the treasures in front of them. She is unable to recall a single detail of those paintings now—not a face, not a body, not a gesture, artist, or title.

There had been music everywhere last night, not just the mindless, tribal bass of the clubs, but music in the streets and coming from hidden doorways, from passing cars and apartment windows near enough to the sidewalk to be scratched by the naked branches of trees that fought to survive in the unlikeliest terrain. It had reminded her of New Orleans. Her ears ring with it all now and she closes her eyes to make one melody come through clear, but all she can summon is Oliver Pleasant playing "Crepuscule with Nellie." *Thelonious Monk, you beautiful, crazy son of a bitch!* she hears her father shout the way he would some nights.

A few feet away a toilet flushes and her waiter comes through the door wearing only blue briefs with a trickle of his business on the front; he pulls his hair back into a ponytail, exposing the two hoop earrings he wears. She grimaces as her stomach turns over again. He is tall, seems even taller from her perspective, lying as she is practically on the floor, and his rippled skin has become a broad expanse now released from the constraints of clothing. He is tattooed. The left arm, from shoulder to just below the elbow, is a series of designs in crisp reds and blues with highlights of white and yellow. An octopus, all black and gray, covers his wealth of muscled back, its curious tentacles reaching up and over his shoulders to his chest, the tip of one tentacle—becoming blacker where it narrows down to its pointed end—teases the silver barbell speared through his right nipple. "Turn around," she says, and he does, because it's more demand than request. "Let me see what all you got there." The tentacles wind down and around his hips and disappear into the blue briefs. Agnes is certain she knows just where those tentacles end, yet she can't, for the life of her, remember where or how. She shifts her weight below the sheets, and the soreness she feels lets her know those tentacles grasp an impressive treasure.

"Good morning," he says. "Everything look okay?" He falls back into bed beside her and picks the cigarette from her fingers, taking a long, dramatic drag from it. She takes another from the pack and lights it.

She shrugs and says "Hello," and thinks what a stupid, simple thing it is to say, as close as they've obviously been. Outside, a garbage truck's hydraulics squeal as it fills itself with an entire building's worth of refuse. "I'm cold," she adds.

"Do you want some coffee? I mean, I don't have any, but I could run out for some. Starbucks is just on the corner."

She looks to the window, the building across the narrow street almost close enough to touch, and up to the gray sky beyond. "My apartment in New Orleans is about sixteen times this size. The doors open right up to a balcony that overlooks Royal."

"Sounds nice. I've never been."

She thinks of Sherman, up by now and shuffling through the Quarter with his saxophone over his shoulder, heading to one of his regular gigs where tourists will drop money at his feet as they wait on beignets and alligator hash. He'll be distraught that he hasn't heard from her; he's like a little boy. But then, Agnes has never noticed much difference between her boys and her men. "You should go. Sometime."

"What are you in New York for? You never did say."

She shrugs again.

"I don't think I've ever seen a girl drink as much as you did. Jesus, downtown is going to have to re-up on booze before tonight. And you talked, too, a lot about music—'the music of the city,' you called it."

She blushes at the thought and tries to recall the night again, purge it into the present, but only comes up with the taste of bacon. "Bacon."

"You're hungry?"

"Did we already eat breakfast?"

"Yeah, well, about 3:00 a.m. we stopped at Junior's. Not sure I've ever seen a girl eat like that, either. You put away an entire number four and then ate half of mine. Caitlynn and Eric loved that."

"Who?"

"We met up with them last night. My friends?" He stares into her blank face. "You don't remember much of anything at all, do you? Maybe you shouldn't have mixed the rotgut I bought you with Ben's high-end scotch."

"Maybe you should mind your own fucking business." She looks back toward the gray sky, smokes some more.

The first time he'd seen her in the club, Andrew had thought Agnes to be frail. That was a mistake, the pale skin and thin frame equating to weakness in his mind. Now he knows her as someone comfortable in the night. She'd moved along New York's streets at ease, to the point that he sometimes had to rush to keep up with her. Outbursts like this one, telling him to mind his business, appear to be the norm for her; she takes nothing off anyone. He's not sure he's ever known a woman with the inner strength and conviction of Agnes, certainly not any women in his family. It's that strength, he thinks, this inability she seems to have to give a shit what anyone might think about her, that is sexier than any physical attribute.

He falls back on the bed to stare up at the ceiling. "You want to eat?"

The thought of food makes her queasy and she rises to go to the bathroom, naked in the dim light of his apartment, which she realizes consists of only the one room and a bathroom. He watches her walk away from him.

"I want coffee," she says. "Why don't you be a dear and reach across the street there and see if your neighbor's got any."

In the bathroom, little more than a closet holding a toilet and stand-up shower with a *Star Wars* curtain, she looks at herself in the mirror beneath a bare bulb. She looks at the circles under her eyes, her thin lips cracked from the cold night, and her hair knotted from wind and fucking. This isn't the image of her New York self that she'd pictured back home. In the hospital, yes, maybe, but once outside those hallways, she'd expected only glitter and glamour. She straightens up and notices the angry purple and red of a hickey next to her left nipple. "Great," she says to her reflection. She lowers the seat and pees, self-conscious of the sound with Andrew on the other side of the door. All she wants is a shower, but she's scared to even look behind the curtain at what hygienic atrocities R2-D2 and Princess Leia might be hiding there. She thinks of her spotless hotel room with its clean sheets and toilet sanitized for her protection and lets out a sigh that tastes of bacon, cigarettes, and scotch. No toilet paper. "Great," she says again.

"I thought you said you're from Memphis," he says when she returns and begins searching through the sheets.

"I am. Where are my panties?"

He pulls them from under a pillow and holds them out to her. When she reaches for them, he grabs her wrist and pulls her down on top of him. "What about New Orleans? You said, 'my apartment in New Orleans.' . . ."

He has his hands on her ass and she feels the cold metal of his thumb ring against her skin. "I've been there the past couple of years."

"Doing what?" He kisses her neck.

"Andrew, come on, I need to go." She tries to push her way up but is no match for him.

"What do you do in New Orleans?"

"I play piano."

He stops his aggressive affections and looks at her. "Yeah?"

"Yeah." She's giving in to his kisses and touch and feels him stiffen beneath her, the smell of sex from the night before everywhere.

"You any good?" He pulls her legs apart and strains against her.

"Good enough." She traces one of the octopus's tentacles with her finger. She doesn't have a tattoo of her own and has always found it odd that people are so willing and quick to alter their bodies permanently when her own body is being altered beyond her control.

"Why did you come to New York?" he says.

She licks the sterling-silver jewelry piercing his chest. "Shh . . ." And she begins the quest to remember where those tentacles might lead.

3.

The riverboat didn't immediately point north. It traveled south to New Orleans as though siphoning blood through a vessel back to the heart, enriching it before pumping it out once again. The trip farther south made Oliver feel as though the captain had taken his musical career into consideration on the trip's itinerary. Oliver didn't know about jazz other than what he'd heard the man playing in his parents' restaurant and what the train porters spoke of at their stops. He'd never even been outside of Winona.

"When that paddleboat pulled up to the port of New Orleans," he tells Frank, who is sitting across from him at Junior's Diner, "it was like my spinal cord had finally connected to my brain so that all my senses came alive. There was music playing from the very minute we tied up. Music coming from the docks and the saloons and whorehouses, almost from the murky water itself—it filled the air and gave me a place. It felt like home, I guess is what I'm sayin. It put me in a mind I never had except those nights in my folks' restaurant when the joint was shakin and everything just seemed to hum and stomp with the music. But it wasn't only in the cover of dark like when we had to sneak around back home; no, it was during the blue early morning hours, the bright white of day, and suppertime, too. Music—always, baby, and forever."

Mr. Fairbanks, the musical director of the River Star Cruise Lines, and his wife had a house in New Orleans, in the Garden District, and it was there that they took young Oliver when they disembarked. The trolley—it was Oliver's first time on a streetcar; New Orleans would become a treasure chest of firsts for the boy—carried them down a street called Canal, though there was no water.

"It was a grown-up street with buildings and men in suits and hats," Oliver recalls, "but there was still music, even on this workday. In the middle of the day!"

The music was accentuated and brought to life by the swaying and rocking of the trolley car.

Madame Fairbanks ushered him off the trolley and to a low, ornate iron fence and gate. Oliver didn't enter right away; he could only stand, staring up at the towering lady in front of him. "Lady" was the only term he could think of for that austere house, so strong yet so fragile with its pale blue coloring and white gingerbread details. A porch the width of the house held rocking chairs and was shaded from the midday sun by an overhang. The rest of the small front yard was protected from the summertime sun by a massive oak tree in the neighbor's yard, its Spanish moss hanging from branches and trying in vain to reach the coolness of that porch.

"Come along, Oliver," Madame Fairbanks called from the porch. She was a light-skinned mulatto with a hint of the islands around her eyes and nose. Oliver was unsure of her age—Madame Fairbanks seemed ageless in her high-collared dress and smooth skin—but she was beautiful at any age. Beautiful, yet stern. Once Oliver entered the house with its formal rooms and towering ceiling, he was welcomed by a wide and low piano. It was the only grand piano he'd ever seen and he stood for a moment and stared into its mouth and the rows of teeth and muscle there, just as he'd stood and stared up at the riverboat when he'd first arrived at the docks, at the skyscrapers from the trolley, and at the roof-line of the Fairbanks House. New Orleans would hold him in awe the rest of his life, upon every return and with every memory no matter where he laid his head at night. When he couldn't stand it any longer, when his fingers itched until he feared they might fall from his hands, he slid onto the bench to pound a rag, one of Mr. Fairbanks's own compositions. He was stopped midway through the first bar by Madame Fairbanks pulling the cover over the keys, nearly severing Oliver's fingers. "Not here, not a note of that devil music in this home."

"It was made known to me right off that, while Fairbanks was lord over the boat and the music and his musicianers while on the water, it was the madame who ruled in her house. And she wasn't havin none of my shit in her parlor. Always thought it odd since it was the music that paid for the house in the first place," Oliver says. "But that was her castle and she was the moat between me and any pleasure while under her roof."

Frank laughs, as he has several times already, feeding Oliver's need to tell a story just as Oliver feeds his face with a plate of his usual bacon. Frank has hung on every word, ignoring his own plate while his coffee has gone cold, and is practically falling on the table as he leans in, scribbling to keep up with Oliver's voice. Oliver seems to have a renewed vigor in the morning, not the tired, slightly slurred speech of his postshow reverie. This story is everything Frank had hoped for, everything he'd told Karen it would be, meeting the inflated expectations he'd given her in their kitchen that night over spaghetti.

He'd spoken to her on the phone the night before, when he'd returned to his hotel from the club. Drinks with Oliver had gone late, later than he'd expected, but he wanted to check in with her, to get points for the call whether she answered or not. If she hadn't, he thought, the subsequent points would be worth more when he pouts about missing her. But she had answered and they'd talked of mundane daily events—he told her about his flight and she of the hormones making her feel cramped, as though she were having her period. He didn't tell her specifically what he and Oliver had talked about, only that he'd spent time with him after the show and he'd talked of the past.

As Oscar talks now, Frank makes mental notes of highlights to feed to Karen.

Mr. Fairbanks was as light skinned as his wife, and though the two didn't have any children of their own, Oliver was sure that if they had, their offspring would have been as white as the passengers on the River Star Cruise Lines. It was this paleness of skin, Oliver would learn, that allowed Fairbanks his exalted position on the line, the home in the District, and the couple their place among New Orleans high society.

"The Fairbankses, they had a neighbor, a widow several times over, name of Madame Margeurite Sherman Ragghianti Fontaine, and she had a girl named Lucille worked for her. Lucille used to hand me corn bread over the fence from porch to porch. That corn bread was better than my own mama's, though I'd never say so in public and you better not put that in any newspaper, neither. Anyway, Fairbanks, he'd take me into neighborhoods I never even dreamed of, whole blocks full of colored folks doin as they please— shootin dice, drinkin, howlin at each other. And in one of them neighborhoods there was a club—hell, there was a club on every goddamn corner, some barely more than a Chinatown bodega in size—but only one of 'em had Marcus Longstreet on piano. Marcus was the husband of Lucille with the corn bread."

"Marcus Longstreet?" Frank repeats, making sure to spell the name correctly on his notepad. "I've never heard of him."

The waitress comes around to refill coffees and Oliver winks at her, taking a moment to smile and see that she notices him.

"That's because you learned what you know from books and the television," he continues once the waitress has laughed and touched him on the shoulder. "Now, I don't mean no disrespect because that's all Marcus Longstreet ever got. Ain't nobody heard of Pops Longstreet, but he was the best New Orleans had. Shit, he'd a been the best New York had, better than Basie, better than Tyner, me, Gil. . . ."

"Better than Duke?"

"Watch your mouth, boy. Don't you blaspheme in here." Oliver takes a long pull from his still-steaming coffee. Frank wonders how it doesn't burn the skin off his tongue, it's so hot. "Marcus was like nothin I'd ever heard or seen at that point, a real showman talkin and laughin with everybody in the room. Not like the man at Sheffield's I first saw; he played the piano. Marcus, though, he played the *room*. He sat stick-straight, sippin on liquor and maybe havin a better time than anybody else. There was a real joy in him and it came out in his music. And there I was, all of sixteen and sittin in a cramped little saloon with Mr. Fairbanks, who, I think, had to get out from under Madame's hand and knew I probably did, too. And I did. Lord, I did, and I thank him for that escape to this day. Didn't know how much I needed it until we walked into that club, neither, and that music hit me in the face like a slap. We was in New Orleans for a couple weeks while the boat resupplied, cleaned up, and signed on new passengers. That was one long stretch, though most of it, as much as I could get away with anyway, was spent at Marcus Longstreet's piano."

This isn't entirely true. Oliver spent much of that time in the Fairbankses' parlor laboring over textbooks and Madame Fairbanks's favorite book, the Holy Bible. She'd made a promise to Oliver's mother, she'd told Mr. Fairbanks, "and I can't let his lessons get away from him."

It was on those afternoons in their home, so humid and with windows open, ceiling fans barely moving the heat around, that Oliver would slip away from his books and out onto that grand and shaded porch that felt to him like a stage to the world. There, he'd take a square of corn bread wrapped in wax paper from Lucille. He'd eat that bread while Madame took her daily bath upstairs or met with her garden club in the backyard under the shade of a wisteria trellis. He would fold the paper neatly when finished and tuck it away in one of those books. He often wondered if Madame ever came across all that wax paper.

Madame disapproved of his trips to the bars with her husband, but Fairbanks insisted it was as much a part of his education as mathematics or Deuteronomy. And it was, Oliver knew. Longstreet's piano was more instructional than any dusty book off any library's shelf. His most important lesson of those weeks in New Orleans, though, began one afternoon when Oliver sneaked to the front porch, his mouth already watering for Lucille's corn bread, and was handed that oily package, not by Lucille herself but by her eighteen-year-old sister, Leona.

"She was somethin, Leona. Not so much to look at, I guess, thinkin back on it. She had dark eyes that bugged out some, and rough skin with a wide nose. But when her full lips parted to smile and she showed off her teeth, just as white as piano keys and crooked as garden path stones, son, I knew I was sunk. Thick trunk, too, just like that old oak tree out front Fontaine's house." Oliver laughs at his own words and memory. "And then she leaned out to hand me the bread and I caught sight of some flesh hangin from her apron top—she helped her sister with the wash every Thursday—and I thought I was gettin a free glimpse of heaven. I was, too, boy. Our hands touched when she passed off the bread and it was electric. She smiled again and went back inside. She smiled like she knew exactly what she'd done to my sixteen-year-old self. Christ, all I wanted to do then was go back inside and play that piano."

"What'd she do to your sixteen-year-old self, Licorice?"

"Shut up, boy; eat them home fries."

Frank looks across the table at this duo—an elderly, broke, overweight living jazz legend with diabetes and the skinniest kid Frank has ever seen. *Is this boy part of the story?* he wonders.

The very next night was the next time Oliver saw Leona, and the first time he spoke to her. It was at the bar with her brother-in-law's piano filling the room, mixing with cigarette and cigar smoke, and the laughter and call of men to women and back again. She was dancing, her body moving like pine trees against a wind. She held a highball of whiskey in one hand, its coppery color catching the low light, and a cigarette between her plum-colored lips. He watched her slide over to Marcus and expected him to tell her to go home, maybe stop the music altogether to tell her she's too young for this music, for the liquor and dancing like that. But she backed up close to him, the wide hips of a young girl already a woman swaying this way and that, and Marcus leaned into her and grinned. His smile was all teeth and squinting, and made Oliver feel happy from across the room. The music didn't stop, never did, and instead seemed to be played just for Leona. The crowd moved in around the piano, its player, and his wife's little sister until Oliver lost sight of it all so that he had only the calls of the musicians and the heat of the room to orient himself in the darkness and smoke.

And then she was sitting beside him. "What you drinkin, sugar?" Her voice carried an age beyond her years. Her body, with its scent of sweat and smoke, smelled like experience itself.

"Root beer."

"Root beer? Ha!" She threw her head back the way Marcus did when he played and let out a bark of a laugh. "Drink this." She slid her highball over to him.

He looked around and didn't see Fairbanks anywhere. Oliver picked up the glass and sniffed. The amber liquid smelled metallic, as though it had been mined from the earth just to be trapped in a bottle. He sipped and swallowed, and the pinpricks burned down his jawline and throat but were warm and comfortable in his belly. He coughed, only once, and wondered if this had the same taste and effect as his grandma Hillbillie's home brew.

"Where you from?"

"Winona."

"Winona. And in what part of the world would I find Winona?"

"Up in Mississippi."

"Mississippi? Y'all still slaves up there?"

Oliver thought of Sheffield and the hungry men standing around his mama's back door for a piece of fatback and a broken-off hunk of bread. "Mostly."

"Well, you in N'awlins now and free to be. Free to be . . . what they call you, sugar?"

"Oliver. Oliver Pleasant."

"Pleasant. Well it's right there in your name, ain't it? I'm Leona. What you do, Oliver Pleasant, besides eat my sister's corn bread and drink my whiskey? What you doin in my city?"

"Play piano on the River Star Cruise Lines with Mr. Fairbanks. We layin out, gettin back on board next week to see Memphis." Oliver sat up straighter, puffed his chest out the way his grandson would almost seventy years later, and he felt for the first time like a man seeing the world and making his own way.

"Piano, huh?" Leona got a gleam in her eye then, a near smile on her face that showed off half her crooked teeth. "Drink that up, baby, and come with me."

* * * * *

Oliver finished what was in the glass in one gulp, feeling the same pinpricks and burn, before he was being pulled across the dance floor and in and out of gyrating, sweating couples like Oliver knew from his late nights at his parents' secret dances. Leona pulled and wouldn't let go, didn't let go of his wrist even when she stopped him beside Marcus's bench.

"Cousin Marcus, this here is Master Oliver Pleasant from Winona, Mississippi—son of freed slaves and piano player on the River Star Cruise Lines," Leona said over the din of the crowd when Marcus had come to the end of his tune. "Why don't you let us see if he any good on dry land?"

Marcus stood. He was much taller than Oliver had expected. He was dressed impeccably in a steel-gray suit and bowed deeply to Oliver, taking a handkerchief from his breast pocket and making a show of dusting the bench before gesturing for Oliver to sit.

Oliver began playing with a fever after too many days of not playing at all and studying books in the shadow of the Fairbankses' piano. It had become too much for him; the wanting was a physical pain of the sort he'd felt lately lying in bed and wondering what the touch of a woman might be like, feeling his childhood urges strain against his bedclothes to reach into manhood. For the past twenty-four hours that need had found a face: Leona Thibodeaux. He played that piano for her as though she were the only person in the room. Feeling the keys at his fingertips and pedals beneath his toes was as satisfying a feeling as anything he could imagine, and he gave himself over to it, mind, body, and spirit. Oliver jumped when the horns came in to accompany him, the close report of the trumpet blast bringing him off the bench and eliciting laughs from Leona, Marcus, and Fairbanks, whom Oliver noticed just to the side of the bandstand, a whiskey in one hand and a woman in the other.

The crowd was moving again, all sway and black, jumping and hollering like the crowd he knew from Winona rather than the staid white faces of the riverboat. The cruise guests had cocktails on the upper deck every night before supper, and Oliver would play a lively number while watching the riverbanks roll by, catch glimpses of small towns in the fading light and boys out fishing for catfish. Dinner was less laid back, the diners retiring indoors to white tablecloths and black men serving with white towels draped over their forearms. Oliver's music then became background, fading into guests' semiconsciousness like the cocktails into their blood and passing fishing skiffs into the paddle wheel's long, purple wake.

This crowd, though, was alive and Oliver fed off it until he thought he'd sucked that teat dry. He finished in a flourish, his confidence from the shoutbacks and those sips of whiskey growing into its own sort of manhood right there in his belly. He wanted to impress Marcus and Fairbanks, of course, but mostly he wanted to impress Leona. Oliver had found the reason that man takes up an instrument, a paintbrush, a pen, or a hammer and nail to create something out of nothing: sex.

He stood, sweating and breathing hard as though he'd just run a marathon, to the cheers of all around him. Even Marcus wore a knowing grin. Feeding off the crowd, Oliver felt invincible, unstoppable, his own music ringing in his ears. And then Marcus sat back down and launched into the very same tune—one of Jelly Roll's—that Oliver had just finished. Marcus played it as though Jelly himself were on that bench, and when his horns came in there was no flinch, just a racing ahead, a sound so full that it lifted the entire room up over Oliver's head and spun it around. In fact, he found himself looking up at the rafters and blue smoke hanging around there; he was dizzy from the experience. He heard the laughter, he the butt of the joke. And then he laughed along with them at a lesson learned. There would be many, he knew, and they would be carried out publicly as this one had been. Lesson number one from Marcus Longstreet: *You ain't shit, boy.* Oliver laughed despite himself.

Oliver looked through the dancing, swinging masses and found Fairbanks's eyes, saw the twinkle in them as his boss raised his whiskey glass in commiseration.

Then he felt Leona's hand on his lower back, felt it slip around and into his pocket as she pressed in behind him. He felt the closeness of the crowd, her whiskey breath on his neck. He felt her hand in his pants pocket, groping, searching, and promising a lesson he'd been hurting for. It was a lesson he'd carry with him from New Orleans and into adulthood.

* * * * *

For the next few nights, Oliver and Leona managed to meet up—sometimes upstairs from the club where Marcus played in rooms meant for storage, poker, and whores, sometimes in the dark recesses of public places that make up a labyrinthine city like New Orleans. Once, right alongside St. Patrick's Church. It was a passion that grew from that first night when Leona pulled him outside, just as she'd pulled him across the dance floor to the piano. Right out into the back alley they went, where the paving stones glistened with a recent rain and the light shot silver streaks from building to building. She pushed him back against the damp wall and fell to her knees. Oliver stood stock-still, trembling, so much more nervous than he'd been to play the piano in front of a crowd. His nostrils filled with the aroma of New Orleans after hours, its refuse and spice. He looked up and could make out the few stars in a hint of sky just past the yellow back-door light and wires strung overhead. He felt her crooked teeth on him, and what he felt then, and what he would recall for days after climbing back on to that big boat to paddle upriver, was music itself. It was a feeling he swore to himself he'd never let go.

During the days, Leona went to work with Lucille, and while Madame Fontaine was at her bridge club or her garden club, Leona would ask Madame Fairbanks if that strapping boy who was staying with her might come next door to help retrieve a pot and pan from way up high. They would fall into a bed unused for decades while Lucille, unknowing, was across the house scrubbing or hanging laundry to dry out back. With the afternoon light pushing through gauzy window coverings, they were fast and passionate, and when it was over, Leona helped him tuck everything back in place, arranging his shirt and tie as though he'd done little more than reach down a pot and pan.

"That girl taught me music," Oliver says, "but it wasn't so much her touch and taste, though that's a damn big part of it. I learned what it's all about when I left that city the first time, because she was still there. She was on that dock, not makin herself known, but just a face in a sea of faces. It brought out a whole new emotion in me, one of loss, and all good music, true music, has some loss in it. Love, to be sure, and sex, whole lot a sex give it tempo and drive, but everybody knows loss and so that's what they connect with. It was somethin in my chest I didn't feel even when I left my people in Winona. It was new, like Marcus's music sounded new, like the taste of whiskey was new. And you know somethin? It was just as excitin to me as all that other shit."

"Ever see her again?" Frank says.

"Naw. Looked, but them boats was slow goin and we went way up north with all the stops along the way. Made it up to Chicago then, my first time. By the time we made it back that far south, I was a year older and then some. And I'd had plenty more of some on that trip." Oliver laughs and looks over at Winky, who's working to cut his link sausage with a butter knife. "Boy, what I tell you? Pick it up.

"Anyway, that next trip to New Orleans I didn't stay in the Fairbanks House, but with a trombone player name of Hamlet Giraud. . . ."

"He was in your quintet on the Verve recordings."

"That's right, young man, that's right. We played all over together, too—New Orleans, Cali, Chicago, Europe, right here. I met him on that boat, headed down to New Orleans 'cause he had a place in Tremé, and I crashed there. Looked around for Miss Leona but didn't see her. Marcus Longstreet still there soundin good as hell, though. He said she went over to Tallahassee see about a boy over there and he ain't seen her since. I missed that old girl, but I found plenty new."

Frank scratches in his notebook. He's becoming an even bigger fan of jazz and had been up all night reading what he could find on the subject, and on Oliver in particular. He plans to go back to the bookstore in Greenwich Village this afternoon to browse the music section for more names and facts. More than anything, though, he loves a good story and an interesting character, and his experience and novelist heart tell him when he finds them.

"You can't use none a this, can you?" Oliver says, finishing his coffee.

"May have to leave out the bit about the back alley, Oliver."

"Hmm. Damn shame."

He wishes he could use the story, that it was appropriate for a newspaper. He feels he could fill a dozen more notebooks with the history of Oliver Pleasant. He wants to know about Oliver's arrival in New York, his other female and musical conquests, whether the mysterious story behind what happened to Hamlet Giraud is true, and who the hell this kid sitting with Oliver is.

"Him? He my neighbor, Winky."

"Name ain't Winky."

Oliver laughs at what he considers their banter. It's not what he'd had with Hamlet, but he'll take any consistent call-and-response like he used to have on the bandstand.

"Can I call on you again, Oliver? Maybe we could get together and talk some more?"

"You call me anytime, young man. Come on out and see me tonight, too. Tell 'em you there for me, you on the list."

Oliver loves telling stories, loves having his mind travel back down dusty roads and debris-littered waterways to moments he'd thought were forgotten. Leona Thibodeaux. My God, that was so many lifetimes ago, he thought he'd never remember it, despite his promise to his teenage self that those weeks in New Orleans would stay with him forever. How much has happened since then? Travel, Francesca, kids, recording, fame, music, music, music . . . and yet here Leona had been this morning, right here at breakfast in New York City.

"Some things, they never gonna leave you, Winky," Oliver says to his guest after Frank takes his leave. "Good food, good drink, good woman, the right song. Never. Stick with you like them flapjacks on your ribs."

"I don't even know what you're talking about, Licorice."

"You will, son. You will."

4.

Darkness. Closeness. Noise: loud clanging like the trolley on St. Charles or her friend Ché on his cowbell—such awful rhythm for a percussionist. A beating, in and out, in and out, in and out. Steady. Agnes retreats inside herself; it's all she can do once slid into the MRI tube as she's been over and over again the past few years. "You think I'd be used to it," she'd said to the tech, but you never get comfortable with being buried alive. "Is it like being swallowed?" Sherman had asked her once when she'd returned after a trip to Tulane. Yeah. Yeah, it is. She swallows hard, knowing she has almost half an hour to go on the inside. She tastes scotch and cigarette tar on the back of her tongue, the grittiness of a fingertip full of Colgate in her teeth. *I can't believe I lay around that shitty apartment fucking and drinking shitty Starbucks coffee all morning instead of going back to my hotel,* she thinks. *Smells like a bayou cathouse in this tube. I can't believe he needs another scan.* Agnes had had all her records sent to Dr. Mundra, but, as he explained in that soothing, paternal voice of his, his preference is to have as up-to-date an image as possible.

The first time Agnes was slid into an MRI—swallowed, buried—she was sixteen years old. She'd been told that the machine was a giant magnet and asked if she had any metal inside of her. She thought then of her body as a machine with gear wheels and pistons, and the plugs and clamps she'd seen laid out on an oil-stained sheet her daddy spread on the driveway when he was taking his old truck engine apart. She thought of herself as bionic and with the invincibility of a teenager and, for the first time in a while, considered that the test might be routine, that the film might show that she was as healthy as any teen anywhere. "No," she'd answered, "no metal." Did she have any jewelry, any piercings that weren't immediately visible? "No," she said, smirking and glancing over at her mother, whose raised eyebrows showed mock horror.

She had been taken out of school midday that Friday, something almost unheard of and frowned upon so late in the school year as all focus turned to final exams—as if such benign tests were at all important. Her father had wanted to be there, but he couldn't miss work with the cost of that scan, possibly the first of many and as expensive as a small used car, he'd said. While she waited in a thin cotton gown with a pattern of ducks in flight all over it, she watched her mother behind a levee of paperwork and the tiny vertical wrinkle between her eyebrows that would grow and become permanent over the next few years while the tests showed, just as that first one would, that what was happening in her young body was anything but typical.

That first time in the machine had been the scariest. It was the unknown, except for the familiarity of nightmares, and a nascent fear of enclosed spaces and the wonder of suffocation. The tech, a thin Hispanic woman not much older than Agnes, had told her to keep her eyes closed and breathe steadily and calmly. The first thing Agnes did after the mechanical whirring and movement stopped was to open her eyes. And then she pressed the panic button and the whirring began again, pulling her from the tube. When her head finally emerged, she was looking up at Rosario. "Fuck. That," Agnes said, rising to go.

A smile spread over Rosario's face and she pushed her back gently. She spoke in a near whisper, although they were the only two in the room. "Scary as shit, huh?"

"Scarier."

"I know, baby. What you gotta do, you gotta find some happy place and go there. Close your eyes and sink down there into your mind and into whatever gives you comfort. I went into that tube a year ago"—she shrugged—"worked for me. You got one of those places? Something to calm you?" Rosario was still whispering.

Agnes nodded and Rosario patted her shoulder and reached for the button to slide her back in. Agnes held to Rosario's wrist. "What was your happy place?"

Rosario glanced back through the window and into the control room before leaning down closer to Agnes's face. "Oral sex. My boyfriend's good at it so I just went back to that in my mind."

Agnes was sent laughing into the machine and kept her eyes closed that time. She didn't know much about cunnilingus then— her boyfriends still had an adolescent focus on their own parts—so she thought of sitting on the bench next to her father as he played piano. For the next twenty-seven minutes she went through a list of songs note by note, seeing her father's hands and moving her own in her mind. Even as the clanging and pinging of the MRI's engine filled her senses and worked to push her fear to the forefront of her thinking, the music of Garland, Pleasant, Monk, Evans, and Ellington filled her head and pulled her out of harm's way. Before she knew it, her concert was over and she was being spit out again.

"Find it?" Rosario had asked, her face a blur in the white light of the open room.

Agnes nodded. "What did they find? From your MRI?"

"Migraines, no perceptible cause. I take Tylenol, try to get my boyfriend to work on me." She winked. "Hope that's all it is for you, too, baby."

* * * * *

Agnes stands on the perimeter of the Great Lawn and looks in awe at the expanse of meadow, the trees, and the grand city beyond Central Park. It is the stuff of movies and the stuff of song, and never did a melody mean so much as when she hummed it under a winter-blue sky and with a view such as this. Anytime she's left a hospital (how many have there been?), Agnes has felt the need to be outside, but never as much as after an MRI. To counteract the claustrophobia, she's walked to the park as fast as she could to lie down on her back in the grass and look up at the sky. After the cold metal, the grass under the palms of her hands and against her neck feels like life itself; the sky is a dome of cerulean and the last leaves of color tumble over her as the wind picks up. The day before, she'd needed the grittiness of the Village and a walk through Manhattan's streets to strip away the false sterility of the hospital and its odor of chemicals and industrial astringents. Today she just wants to breathe.

After her first MRI, her mother had wanted to do something special and took Agnes shopping. Her mother suggested they look for a prom dress; she was grasping then for a normal moment, for a classic, cliché mother-daughter moment because she was scared. Agnes's mother didn't know how many more of these moments she might be allowed. She didn't know if she'd have the chance to see her daughter in a college gown or to plan a wedding. Because she didn't know if she'd hold a first grandchild born to her only daughter, she wanted an afternoon of lunch and girl talk and shopping.

The idea was as out of character and out of context for the two of them as a sixteen-year-old with an incurable neurological disorder. Agnes and her tomboy ways, preferring to climb a ladder to a rooftop with her daddy or play a seventy-year-old torch song, her mother more comfortable with a clean white sheet of paper and stick of charcoal, and the mess such an afternoon of creativity might make.

But each went through with it for the other, each willing to suspend routine for an afternoon to make the other happy, until it all fell apart. She and her mama had picked out an armload of dresses at Goldsmith's department store, laughing like sisters at the different styles and wondering how Agnes's thin frame might fill one out, before carrying them back to the fitting room. In that small cube with its floor-to-ceiling door and overhead fluorescent light, the walls closed in around Agnes. She heard the clanging and whirring of the MRI tube she'd left only an hour before and believed the air had left that little room.

"What is it, Agnes? Sweetie? You look pale—are you okay?" her mother said, dropping the dress she'd been holding into a heap on the floor. "Oh, baby, you're shaking like a leaf. Agnes?"

Agnes leaned back to feel the cool mirror on her bare back. She slid down until she was crouching and hugged her arms, skin raised with gooseflesh even as sweat beaded on her forehead and across her upper lip. Her mother opened the neck hole of her T-shirt and slid it back over her daughter's head. "Agnes? Talk to me, Agnes!"

Her mind raced with possible causes for this erratic behavior. Was it an adverse reaction to the MRI, a side effect of the radiation or whatever was in there? Or was this it? The end? And she said over and over in her mind, *Please don't let this be it, please don't let this be it.*

"Mama?" Agnes said, as evenly and coolly as she could, her eyes closed and her right hand trembling as much as her left.

"Yes, baby? You okay?"

"Mama, open the door."

"But your shirt. Here, let me slip it over your arms."

"The door, Mama."

"Okay, okay."

When her mother opened the dressing room door, Agnes shot out like a bullet, running into the prom dress department, past shoes and accessories, through menswear, and out the door into the parking lot. Her T-shirt flapped behind her like a cape around her neck, her bare torso attracting stares from people uncertain of her gender. By the time her mother found her, Agnes was sitting on the hood of their car chewing at a hangnail. Her mother leaned back against the car and they both stared off at the department store doors in the distance.

"I didn't like those dresses," Agnes said, and they both fell into laughter.

They told Agnes's father the story at dinner and he laughed with them until tears came to his eyes, both at the comedy of his daughter streaking through Goldsmith's and the tragedy of his daughter inside a medical machine—and, too, for the fear of the unknown. He didn't laugh at all when his wife told him later that the boy who had asked Agnes to prom had backed out. Teenagers could be cruel, and when word got around that Agnes was having tests done in a hospital, and classmates noticed that her left hand never stopped quivering, rumors of cancer and AIDS and sickness and contagion and everything else children don't know a damn thing about scared that boy off. He came up with an excuse not to go, though Agnes heard he was at the dance with a girl from Dyer County, a girl who may not have heard that he might already be infected.

Her father did finally laugh to himself, however, one day that summer when he came across that boy's prized, restored Mustang at the Hatchie bottoms where kids went to ride four-wheelers and drink, and he slipped it into neutral and eased the front end of that car into the river.

Agnes thinks of all of this now, here, on her back in Central Park. She wishes her daddy were with her, wishes he could have heard Oliver Pleasant play last night. She thinks of how much she's looking forward to hearing him play again tonight. Andrew said he'd reserve a table for her, though he looked hurt by her eagerness, knowing it wasn't for him but for Oliver. Such a soft boy. So many feelings worn right there on his sleeve, tattooed across his thin wrists. She should feel guilty for accepting such kindness even though there are no feelings for Andrew, but she's behaved worse, she supposes.

She suddenly realizes that Landon will probably be calling soon. She still smells Andrew on her and needs to shower, too. She should go. "Just a few more minutes," she says, and stares up at one lonely cloud making its way across the sky, then closes her eyes to it all.

Frank sits on the bed in his hotel room and types the notes from his morning interview with Oliver. He laughs to himself remembering stories of Leona and Madame Fairbanks and wishes he had someone here to share them with. Oliver and the boy were an odd pair; he makes a note of the way Oliver treated him like a doting, though distant, grandfather might. He made the kid eat his eggs and sausage, handing him a napkin and ordering him to wipe his mouth, but then would seem to forget the kid was there beside him for some time while telling lurid stories.

After breakfast, with Oliver's gravelly voice and laughter still in his head, Frank had walked back to the bookstore to see what was on the shelves regarding jazz. "Do you believe in fate?" the old man said from behind the counter when Frank walked in. He was sitting at a wooden desk piled high with paper invoices, catalogues, reference books, and a tall stack of novels at his elbow that he went through one by one, taking notes on them in a yellow legal pad.

"Fate?" Frank said once he'd found the source of the voice among the clutter. "Yeah, sure. I guess."

"I saw you at Pleasant's gig last night."

"You were there? I didn't see you."

"You were busy talking with Davis McComber; I didn't want to interrupt."

"You know Davis?"

"Sure, sure. He's a customer. Good writer, too."

"He is, and young. Did you enjoy the show?"

"Oh, sure, I've never been disappointed. And I sat, as it happens, with the other Memphian—a gracious young lady."

"Is that right? Weird. I'll do you one better: I just left Oliver. I was interviewing him for a story."

"Newspaperman? As endangered a species as jazz artist. As rare in the wild as a seller of books."

"You don't have to tell me; I was laid off last month. This is freelance work."

"No shame there, young man. Talent is talent regardless of the medium."

Frank has *Wikipedia*, of course, and can summon up any artist with full bio and audio clips with the click of a mouse, but he still enjoys flipping through books and the thrill of not knowing what he might find on the next page. As he walks through the bookstore slowly, pulling out books and taking his time finding the section labeled "Music," he appreciates the heft and density of the objects on the shelves. He values the effort that someone put into researching and committing a biography to paper; it is something that can't be changed at the whim of someone else, somewhere else, with their own click of an anonymous mouse. A book is as permanent as our past, as lasting as ink.

As it happened, the music section was large, more than Frank had hoped for, and situated against the far wall from the front counter and door. Frank stood in front of it, staring up at vertical and horizontal spines, some books as large as coffee tables and others mere pamphlets. Bare, World War II–era brick was visible through gaps in blues, opera, and rock and roll. His eyes drifted to the street through the large plate-glass window speckled with flyers advertising readings, poetry slams, and music revues to passersby. The wind had picked up and he watched a small cyclone whip down Bleecker and lift leaves and trash, tossing them into the air before laying them all down again on the hood of a cab. The driver looked irritated, more at the fact that there was no one to blame than for the mess itself. Something was blowing in out there.

"Looks like snow," Lucchesi called from across the store.

Frank had asked about the other Memphian. A young woman, Lucchesi had told him. "Young and pretty, though pale, as if she might benefit from an afternoon outdoors."

"What does she do?" A reporter's questions are like a chef's knives or a cop's pistol, always there by his side and at the ready; always sharp, always loaded.

"Didn't say, though she loves the music. Perhaps she's a musician herself?"

"Here alone?"

"Appeared to be, at least she was last night, though the waiter seemed taken with her. I don't believe I'm so old as to have overlooked that."

"Are you a longtime fan of Pleasant's?"

"Oh my, yes. His wife as well, I guess you could say. I used to sell her books. Francesca Pleasant was a voracious reader."

"She died, didn't she?"

"Yes, twenty-two years ago."

Lucchesi had slipped away from him then, through the transom of the door, taken away on the brisk air blowing through the streets like a wind tunnel. He'd gone back in time someplace where Frank wasn't invited, left the bookshop with only a shell where his body had been. It didn't take an investigative reporter to see that there was something more than books and music between this man and the Pleasants.

"You were close?" Frank said, bringing the old man back to the shop, but slowly, allowing him to lower himself to the floor at his own speed.

Lucchesi smiled and his blue eyes twinkled a bit behind his glasses. "It shows?"

"Most people would have simply said 'about twenty years.' I'm sorry to pry; it's none of my business."

The old man looked to the windows as if Francesca might be there. "She was lonely, Oliver was gone a lot. She seemed to take refuge in her books, as though the characters were more than just paper and print. They'd become her friends, I believe."

"And so had you?"

He nodded and puckered his mouth in further thought. "We had a common interest in literature and we both believed in the magic of good writing to take one away. My wife had passed only a few months before Francesca began coming in, and conversation was easy; we were both lonely. We talked about books, of course, and our favorite authors. The talk led to a weekly coffee at a little shop that used to be next door, and that soon became twice weekly. It was more than a year before I invited her to my apartment just around the corner. Even there we were slow, still talking about books and her children or my late wife, even Oliver and music. It was another month before we both summoned up the courage to go to bed. It's a short distance, it turned out, from the magic of literature to the magic of love."

Frank's scalp was tingling with the story and the pain in Lucchesi's voice. He was touched and thought then of Karen and the distance between them. "You loved her?"

Lucchesi nodded and removed his glasses, wiping his eyes. "And she loved Oliver. And her children, her family. But he spent a lot of time away, months at a time, and, as I said, she was lonely. Oh, I don't mean to say I was *used* only for physical intimacy. There were feelings there, very real feelings, but she never would have left her husband. Even when that woman came from France and threatened everything that Francesca held dear, she didn't leave him. And I knew that, I understood. She filled a void for me, just as I did for her. We became such close friends and were in love on some level. I miss her now."

"Did he ever find out?"

Lucchesi shook his head and put his glasses back on. "I don't claim to understand what happened between Oliver and Francesca. Sure, there were stories of him on the road, of musicians a long way from home—everyone's heard them. Francesca heard them and dealt with them in her own way. It wasn't my place to interject or let him know how his wife spent her time. The man is a great musician and, I believe, a good man. He was lost for a time, but who isn't?

"And all this, by the way, is off the record. Both for your story and for general knowledge. I hope you'll respect the wish of an old man, and a long-deceased woman?"

"Of course. But, I'm curious, the French woman who you said 'threatened everything that Francesca held dear'? Who was that?"

Lucchesi smiled again. "The intrepid reporter. That, I'm afraid, is not a tale for me to tell. But I wish you luck with your story, young man."

Later that day, Frank lies across his bed on top of the spread and thumbs through an encyclopedia of jazz published in 1967. Like cutting through an old-growth tree, he believes he's found a ring closest to the fire with this tome written while so many of the players were still playing, still so alive. He turns to the *P*s and there he is: *Pleasant, Oliver (1921–); b. Wynona* [sic], *MS; performed with* . . . and they're all there. Dizzy, Teagarden, Armstrong, Billie, Coltrane, Miles, Cannonball, Hawkins . . . the list goes on.

He flips through a biography of Thelonious Monk, a newer book thick with the thrill of genius and chronology. Oliver and Monk wouldn't have played together on the same stage, of course, but Frank has always been fascinated by the latter's eccentricities. *Solo Monk* was one of the first jazz albums Frank ever bought. The first, thank God, was *Kind of Blue*. Without Miles Davis's record,

Frank may never have stuck with jazz. He was raised on his parents' Beatles and Motown. His father had a thing for Chuck Berry and that led Frank to the Stones. Hendrix came a bit later, followed by Led Zeppelin and Van Morrison. He moved through punk fairly rapidly and took from it the Clash and the Velvet Underground. New wave was a lean trend for him, but Elvis Costello saw him through it until he landed on the other side with REM, U2, and the Cure.

Jazz, though, took a concerted effort. It was sought out. He'd heard it, as people do these days, in the background, at weddings or in department stores. It was the sound track of film and passed by somewhere on the lower end of the radio dial. But along with college and his want of creativity and his newfound passion for writing came a curiosity and craving for knowledge. So he snuck away from his friends and their Nirvana and Pearl Jam to a used record store down the Highland Strip and picked out names he'd heard . . . where? Someplace over the years. Everywhere, it seemed, once he saw those names on album sleeves: Miles Davis, Dave Brubeck, John Coltrane, and Thelonious Monk.

He closes the book and lies back on the bed. He hefts it up to feel the weight of it, opens it and sniffs (he'd done this in the store as well, before he'd even paid for it), and then places it on his chest. He can feel his heartbeat against it. He looks over to his laptop, still open, and at the letters there on the open document, that crisp white "page." *Times New Roman, 12 pt.* The type crawls across the page like insects. He reaches back over his head to find his phone among the pillows and presses Karen's icon. It rings and he waits and he knows it isn't her he's thinking of, but the novel sitting on an unused desk in an unused room of the unused second floor of his house. He thinks of what Lucchesi had said about "the magic of good writing to take one away" and the power some people, Frank included, place in books.

"We had a habit, Francesca and I," Lucchesi had said, not wanting to end his reverie, just as one might want a favorite novel to go on and on, for those characters to live long after the book is shut. "In the books I gave her, not those she purchased of her own accord, but the ones that I personally chose from my shelves or sought out at other bookstores and from scouts and dealers, I would inscribe with a small 'ML' in a top corner of the inside cover. And she would, upon finishing the book, put her 'FP' on the final page. Whatever was in between, I suppose, whatever world had been created and populated by those characters, belonged to us. It was silly, really, but I like to think of those books, of our initials and our stories, living on today, long after she's gone."

It isn't silly, Frank told him. Reading and literature had brought the shopkeeper and Francesca Pleasant together, two people who were lost and lonely in the world. They had brought Frank and Karen together as well. Fiction, the landscape of make-believe and romance and fantasy, is a force to reckon with and still makes Frank's heart beat quickly when he considers what it might all mean for him.

He first met Karen in the bar near the university. It was the early nineties and she'd worn a flannel shirt tied around her waist and a Nirvana T-shirt—the uniform of the day. She's tall and her height was what he'd first noticed, followed by her hair, strawberry blond hanging down her back and over one eye. He and his friends sat at a small table crowded with empty beer bottles and spent cigarettes, talking of the future and past as if those bottles and cigarettes held the answers. He noticed her when she'd pass by, combat boots heavy on the tile floor, on her way to the restroom. She went a lot.

"I wanted you to notice me," she told him later. "I'd go in there and stand around, check my makeup, and read graffiti—the other girls probably thought I was some kind of pervert—and then I'd hold my breath as I walked past you again, just hoping you'd look my way."

"I figured it for a urinary-tract infection," he'd said, and they both laughed. "Either way, I guess it worked."

That semester was filled with laughter. Frank and Karen would walk the train tracks from the bar, past the university, to the sloping lawn behind the water-pumping station. Karen told him she liked the old building with its soaring windows and WPA-era art deco ornaments. She told him she was majoring in accounting because it's what her father did—"Figures and sums are the family business." But she had a streak of color in her, a coppery stream that cut through the unmoving stone of mathematics and statistics. That stream floated art and music and literature. She had a nascent interest in abstract paintings and alternative music, and a great love for Jane Austen and nine-teenth-century prose. Frank helped to guide her, channeled that stream just as his high school love had for him—through easy conversation both in and out of bed.

His high school girlfriend had left him for a greater love—edu-cation, and Sarah Lawrence College. A long-distance relationship wouldn't work, she'd said, and he'd taken her on her word just as he'd trusted her in all else. Even as he moved on with his life, he ached for her. She left him, but left him with a greater understand-ing of who he was.

It was Karen who showed him who he wanted to be. They would lie back in the grass, the motors from the pumping sta-tion vibrating the ground beneath them, and look down at their school, and they would talk of writing and literature and very little of accounting. They would kiss and touch and he would find the courage to say, "I want to be a writer."

Karen, with a warmth spreading through her chest, would encourage him, wallow in this dream with him as though they were skinny-dipping in the water that flowed behind and below them. "But you should be a reporter, finish journalism school," she said, her bloodline of net pay and bottom lines still coursing through her newly engorged heart. Neither could have predicted the slow crumbling of the fourth estate in their new springtime of love.

In the bar, on the lawn, in her dorm and his apartment, they grew closer, made love, dreamed, and planned. They became inseparable and married only weeks after graduation. He began a novel that same summer, it coming to him in bits and pieces on their drive to the Gulf Coast for a honeymoon. He stayed up late nights typing on an electric typewriter in their small apartment in Midtown Memphis. She went to work for her father's firm and Frank was hired as a copy clerk for *The Commercial Appeal*. When he was eventually hired as a reporter, he saw it as a stepping-stone that would lead him to a larger market or a career as a novelist. He never expected to be there seventeen years later, still as a reporter. He never expected to earn less than Karen, who worked the corporate world as though she were fly-fishing, tugging a line here, dropping bait there, until she'd hooked some of the grander species in the small pond of Memphis. Neither had he expected to be unemployed in his forties.

He *had* expected to finish that novel, and she'd expected to have a baby.

When the first miscarriage occurred, Karen had been devastated. It had taken so long just to get pregnant that she believed she was owed that baby. The early days of pregnancy were spent planning and dreaming and took them both back to those warm spring days on the hill of the pumping station behind the university. They even went there one afternoon with cheese and bread to lie on a blanket and take turns pressing their eager palms to Karen's newly inhabited belly. They volleyed names back and forth—literary names from their favorite novels, musical names from a decade, five decades before. They were run off by a security guard like a couple of college kids, laughing and stumbling down the hill.

When she lost it, when the hummingbird heartbeat had stopped, so did the dreams, the plans. Frank would try to engage Karen, suggesting she read a newly released book or one of her old Jane Austen friends, but she waved him off, saying she had work to do. She seemed annoyed by his constant need for music in every room of the house or the way he could disappear into thought and take notes on scraps of paper or napkins about what he found there in his mind.

They would try again. And again. There were two more pregnancies lost, each met with lower and lower expectations. Those lowered expectations seemed to extend to each other, and one another's needs, over time. Frank still loved Karen with all he had, and she him, but it was a love emptied of passion and spontaneity. As empty as the second floor of their house, as empty as the unfinished nursery and the sheet of paper still scrolled into Frank's college typewriter.

"Hello?"

He's calling from habit and out of a sense of obligation, and he'd hoped to let the phone ring until just before Karen's voice mail picked up, knowing she'd see he called. He puts the phone back to his ear. "Hey! I was about to hang up. What're you doing?"

"Working. Where are you?"

"Hotel. Typing up notes from an interview this morning."

"Oscar?"

"Oliver. Yeah, interesting guy. Where're you?"

"On my way to a client's."

"Which?"

"Spillman."

"Hey, little lady." He says it as caricature in a growly, musky voice.

"That's the one. I'm late, can I call you back?"

"Yeah. I'll be going to his show again, but it won't be until later."

"I'll be going to bed early anyway."

"Feeling bad?"

"A little nauseous. Hormones don't agree with me so much."

Hormones. She's started a round of shots again. *Dammit,* he thinks. *I forgot.* "Two shots so far, huh? Since yesterday?"

"Yep. I'm all hopped-up, crazy and pukey as ever. So come on home so you can get some of this." It's Karen's way of making light of the situation, but it always leaves Frank in an awkward place. He never knows what to say when she detours down that road, whether to console or play along. But he always tries, and usually to disastrous effect.

"I'll want some by the time I get back."

"It'll take you that long?" Karen is always quicker and always more vicious.

"I'm ready now," he says, trying to salvage this, trying to climb his way up. "I'll be ready tonight if you want to get a little dirty online." He says this yet finds his mind is wandering, not to their bedroom but just down the hall, up the stairs of their house, and into the office he hasn't entered in months. He's sitting at the desk and there it is: a clean white sheet of typing paper.

"Too sick, like I said. Sorry."

He is relieved. Relief is not the feeling he wants to have, but it is the one that emerges and he breathes easier.

"Here I am," she says. "I'm late so I really do need to go."

"Okay. I'll talk to you soon. Love you."

"Bye."

6.

Guests are filing in and Ben signals to Marcie to get off of her phone. She turns her back to him and continues her low-volume argument. Ben shows a couple to their table. He should fire Marcie, he knows, for a myriad of reasons, but it is an asset, he also knows, to have guests greeted at the door by those breasts and then escorted to a table by that ass. Marcie is as much a decoration and fixture as the deco wall sconces and ornate millwork on the bar.

"What is it you're waiting on?" Ben asks Andrew as he crosses back to the hostess stand. Andrew is leaning against the bar and staring at the door with a steaming cup of coffee at his elbow.

"What? Nothing, just watching the customers."

"She's coming back tonight?"

"Yeah."

"Does she know your auspicious beginnings yet?"

"Shut it, Ben."

Though Andrew Sexton knows who to ask for when he enters the hushed womb of Brooks Brothers, he never goes there anymore. He knows where and how to order off-menu from Midtown to Chelsea to SoHo. His favorite restaurant, though, serves Vietnamese off the books from a converted apartment over a donut shop in Alphabet City. If he ever needs to get someplace, a car service could be at his door in minutes, yet he's memorized the subway and crosstown bus schedules.

Andrew Sexton was raised among privilege, attending the best schools and running with the most starched of Upper West Side boys and girls. His grooming was looked after and impeccable, and he was raised to take over the investment banking of his father and his father before him. It is a pedigree that boasts founding fathers of banks, foundations, a city, and a country. Andrew wants none of it. "What is it you want, Andrew?" a girl once asked him, a lily-white girl of seventeen in her pink bedroom with fresh linens and a view of Central Park. She was astride young Andrew in name-brand bra and panties, but she wasn't talking about sex. She knew Andrew wanted her—they all did. She wanted to know what he wanted from life, what he might provide her from those steel and glass buildings at the southern tip of her island. She ran the manicured nail of a long finger down his hairless teenage chest and asked again: "What is it you want?"

"I'm going to be an artist."

It was the answer she wasn't expecting; it was the first time he'd said it out loud and surprised even himself when it came from his lips. It would be the last thing anyone expected to hear from a Sexton. And what sort of artist? They would ask. Fine arts? Studies in Rome and Paris? Days spent copying the masters in the Louvre and Florence's Uffizi Gallery, champagne-filled nights in the arms of a baroness? That was all acceptable, though barely—a distraction and hobby for his early years. Abstract expressionism? A bit more difficult to swallow, to convince Mother and Father's friends that it is worthwhile. A rogue figure in the family, yet manageable with a loft in SoHo that is both residence and studio, and a white-walled gallery in Chelsea selling his work for the cost of one of those Brooks Brothers suits. Perhaps a profile in the *Times*' Arts and Leisure section, certainly a mainstay on page six.

"What sort of artist, Andrew?" that young, nubile kept-woman-in-waiting asked.

"A tattoo artist."

All hope is lost. The suits, the restaurants, the cars, the business, the legacy. He has brothers—the legacy of name isn't an issue—but where did it all go wrong? The schools were the best money could buy, as were the friends. The blood, certainly, is top tier. A tattoo artist? "Why, I've never heard of such a thing," his mother said. "No son of mine . . . ," his father blustered. And Andrew, to his credit, didn't ask for suits or food or cars. He didn't ask for help. He didn't even ask for their understanding. Andrew Sexton, of the Upper West Side Sextons, instead held a series of restaurant jobs, paying for his own art lessons, equipment, rent, and board. While a large sum of money sat in trust until he "came to his senses," Andrew was sucked into a whirlpool of drugs and hustling, living for a time off what he could steal or scrounge, and still he didn't go back to his family. Two years were spent in the gutter, making his way from tattoo parlor to tattoo parlor, offering to sweep up or wash windows for an apprenticeship. He'd keep one job for a while before losing it when he showed up to work high, or not at all. Despite the snowstorm of cocaine and, later, heroin, he learned a thing or two. He practiced and got better before losing a week or more to the streets, having to work—or steal—twice as hard to buy his tattoo rig back from hock.

It was a low time for Andrew, the lowest being a four-month stint at Rikers, a fortress his parents probably didn't even know existed. It cleaned him up for a time, but he scored soon after release. Soon after that release, while sleeping days away on a concrete ledge beneath the Manhattan Bridge, he went to work for Ben Greenberg, washing dishes and taking out trash. Ben saw more to the boy than such work, and he also recognized the stench of despair and hopelessness. He reached out and rescued Andrew; the heart of Ira Greenberg still beat within his son.

Ben pulled Andrew up and out of the sewer, cleaned him off, and cleaned him out. He stayed after him to go to AA meetings, to get out in the fresh air of parks, and to work toward his goals. Ben knew talent, not only when he heard it onstage but also when he saw it on a canvas, whether that canvas held oils or was a scar on skin. By staying clean and staying employed, Andrew was able to make new friends, a different sort of friend than he'd ever known—true friends—and he became happy again. It was a happiness not even his father's money could buy; he'd found it on his own. He tried to keep his pasts—both of them—from these friends because he didn't want to know if they were or were not the kind that money could buy, or the type who would run from weakness.

Andrew, of course, didn't marry the girl in the pink bra and panties. A tattoo artist? She was having none of that in her perfect future, though she did that day. It was the best sex she would have for years to come, while leaving Andrew with a taste for something more exotic.

He watches the door like a puppy waiting for his master to return home. It has been five years since that girl asked what he wanted and he's coming close to getting it, working by day for a tattoo parlor in Times Square, inking "I ♥ NY" and "9/11—Never Forget" on tourists. He feels he was on the right track, so close, and then he met Agnes Cassady and now he has a whole new want. *Day to day,* he thinks to himself. *That's how things change.* If he could go back in time and again find himself beneath that perfect and poised girl going moist atop him, he would say, "I want to be an artist, and I want *Agnes.*"

* * * * *

Andrew greets her before she's completely seated, having been shown to her table by Marcie, who gives him a bored look. "Hey," he says, words failing him. This is new for Andrew, a young man who, though he's shaken the ornamentation of status from his surface and had it scrubbed with asphalt streets and broken concrete, can't rid himself of the confidence that comes with wealth. It soaked into his skin like summer sun during a childhood spent in the Hamptons and on tennis courts along the Hudson. Yet in the presence of Agnes, whose indifference he finds so alluring, worn on her collarbone like a fragrance, he has trouble with the simplest greeting. "Good day?" He's missed her, longed for her the minute she'd left his tiny apartment, leaving him alone in his warm, damp sheets.

He doesn't hear her reply; she appears to shrug, to toss her hair, to rub her bare shoulders for warmth. It is all exhilarating to him. "You left pretty quick this morning," he says.

"I was late."

"Meeting?"

She shrugs again. "Scotch? Please?" She puts Andrew Sexton back in his place.

The room is at capacity again. A buzz fills Agnes's ear. It's the excitement and music of the previous nights that has managed to penetrate Manhattan's thick concrete crust, calling to people who want to know for themselves what forces have been moving beneath the surface of their streets and their safe day-to-day lives. Her attention is drawn to the door, where Marcie is turning away a party of four. The man, the leader of his pack, is irate. He is obviously not used to being told no. Marcie, also obviously, is taking great pleasure in being the first to do so.

Despite the standing-room-only crowd, there is the same large, empty table beside Agnes's that has been there the past two nights. The small "Reserved" placard in the center acts as a beacon for the angry silverback at the door who gestures toward it. He is finally intercepted by the bearded man in sandals and directed back outside.

For Agnes, it's the music. Always the music. She hasn't come to New York for the pageantry, to gaze upon the fashions and fashionable or to drink in the elixir of celebrity. The music, ever since she was old enough to reach the keys from a piano bench, has been her life force. In those earliest days, the sound of the piano was intertwined with the closeness of her father. Memories of his music from that bench and his smell of coffee and sawdust are all the same to her. It's what she missed the most back at home for the funeral. She sat on the bench in the family room of the old farmhouse playing the slow numbers that were her father's favorites. She slowed them down another half step for the day. Still dressed in cemetery black, her mother sat beside her. Agnes laid her head on her mother's thin shoulder and they both cried silently while Agnes played, the music the embodiment of a husband and father who had left the room too soon.

The two women had traveled to downtown Memphis, whisked away from Tipton County and the buzz of cicadas by a Town Car, to a white-tablecloth restaurant and Landon Throckmorton. He charmed her mother, rising when she arrived and gently kissing the back of her hand. He expressed remorse for the passing of her husband and asked after him, and he listened intently and genuinely as Agnes and her mother traded stories.

Her mother described a simple man, a handyman by trade who was good with his hands. She'd meant at his work and the way he could repair anything, but she blushed all the same. She spoke proudly of her husband, unashamed of his simplicity or his work measured more in the sweat of his brow than any pay by the hour.

Agnes told Landon that the evenings were her favorite when he'd come home from a long, hot day of patching rotted windowsills and changing locks. He was tired, his hands mottled with paint or grease, and he'd sit at the secondhand Cable-Nelson console piano and play tunes by McCoy Tyner or Bill Evans.

"How was work, Daddy?" Agnes was always on the bench beside him as his head would sway, tilted back just a bit. Sometimes he closed his eyes.

"Crows cawing."

"What about?"

"Don't matter, just listening to themselves. Each one trying to be louder than his neighbor. Look at me! Look at me!" He'd imitate a bird, flapping his arms out to the sides like wings and nudging Agnes, who giggled in delight. She could picture her staid and heavily rouged piano instructor perched on the music stand in her conservatory, shrieking like the big blackbirds that alighted on the barn where Agnes's father kept his tools and the small, green tractor he used to mow the lawn.

Her daddy played soft on those evenings, maybe to counter the volume of his day spent with ripsaws and hammers, and the incessant complaints and demands of his clients. Agnes liked it. Loud or soft, she loved listening to him play.

Agnes was as grateful to Landon for the night out and her mother's much-needed distraction as she was for the passage to Memphis and all else he'd arranged. But her mother questioned Agnes's relationship with the older man later at home as the two women lay curled in Agnes's parents' bed watching a late-night talk show. "Friend," Agnes said. "Sometime employer."

On the train back to New Orleans, she sat cross-legged on the bunk of the train compartment and watched him as he read, just as he had for the entirety of the trip to Memphis. Her book, one suggested and loaned by him, lay open in her lap while she watched this man, almost fifty years her senior, and wondered what he wanted, what the needs might be for a man who seemed to have everything. She grew restless and left the compartment to walk the length of the train, stopping periodically to sit in vacant coach seats and stare out of windows at passing towns that vanished into thin air, she imagined, as soon as they flew from sight.

Landon had brought a bottle of wine and they shared that back in the compartment, watching the kudzu-covered trees and lamp-posts glide by. They discussed Memphis and New Orleans and all that lay between the two. Landon never touched her on the train, never asked for more than conversation and company.

To grow so close to a man without the inevitable physical play was anathema to Agnes, who collects men and wears them like a carnival mask—not to hide who she is from others but to show herself who she might be. The doctor's wife one week, a long week-end as the judge's girl, the mistress of a venture capitalist, and play-thing to a chef. She's had them all. She gathers them in and holds on to them until she's finished. And by then, they want her. They want to hold to her, to lock her in a room to play piano for them, to love them like their wives or girlfriends or boyfriends can't, or won't. She doesn't need them; she needs the music and the fleeting feeling of being in control. She wants to be an adult while she can, to learn what it might be like to be married to any one of them just as her mother wanted to know what it was like to shop for a prom dress with her daughter and to give her away as a bride.

It's a normalcy Agnes feels is due her. She'll be dead by the time she's twenty-five. This she knows. How? From a dream. A premonition. A high priestess in a low place along oily voodoo streets of New Orleans who reminded Agnes of the things that come to a person in and out of hospitals, lonely in those exam-ination rooms or as a budding teen when ostracized by her peers. Holding to any one of these men for too long—for a month or a season—would mean giving them a lifetime: her life. She wants experiences, craves the myriad spices, tastes, and sensations. Dr. Mundra can't help her, none of them can; only her own will and curiosity can make her whole.

Now, as Agnes sits in the bar at the Capasso, Andrew aches for her. He watches her, taking in her bare calf and the way her shoe hangs from her toes. He wants those legs wrapped around him again. She flips her hair to look back at the front door and he lets slip a moan from his throat for the tendons there, bending and twisting with her backward glance. In her hand is the scotch and he sees the slight ripple of the glass, the faintest vibration he'd noticed that morning in his bed as her hand moved down his chest, his stomach, and between his legs. He can't purge the memory of this woman's body and touch and smell from his mind.

And she knows it. Agnes can feel his gaze on her and it only makes her less inclined to look for him among the crowd. But she does wonder where he is, and as she scans the room back to the front door for any sign of Oliver, she lets her eyes wander to the periphery. *There he is, by the bar waiting on a drink order but watching me. Sweet boy.* She wonders how lonely she is, whether she'll go back for more tonight, though this time it would have to be in her hotel room and not the dungeon of his flat. She can almost see them together once again, feel his weight on her, moving more and more quickly, when suddenly the piano catches her by surprise. It's something slow and light played in C. Where had he been? She's been watching intently for Oliver Pleasant but hadn't seen him at his booth or crossing the room. She'd been distracted by her tattooed lover. She decides to forget Andrew Sexton for now, for the duration of this tune, this show. She'll decide on him later, after the music has washed over and through her. That might, once again, be all she needs.

* * * * *

When the set is over, it's the bearded man in sandals who brings a scotch to Agnes. She sees up close that his beard is shot through with gray and he wears a small gold hoop earring. He smiles familiarly as he greets her. "My name is Ben Greenberg and this is my club. My friends call me Benji." He offers his hand and she takes it, noticing the small tattoo of a music note on his wrist. She feels nothing at all for this man and can sense it is mutual, and she is at once relieved and at ease. "I've seen you here every night of Oliver's show," he continues. "I can't get busboys to show up so regularly."

"I'm here for Mr. Pleasant, for the music."

"We all are. Would you like to meet him?"

"Oh, I couldn't. He seems tired tonight."

"I'm sure he is. You're a musician, right? A pianist?"

"How did you know that? I mean, I do play piano, but not in New York, not like Pleasant."

"One doesn't spend as long in this business as I have without being able to recognize a player. Come on, let's get you over there, Ollie always has time for a fellow musician."

Ben introduces her to Oliver Pleasant, who sits like a boulder, a backdrop to the still life of Campari, foreign cigarettes, and silver lighter in front of him. He beckons her to sit and thanks Ben, who makes his way to another table.

"Where you from, Miss Cassady?" Oliver says.

"Memphis?"

He blows a tired stream of smoke. "Is that right?"

"Well, Tipton County, just outside Memphis. Close enough to smell the barbecue, though."

"Memphis. You know that young man there? The one with the notebook? He from Memphis, too."

She follows the direction of his index finger across the dimly lit room. "No. No, I don't know that man."

Oliver manages a smile and says it again. "Memphis. W. C. Handy . . . The Peabody Hotel."

"Now those I know. Yes sir."

"What you doin in Manhattan?"

She shrugs, glances sideways, and sips at her scotch in the same manner as she'd noncommittally answered Andrew's question earlier. But Oliver is more worldly and has communed with women in faraway places, and he knows when an answer isn't.

"Ain't nobody's business. You like the show?"

"Like it? It's been wonderful, every night of it." She wants to tell him that she plays piano as well, that she grew up with her father playing Pleasant's songs and that hearing them again, here, live, is like having her daddy back, if only for a night. She wants to thank him for those songs, for what he's given the world. She feels all of these things bubbling up in her, but Oliver is some-place else, looking down at the smoke as it curls off his cigarette. "It means a lot to me to be here," she finally manages, gulping from her glass and looking for a passing waitress, Andrew, or Benji to have it refilled—even Marcie at this point, such is her discomfort with being here while Oliver so clearly is not.

It's the same beat and weary look that was in his eyes when he'd taken the stage earlier. He'd sat there alone and merely played with a few keys in C here and there, pushing at them like a child with a plate of unrecognizable food, not knowing if it might taste good or even be edible. He talked in circles; he spoke low so that the crowd hushed with him, not completely mute, but respect-fully quiet so they could hear what it was he was talking about. He talked about books and about California; he spoke of cold-water flats and babies and loss. The words meandered as much as the tune until the melody finally started to coalesce, as did the talk, and he spoke of his wife.

He said he'd married so long ago, he believed that maybe he'd always been so. "I been knowin her forever," he said. "I ain't never not known her, but I lost her and that feels new to me, like it just happened this night. Wish she was here. Lord, I wish for that. Wish they all was." The tune took more shape, like a balloon filling with air, and there was a palpable fear in the room that it might overfill and destroy itself. Agnes had seen the man in sandals—the man she now knows as Benji—standing close by, his eyes on his friend. The song was so slow and beautiful that Agnes had only wanted to put her head down on the table and close her eyes to it. "I brought

Francesca back from Sacramento, California, and married her. That was a beautiful week for me and I wrote this here song for it, for her. Guess I ain't played it since she left us. When was that? Benji, baby, you know? You recall? Today? Was it today or was it two decades ago? Let's see now if I can get this song out, see how she goes." The room had quieted more so that even the servers stopped, and it was understood by everyone that they would wait on drinks and food. The silence was such that even the kitchen seemed to have halted its industrial gears.

When he'd finished, he'd pushed his porkpie back on his round head and mopped his brow, his chin, his eyes with that blindingly white handkerchief. No one applauded because it wasn't for anyone else. This was Oliver talking to Francesca, and there only happened to be a room full of people by accident, a room full of people giving those two their moment together. The band stood just off-stage and seemed to await his invitation to enter that space of the piano. The horns held their instruments in folded arms and each of them bowed in reverent silence until Oliver nodded to them, and only then did they join him.

And when they did, Oliver led them in a wild swing as though to shake the sadness from his mind and air out the room, as though it would shake the plaster from the walls and ceiling. Those young guns on horns, drums, and bass sucked wind for the better part of an hour trying to keep up with that old man.

Now, in his booth, a neglected cigarette burning down to ash and Campari going to water in his glass, he still looks as though he's with Francesca someplace, maybe back in Sacramento or up in that cold-water flat. He looks to Agnes as though it's exhausted him, all of it—the frenetic pace, the long hours, the booze, and the memories.

"You play?" He says from nowhere, as though that's what he's been wondering as he sat there in silence.

"Oh, well, a little, yeah. My daddy played and I took lessons as a kid."

"That's nice. Nice. Jazz?"

"That's what my daddy played, yes sir. I was raised on it, all the best—Bill Evans, Brubeck, McCoy Tyner, Duke, Peterson, Basie . . . you."

"That's fine, real fine. You got to have that foundation and it sound like your daddy did right by you. He still with us?"

"My daddy? No sir. He died a couple years ago while I was down in New Orleans. That's where I live now, playing in the Quarter and places."

"New Orleans you say?" He seems to perk up at this and she notices his slight gesture to a passing waitress at Agnes's empty glass. "I spent some time in New Orleans now, yes ma'am. Good times."

"Did you live there?"

"Well, no, not so I had an address or nothin, but I think we all live there, part of all us musicianers. Don't you think? Ain't all this"—he moves his thick hand across the table as if to take in the room—"born from New Orleans? Wouldn't be no Capasso, wouldn't be no Benji Greenberg, wouldn't be no Oliver Pleasant or Agnes Cassady without New Orleans. Wouldn't be no jazz."

A waitress sets a fresh scotch in front of Agnes just as Oliver holds his glass up for a toast and the two clink glasses. "To New Orleans," he says.

"To jazz," Agnes offers.

The two talk of music and lightly of travel and New Orleans. She talks of the past—not hers, but the music's. She tries to speak knowledgeably about history and make it clear that it comes from so much study, so much curiosity, and her father's vault-like memory of names and numbers. Oliver had lived through these times and she wants him to know she respects that. Oliver nods and smiles. The girl knows her stuff, he can hear that. Once the scotch has worked itself through her tough exterior and stiff nervousness, loosened her up so her mind moves more like a wave machine than a grandfather clock, she talks almost nonstop. She takes one of his Gitanes from the pack on the table without asking and lights up, laughing and apologizing only when the thick smoke chokes her and she realizes what she's done. He waves the apology off, always happy to sit in public with a pretty girl.

Oliver has come to know loneliness like a growth, something he has to deal with every day, always there and up front when he looks in his filmy morning mirror. He's relished these past few nights with other musicians and his friends who have stopped by to pay their respects—Sonny Rollins stopped in, as did Jimmy Heath, Joe Lovano, Diana Krall, even Tony Bennett and the Marsalis boys—but he misses the touch of a woman. He's afraid he may forget that warm sensation eventually, just as he's begun to forget his earliest compositions. Forgotten, even, what he'd had for breakfast or just how bad his morning piss had hurt.

Sitting and talking with Agnes brings back that warmth like the first sip of whiskey taken in forever. He's enjoyed the nights in his oversized round booth in the back of the club, plush and comfortable like nothing he knows of in his own home and the world outside Benji's. He wears his ever-present porkpie atop his head, covering the baldness there. He's not vain, but has always liked the hats and has a collection he's taken from friends over the years, stolen them until they came to expect it, hope for it, even. It was like a badge of honor for Oliver Pleasant to be wearing one of your lids onstage or in an album cover photo. He has one from Count Basie, Ornette Coleman, a couple from Oscar Peterson, and even one from Frank Sinatra.

As people wander to and from the bar, and in and out of the club, they stop to say hello to Oliver and introduce themselves as fans. He accepts their hands politely but does not acknowledge Agnes to them until his band drifts past from backstage. He calls them over one by one to introduce "a fellow player," a phrase which flushes her face more than the liquor or the French cigarette. Each member leans in too close to her, sits right up next to her with their thighs touching, putting their arms around her to say hello, ask her where she's from, ask her where she's sleeping, before Oliver sends them on their way like a mother shooing her kids away from a freshly baked pie.

When they've gone and the room has cleared a bit, he offers her some of his Campari. She sips from his glass, lingering and swirling the fragile aperitif glass in her hand, stopping to watch the whirlpool she's created. She tells him then about pain, about a dusty hand-me-down piano back in Memphis so infused with the blues of the South that some nights she'd swear she heard it crying in the other room as she tried to sleep. She tells him about the disease that's consuming her slowly, gripping her nervous system like the law stepping on a criminal's neck, how unfair it is that it would begin its death march with her left hand and bring with it a pain in her skull, loss of feeling, and tremors. She places the glass back on the table and he covers her hand with his large paw, holds it there to feel the trembling. She, in turn, feels the warmth, not just the physical heat of his hand but the tenderness he feels toward this woman who will never know her potential, a music that will never find its natural height. A music unknown is one of the most melancholy things Oliver has ever considered.

He doesn't know if she can play or not, doesn't care. Oliver hasn't heard anyone talk about jazz and the need—the ache and hunger—to play in a long, long time. Most of the musicians he's played with toward the end of his career were more interested in when the paycheck would arrive and for how much, when the dope would arrive and how much, and the same for the women. But this girl feels pain and, he believes, she can play through that pain.

Not knowing just what to say and hesitant to drink from his own glass she's filled with such sorrow, he tells her some stories of the old days and their characters. He tells her how the young cats, the idealists, the innovators used to meet at Gil Evans's place on Fifty-Seventh not far from the Capasso where they sit now. "Everybody would be there," he says, "Gil, Max Roach, George Russell, Lee Konitz, even Bird would stop by, usually just to impress us.

"Gil's flat was in this old building right behind a Chinese laundry and all the pipes from that building ran through his little place that wasn't more than a damn closet with a sink, toilet, piano, and bed. We'd bring in crates and boxes and whatever we could find to sit on. Bottles and stories got passed around. New ideas, Russell's 'Lydian Concept'—that shit was far out then but most a them cats dug it . . . or said they did."

He gets her to laugh eventually with stories of the Chinese laundry owner's wife, who would cook them something to eat, even at four in the morning when they'd all finished their sets and gathered to talk and blow and smoke the dope that the laundry owner supplied. "She didn't understand a word of English, especially the shit we talked because that wasn't exactly the Queen's English. We'd ask her to blow, nudge each other, cacklin like a hutch full of goddamn hens until Bird or somebody offered their horn and she blew on it so it made a noise like a dyin cat. Then we'd all laugh and tell whoever's horn it was they could learn some shit from Chen or whatever the fuck her name was."

Agnes eats these stories up and washes them down with her scotch, the earthy taste quickly washing the sweet Campari from her tongue. She wants another cigarette and asks this time; Oliver obliges.

"How long ago did she pass, Ollie? Your wife?"

"Twenty years."

"You said up there that you wish she was here, said you wish they all was. Who's 'they'?"

Oliver takes another cigarette for himself and takes his time lighting it, blowing the smoke, and tasting.

"I'm sorry," she says. "It's none of my business. I just heard you say it."

"Guess I was talking more to the piano than anybody."

"It's okay."

"My kids. I got two boys—twins—and a girl. Don't see them too much."

"They live far?"

"Girl, Charlene, she in Brooklyn. Boys all over, musicianers, you know. Hell, you probably seen them in New Orleans."

"I would've gone to see a Pleasant. Don't recall them there."

"Use their mama's birth name: Zanone. Wanted to make it on their own. I respect that."

"Pianists?"

"Trombone. Tenor sax. They good, both of 'em. Play here sometimes when they come through, thought I might see them one of these nights. Hopin to see all of them. Damndest thing, though, my grandson stopped in last night. Tells me he's a musician and wants me to come see him and his boys play."

"Jazz?"

"Please. Hip-hop. You believe that shit?"

"I don't." She thinks. "But then, I don't get out much."

Oliver laughs and drains his glass. "You ever been to Paris, Miss Cassady?" he asks.

"Ain't been nowhere but Tipton County and Orleans Parish. Except here. What county is this?"

"Hell if I know."

"What's Paris like, Ollie?" She lays her head down on her arm, un-self-consciously and unaware now of her surroundings.

"Paris like a woman. Well, it's like bein in love with a woman. You ever been in love, Miss Cassady?"

She shrugs as best she can in her position. "Most days. Nights, anyway. Tell me about her, tell me about Paris."

"It was tamed by then, late forties, fifties and such. Men came before us, Bechet, Armstrong, and they tamed her, though it cost them all somethin. By the time we lay down with her, she was eager, swallowed us up, boy. We could play all damn night, any night, and she'd be clawin for us by lunch."

"You live there?"

"Off and on. Kept a place there, anyway. Kept a woman there."

"Francesca?"

"Hmm? No, no, Francesca was here. I kept a little fifth-floor flat and it's where I stayed when I was in town. It was quiet and gave me and the other cats a solitude we needed. Musicianers seek spotlight and recognition onstage, but when it comes time to wind down, we want it quiet and out of the way. Maybe not so quiet, now that I think on it; it was a rare thing if any of us went to bed alone. This little apartment was in the center of the Latin Quarter, and the inside and out was wrought iron and plaster with good windows that caught the breeze from the Seine. It was high enough up off the street to filter out that early mornin sidewalk noise below, too. I sure miss that flat some days.

"I had this old girl name of Marie there and she'd wait for me to come back overseas like a dog waiting on a bone. That old girl was hungry. She wanted me to move there, which I wouldn't; I couldn't with so much of my life, Francesca and the kids, bein here. But if I was there for two weeks, four, two months, she didn't care, she wanted us to live like husband and wife. She got it, too."

Despite the family he had back in New York, Oliver looked forward to those times in Paris as well. Marie was beautiful and worldly, and when Oliver was away in America, she worked in Italy and Spain as a photographer for the fashion industry. Even in his infidelity, Oliver was monogamous—a taste of the same fruit, just from a different orchard. As much as Marie enjoyed her time with

Oliver, the late nights at Paris's jazz clubs and cafés; drinks with other musicians, artists, and writers; early morning walks along the river to their little apartment where they would make love as the pinkish light of day was just beginning to break over the horizon—as much as she enjoyed the life, Marie was a jealous woman.

"When me and Marie weren't around, them other cats might stay there. There was this other little girl over there, Giselle," he says, pouring a sip more of Campari into his glass. "Giselle looked after the flat and whatever musicianer might be there at any given time, makin sure they had food and drink, and that the place stayed clean. Her daddy owned the building and ran a patisserie on the ground floor. Giselle was legendary for fightin off American boys who ended the night alone, or those that didn't but wanted a little extra taste anyway. 'Juste un peu plus d'amour, mademoiselle?'"

Marie could cope with Francesca, the American wife, the public face of Oliver at home; that was the way it had to be. The other girl, however, the Parisienne, was a different matter. There was only room for one and Marie resented this intrusion. There were nights Oliver was in Paris and Marie had to be away, mostly for work or to help look after her ill mother. She fretted these nights the way Francesca must have back in the small Harlem apartment she and Oliver had at the time. Marie clung to wild fantasies of Giselle entering the apartment and of her slipping into bed with Oliver, who would still be wound up from the night's show and all alone. The thoughts were enough to send Marie into a blind rage. To make her presence known, on mornings she was there, when Giselle would let herself in and spread food on the small table beneath the window and boil water for coffee, strong and thick like Americans take, Marie would rise and parade nude around the apartment. She would flaunt her beautiful body, her long legs and full breasts, inspecting the fruit Giselle had brought, "the pears are not so ripe"; stand full in front of the balcony doors and comment on the weather, "it will rain today"; and leave the door to the small water closet ajar as she washed the previous night away with a rough washcloth.

"Did you love her? Marie?"

"I did. I think I loved all those women at one time or another. They gave me somethin to play for, somethin to go on workin for. I knew I wouldn't have them all, not for long, except Francesca. Almost lost her a time or two, but she stayed with me. She's my muse."

"What happened with Marie?"

Oliver stares again at the smoke from his cigarette, curlicues reaching for the light. He picks up the cigarette and sets it back down as though the weight of it is too much. Settles, instead, on another taste of liquor.

"Oliver?"

"Well, that's another story, sugar. Another story for another time. Another time from another life.

"Tell me what you know about love, Agnes Cassady."

Agnes has to think about this. She thinks about it every time it comes up, which is more than you'd suppose down there in the Quarter, though it's usually in the form of "Are you married?" "Got a boyfriend?" "Want one?" She smokes the French cigarette, pulling it in deep without concern—it's one of the perks of knowing life's limit ahead of time. She blows the smoke out in a sharp stream, splitting Oliver's tired cloud in half. "I loved every one of them," she finally says.

Oliver laughs, a deep growl of a laugh. "How many?"

Agnes shrugs. "Not enough, not for a lifetime."

"How old are you? Talkin about a lifetime. What you know about a lifetime?"

"Twenty-two. But I'll be dead by the time I'm twenty-five."

The words strike Oliver like a slap across the face; he doesn't speak of death if he can help it. It's a fear he carries around with him in his breast pocket. At eighty-five, Oliver lives in the same neighborhood as death, can see it sometimes out of his window, lurking across the street, hears its feet shuffling up and down the sidewalk outside his door. It sits on his stoop and waits. That knowing, deep in the soul, that there's something swirling about in a room or out in the city that can take you any time it wants makes a man sober. Giving voice to it, the way that Agnes just did, is just inviting it to sit down with you, begs it to reach across the table and into your breast pocket to take what it wants.

"Dead?" he says, whispering without even realizing. He pulls his porkpie down low over his brow. "What you talkin 'bout, dead? You young, girl, the thick of your life."

She mashes her cigarette into the crystal ashtray. "It's eating me up, Oliver, killing me from the inside out. Look at it!" Agnes thrusts her hand up in front of his face and they both watch it tremble, the shadows changing and dancing between her fingers and on her palm. "There are times I can't control it at all, times I can't feel the fingers. And the pain that comes with it, from my neck to my shoulder and down that arm, back up to my brain. It's blinding, it's torture. There are times I just want the lights to go out. Goddammit, I just want it to stop. And I used to be able to stop it— that's what scares me the most, because I can't anymore. Time was I could sit down at the piano and play and the shaking would stop and the pain would stop and the wishing for death would stop."

Oliver is nodding his head, but still staring at the hand, at the thing in front of him he thinks might just reach into his breast pocket. "I know it, darlin. I know what it's like for the music to take some pain away. I've lived a long time, lived through pain and hurt, and I know what it is to have it go, how good it feels to have them scales take over the empty place inside, fill up what the pain left behind."

"That's right. That's right, it fills you up so nothing else can get in there, not pain anyway. You known pain, Ollie?"

"I know pain."

"You know what it feels like to want to die?"

"I know, baby. I know. But you ain't got to. What the doctors say? What they call it? Got to be medicine for it. Shit, there's medicine for everything now, head medicine, arthritis medicine, dick medicine, mood medicine. . . . They got somethin for you?"

"They don't know. It's why I'm here, see another doctor, another hospital. Shit, Ollie, I've spent years of my short life in hospital rooms, doctors looking at me, poking at me, fingers in here, fingers in there. I just want to live and love the last few years I got."

"Live and love, ain't that somethin. Some people live a hundred years don't figure out the secret to it all is just livin and lovin. How many you loved, Agnes? You gettin close to a lifetime, ain't you?"

Agnes laughs and sips her scotch. She looks across the room at Andrew Sexton stripping tables of their coverings, throwing spent silverware in a bus tub, and snuffing out candles. Church is over. "Every one of them. Every man I take to bed I'm in love with, love them just for being with me, helping me feel alive and making me forget the pain, the death for just an hour or two, same as music." She chokes on the feeling in her throat and gulps her drink. "Same as music was."

"Ain't no more?"

Agnes slowly shakes her head back and forth. "Ain't no more, Oliver Pleasant. I can't hold it still enough to get through a song. Hurts worse than telling a man I'm not in love with him anymore, hurts more than the needle from my spine to my brain. It's a pain I wouldn't wish on anybody."

"Agnes Cassady," Oliver says to no one, almost whispering it to his glass. "Poor, poor Agnes Cassady." He covers her hand with his again so she can feel the rough palm against her knuckles. He presses down, flattening it to the table firmly, yet gently, and stops the trembling.

A tear rolls down her cheek as the main lights in the club come on, exposing them in a harsh glare and signaling it's time to go.

(INTERLUDE NO. 3)

NEW YORK CITY, 1938

a conversation between Oliver Pleasant and Winky
Central Park
New York, New York

"I ever tell you about my first night in New York? Winky? Where you at?"

"I'm here, Licoricehead. You never told me about it. When was that? Were there dinosaurs?"

"You got a mouth on you, boy. It was a cold night, colder than this here. January 16, 1938. I was seventeen years old."

"You're the dinosaur," Winky said, laughing at his own joke, wittiness becoming a new taste in his mouth.

"We came in on the train and, first thing I know, my man Hamlet's tuggin me out of Penn Station into a cab and up to Harlem. We go round to the Savoy and there must be ten thousand people outside that place. Looked like a revival, or a riot, except everybody's dancin and drinkin and foolin on each other. Hamlet, he pulls me round back through an alley and knows the brother at the stage door who lets us in. And in we go, to church. You listenin? Winky?"

"You said 'church.' What church was it?"

"The Church of Jazz, the Church of the Music of the Day and a Lifetime. Our Lady of Perpetual Hep. Come over here now; I'm talkin about the Church of Swing of New York City, boy."

Winky rolled his eyes and threw down the stick he'd been using to try to break the frozen crust of Central Park. His breath showed white and heavy in the frosty air, and he shoved his hands into the pockets of his thin coat and slumped down once again beside Oliver.

"Now, that night was a historic night. Me and Hamlet, we stood just offstage and watched Chick Webb and his orchestra and Count Basie and his in a cuttin contest like I ain't never seen. It was a heavyweight bout, a title match."

"Cuttin?"

"Cuttin, boy. Cuttin, to see who's best, who could hold title to the King of Swing. Basie, he'd just been down at Carnegie Hall— that's another church down in Midtown—playin with Benny Goodman and some other cats, but he'd hightailed it up to Harlem and was givin them people, all of us, a show. Givin Chick a show, too, son. They was cuttin each other with knives like you ain't never seen."

Oliver was getting excited and his breath came out in short, quick blasts of exhaust. He wrung his hands together, both for warmth and from excitement, and it looked to Winky like he'd left the park. It was like Oliver just lifted up and floated right out of there on clouds of exhale and memory. Oliver's eyes bugged out and glazed over at the same time, and his foot tapped as though he had a beat in his head and in his heart.

"Who won?" Winky, too, was excited, as though he were watching a boxing match on television. "Who got cut the worst?"

"Well, that's arguable, still talked about and debated to this day. Some say Chick, others say Count. I guess, I suppose maybe it was Chick—it was his house after all. Any tie gonna go to him. Hell, maybe it was the people won, those of us watchin, 'cause we witnessed history that night. We saw some of the best swing ever, some of the best musicianers in the world—then and now—playin that night. And it was my introduction to New York City. It was my first hint at what this could be, where the music could take us as a people—not just blacks, but all of us. Them people in the audience in the Savoy, and, hell, out in the street, them that couldn't get in, it was like they was lifted up all at once. They danced and they laughed and they was sweatin like I ain't seen since my time as a boy playin for the colored who came to my mama and daddy's to dance and drink or around Longstreet's piano down there in New Orleans. As a boy, I didn't know if it was the music or the drink did that to them. That night at the Savoy, though, I knew. It was the music, the music has a power, son. It's a power you can only find in the darkest saloon or the most holy church.

"After that show, Hamlet hustled me and a couple girls he picked up I don't know where into the back of a cab and told the driver, 'To the Village!' That driver didn't look so happy about havin a couple Negroes with white women in the back of his cab, but he drove on anyway. I didn't know what village Hamlet was talkin about. Didn't know how Hamlet knew to go to Harlem and the Savoy or how to catch a cab and where to go next, but he must have learned it somewhere between Vicksburg, Mississippi, and New York City.

"Manhattan opened up to me like an amusement park on that drive. The driver took us all the way down Broadway and the lights and people were like nothin I'd seen before. It was like they was all celebratin somethin and I asked the driver what it was was goin on and he just looked at me in the rearview like I was out of my mind. And maybe I was, because them lights was out of this world, son. It was all tinsel and gold and you could just feel the possibilities comin at us through the windshield.

"Anyway, them girls wasn't white so much as they was Puerto Rican, even talked with the rolling *R*s and had big brown eyes and soft hair. We was all wedged into that cab half on top of each other and, God forgive me, but the smell of them big girls, their perfume, I guess, put me in mind of my mama's church on Sunday morning. It might not have been the same musk, but it was close and hot as hell and stirred something inside me, that's for damn sure."

"They swear a lot? You swear a lot."

"They was Puerto Rican, so yeah. All Puerto Rican girls cuss."

"There's a girl in my class at school, Rosie, she's Puerto Rican but she don't cuss."

"She will, you wait.

"So we get down to Greenwich Village and find us a jazz club but there ain't nobody down there. They's all up in Harlem at the Savoy, so we get a good table, the four of us, and we have some drinks and everything's feelin good. And then this cat gets up onstage and starts playin the drums. Real soft, too, with brushes, and the other folks in the club, what few there were, was just lookin around waitin for more. After a while, after quarter hour of this, a cat comes in wearin a suit and shades and he's talkin to the bartender about what he just seen up in Harlem—the very same show we was at. And this cat gets onstage and takes a bass out of the case he was carryin and starts playin along with the drummer. They don't even speak, just fall in together on some tune or other. Little bit more and another cat comes in, this one with a fat cigar in his mouth, and makes a beeline for the piano, where he sits to play. Then, later, some horns come in. The whole band filled in like that, all tricklin down from Harlem. I guess maybe that's how jazz got to the Village—it trickled down from the top of the island like an hourglass, only with black sand.

"Time was another thing that got me that night. It was like it stopped, like the nighttime might just go on forever. There was no windows, of course, and the club was dark as hell and I spent most of that night with my face in one of them girls' hair, I guess, and listenin to music, but the night was eternal. Forever, boy. Nobody asked what time it was, nobody seemed to have to be nowhere. Hell, maybe no place else existed outside that club.

"When that music finally did stop and we stepped onto the sidewalk, swayin this way and that from the drummer's time and good liquor, it was *still* dark out. Hamlet found us another cab and we headed back uptown to Spanish Harlem; neighborhood was barely a couple blocks in them days and just a few streets up from here. Took them to their building, where we figured we'd invite ourselves on in—you know what I'm talkin about?"

"No."

Winky wandered away as though he didn't care to know. Oliver didn't notice his audience had gone.

"You will, just wait.

"But here's the thing. On the stoop of that building was a man, and that man said them were his girls. 'Both of 'em?' I said, and he just grunted. 'How you gonna have two women?' Hamlet asked, gettin up in that man's face. Man stood up then, tall son of a bitch, and said that them girls worked for him and, near as he could tell, we owed him about twenty dollars each. 'Twenty dollars?' Hamlet shouted. 'Where the hell I'm a get twenty dollars?' And then Hamlet and I looked at each other and we just seemed to know, to understand—we was like brothers that way—and Hamlet gave that tall motherfucker a shove and he went backward onto them steps and we ran like hell." Oliver doubled over in laughter at this. "But not before he gave one of them Puerto Rican girls a grab on her big ol' ass. And that pimp chased us back to lower Manhattan. Don't know how we lost him; he must've grown tired. Or maybe we sank back into the eternal dark.

"We wandered, ended up in Battery Park when the sun finally did show up. We watched the light come up there, over the water and shine off the lady out there in it, and you know what it was like, Winky?"

"Guess I'll find out." The boy had grown weary of so much talking, which became more difficult to hear over the rumbling of his empty stomach.

"It was like church, like the whole city was church."

Oliver looked up into the light coming through the trees in the early morning, disbelieving it could be the same sun that had shone on him and his good friend. He couldn't believe his friend wasn't there with him as his life prepared to change once again.

"That was my first night in New York. It was holy and it was sinful. It was a blessed time in a searing pool of brimstone. I didn't know it then, though I was startin to feel, that it was everything I wanted. Sure do hate to leave it all. Sure do."

Winky, who had been alternately digging in the dirt, chasing squirrels, and only halfway listening to what Oliver said, climbed up on the bench next to that big, round man and stared, too, at the new light.

NIGHT FOUR

1.

Frank is pulled from sleep as though from under water. Breaking the surface, he gulps air and then, realizing where he is, feels foolish, feels the other side of the bed, but finds he's alone. This is nearly as surprising and disorienting to him as the sense of breathlessness he'd felt only moments before. He and Karen have spent only a handful of nights apart since they were married seventeen years ago. It makes this trip all the more difficult and, Frank has thought the past couple of days, necessary.

The first night they spent apart after the eve of their wedding day came within the first year of marriage. Frank was a young reporter then and his work hours erratic as he paid his dues at the beck and call of police scanners, murderers, victims, and their inconsistent states of consciousness, and editors' even more inconsistent nerves and bowel movements. He'd worked a week and a half straight of late nights, staying in the newsroom until just after the presses ran in case there were last-second corrections to be made. He was young and eager to please, eager to show his worth. Many of those nights he'd ended at the P & H Café just down the road from the paper in a smoke cloud where the copydesk, designers, and reporters too locked into routine to not work that last shift met for beer and commiseration.

Karen was lonely, Frank sees that now. He rolls over and counts the skyscrapers visible across Manhattan from his bed and thinks that Karen didn't have as many friends then as rooftop spires he counts. She was working just as hard as he was, but it was "regular work," as he called it—nine-to-five, grab-a-lunch-at-noon-with-the-girls kind of work. And that one guy. His name was Chad and he worked in Karen's firm. Chad. *The fuck kind of name is Chad?* he thinks even now. She'd gone out that Friday night with everyone from the office because she knew Frank would be working late, and because she didn't care if he was working late or not by then, she was going out. She'd sat at home for eleven nights counting and wasn't about to have another dinner alone, did not intend to watch *Law & Order* and then drift off to sleep with Jane Austen instead of her husband again.

So she went out. And it was early the next morning when she came home. She said the girls had all ended up at Amanda's house and that was probably true. He knew back then that it was probably true and as he looks at his fleshy, lined, forty-year-old face in the bathroom mirror of an inexpensive New York hotel now, he still knows it's probably true. But he didn't care then; he had just wanted to hurt her and had accused Karen of spending the night with another man. Chad. They'd argued and she'd told him to call Amanda if he didn't believe her and then flew into a rage when he picked up the phone. He wasn't going to call her; he was bluffing. They didn't speak that day and slept apart that night, though under the same roof. They were in their small apartment then and he'd fallen asleep in a chair in the living room where she left him. Eventually they made up, but the scar was there. It became a raised white line of suspicion that, over time, they may not notice, but every once in a while a fingertip grazes it or its ugliness is caught in the reflection of a mirror.

But it's not all cold, the scar has faded, and Frank and Karen do love each other. They wanted to have that baby together and to fill up their house with children. A family would help to erase the scar even more, they both know, and so they've tried and tried and tried until they've both grown so very tired of trying, and yet they still do.

He lies back down on the bed, dripping water from the shower. He just wants to crawl back under the covers, sleep for a day and a night, but he's got a breakfast date and knows he shouldn't skip it. His notebook is peeking out from the back pocket of his jeans, which are lying balled up on the floor. He reaches for it and sees written in a handwriting that resembles his own, but not quite: "Internat."

"Internat?" He says to the notebook. "What the hell is an 'Internat'?"

He'd gone out with Davis McComber after Oliver's show the previous night. Frank had wanted to sit and talk with Oliver some more, but he had company, a young woman who was pretty but so very pale and thin. Davis took Frank to all the haunts of lower Manhattan, rushing past some to tell him who'd played there— Van Morrison, Morrissey, Elvis Costello, Blondie, Miles Davis, Nirvana, and Mos Def—and into other clubs where he was greeted at the door by name and never charged a cover, and he seemed to know everyone everywhere. Those in the crowds, young and old, said hello, holding up beer bottles with apathetic acknowledgment, as if they knew he was only passing through. Catching and holding Davis in conversation last night would've been like catching water in your bare hands. He read handbills posted on doors and strained to look over heads to see who was onstage before turning around to dart out the door again with Frank following. Davis kept apologizing and cursing the fact that they were sticking to the Village and SoHo while completely disregarding Harlem. "Harlem's got some good shit going on. Good shit. Not like the old days, of course, no house parties and all-night cutting contests, but some decent clubs with old-timers and new guys. It's making a comeback. But what the fuck am I talking about, you're from Memphis, you know from good music. Clubs on every corner there, every half corner, I bet. Soul, rock, funk, R and B, alt country. Home of Ardent down there—Big Star, 'Mats, Jim Dickinson. I got to get down there."

Davis seems to think any city, any area of a city, with a musical heritage oozes with chords and a backbeat, that simply by having a front door and an address, whether a dry cleaner, grocery store, diner, or bar, they are obligated to host live music shows. He expects it. The world, he believes, expects it, and it is, by God, that city's duty to accommodate.

And it is Davis McComber's duty to report it all. Frank watched as Davis scribbled notes and asked questions. There was a story everywhere, in every dive, on every stage, and in every note. "Is this how it is? Is this the life of a freelancer?" Frank had asked, his head swimming from alcohol and environmental stimuli.

"Nah. Well, yeah, for me," Davis said. "All this could be written from my apartment using Google. I know the fuckers who do it that way, but I've got to get out. I need to put my feet on the street and get my ears onstage with the players. That's where you find the details."

Details. Frank's mind flew back to journalism school and Professor Jordan, who must've seen all this coming—Frank's career, his being laid off due to a decrease in ad revenue and proliferation of online news sources. Had he also seen Frank's malignant contentment and his laziness adding up to little more than a still-empty sheet of typing paper in an unused home office? Davis is excited, and excitable. He sees the details in the stories and the stories in the details the way that Frank used to on those late nights in the newsroom and nicotine cave after work.

"Why?" It was all Frank wanted to know. "Why do this when people can just Google and fill their cloudy heads with the crap that ad executives are telling us to consume these days?"

Davis shrugged. "I figure it's the least I can do for them."

"Them? Who?"

"Readers." He shrugged again. "Music fans. Little dudes sitting in Iowa or some other fucking place who don't have clubs or live music, places that aren't the beginning of anything. Except maybe corn or something. This shit goes out everywhere." He wiped his open hand across the sky for Frank. "Every-fucking-where. Don't need a subscription for this, just electricity. Figure they have electricity even in Des Moines."

The electricity of Davis McComber shocked Frank. It was like time travel back to his own first years as a reporter when the story was the thing. He'd forgotten what it was like to give people a story just for the story's sake, just because they might not be able to experience whatever it was he'd just experienced. Maybe all his colleagues had forgotten that as well. Getting it back might not make up for lost ad revenue or increase circulation, but Frank was done with all that anyway. Maybe, though, that electricity could jump-start his own heart, kick-start his own writing. He pulled his notebook from his pocket and, in a boozy, bleary-eyed hand, wrote: "Internat."

Frank had followed Davis's meandering walk and talk for as long as he could, his head a mash of jazz, alternative, punk, post-punk, grunge, and straight-ahead rock and roll. They'd had a beer at every stop and Davis had produced a half-pint from his jacket at some point for the walk between locations. At 2:00 a.m., Frank had wandered away. He simply didn't turn a corner when Davis had and, instead, kept walking straight ahead. He called out, he'd tried to tell Davis goodnight, but Davis was already on to the next thing, the next sound, scribbling words of detail into his composition book and sipping from a nearly empty bottle of bourbon. Frank, disoriented and half drunk, was heading in the opposite direction from his hotel.

And now Frank is on his way to breakfast at Junior's. It seems a long way to go for eggs and bacon, but it's really the coffee he's after. The coffee and the company.

* * * * *

Oliver and Winky sit on their bench at the top of the park. It's cold and the light is just starting to spread through the trees at the far south end, just beginning its reach into this sanctuary where animals and leaves and people are coming to life, grateful for its warmth. Winky watches a nearby squirrel and spots a rock at his own feet. He thinks maybe he can snatch up that rock and throw it before that squirrel knows what's happening, but Oliver breaks his concentration. "You ever go to church, Winky?"

"Church?"

"Yeah, you know about church?"

"I know about church." He shrugs and adds, "Don't go." The squirrel has moved on, scared away by a jogger in spandex puffing like a freight train through the frosty air.

"I used to go with my people down in Winona. Little wood building, one room, woodstove to keep us warm in winter, ladies with hand fans movin hot air around in summer. Preacher would get up on that stage and scream and dance, sing to the Lord and curse at us."

At this revelation, Winky whips his head around to face Oliver. "Cursing? A preacher?"

"Shit yeah, cursin. God in the South is angry, boy. I was thinkin this morning about that smell, though. That smell of church I think is what I miss. Perfume and dirt from the fields, tobacco, and maybe a little hint of Saturday night's sin." Winky has wandered off looking for more squirrels to toss a rock at, or maybe a jogger. He's come to learn during his mornings with Oliver that Oliver isn't really talking to him. He doesn't know whom it is Oliver is talking to, but it isn't a little kid from Harlem. He'd stuck around the first couple of mornings but couldn't make heads or tails out of what Oliver was going on about. Moonshine, dice, dancing, girls, cats, swing. None of it makes much sense to a ten-year-old boy. He just wants to learn to play the piano and he sure as shit doesn't know what church has to do with it. So he's let his imagination and then his feet wander, and Oliver becomes just another crazy old fool of the city, sitting on a park bench talking to himself.

"I ever tell you about my first night in New York? Winky? Where you at?"

"I'm here, Licoricehead. You never told me about it, no. When was that? Were there dinosaurs?"

"You got a mouth on you, boy. It was a cold night, colder than this. January 16, 1938. I was seventeen years old."

"You're the dinosaur."

Oliver tells him about a wild ride in a New York City taxicab that takes him from the glass and steel splendor of Penn Station, he says, to the brick and soot stylings of Harlem. It was his first time inside the Savoy and his eyes were opened, he tells Winky. "And in we went, to church. You listenin? Winky?"

"You said 'church.' What church was it?"

Oliver tells him about churches, about a religion the boy didn't know, that of music and heart-stopping swing with people who all feel the same way, believe in the same god. There it is again, cats and booze and girls, and Winky's mind flies away with the pigeons.

"You ain't even listenin," Oliver says, disgusted with this disinterested boy. "When's the last time you made it to church?"

"Papi's funeral," he says in a hushed voice as though mass has begun, and fills his cheeks with air to help hold his emotion in.

"Papi?"

"My daddy."

"Your daddy dead?" Oliver looks down at him now and it's as though he's seeing this little boy for the first time.

178

Winky nods and wipes his nose with the back of a gloved hand. "How he die?"

Winky squints up into the sunlight coming through the trees. He looks south and points, as if toward the sun. It's cryptic, but Oliver knows.

"Towers?"

Winky nods again.

Oliver recalls that day. He was home, in the relative safety and the dark warmth of his sitting room, when he heard the commotion from outside. He looked out to see people talking on the streets, people who never would have given each other the time of day normally, all excited and pointing. Then he saw the crying and the fear on their faces. The small television on his kitchen counter told him the rest.

Over such a long lifetime, Oliver has seen pain and loss. In Winona, he'd seen a black man dragged through the street by a mob saying he stole from a white man. His own mama and daddy had to sneak around just to act like human beings. The South was long on sorrow, and Oliver and whatever band he was playing with saw plenty of it, received plenty of grief themselves. They were made to enter through service doors, eat in alleyways, and stay in motels that weren't fit for animals—or sleep on the bus parked on the street outside a white hotel. It's not just here, though; he's seen wars come and go—kept out of them, thank God, because of his busted-up leg.

America can fight evil the world over, but she's not all smiles. Oliver was in hot and humid South Carolina in 1955 when he heard about Emmett Till, poor little black boy visiting Mississippi who was murdered for, they say, flirting with a white woman. "Flirting with a white woman," Oliver says now.

"What?"

Oliver just shakes his head as though to say "never mind." This boy is almost the same age as Emmett Till was. Lost his father—Winky practically just a baby then—in more ugliness, more hate, all in the name of what a man thinks is right or wrong. Same hate that causes a war, same hate that leaves a little black boy to die in a ditch.

Oliver has seen too much of it. Too goddamn much in a long life. He's lost his wife, lost his best friend in an accident that still haunts him and hurts his heart, and he's all but lost his own children even though he can almost see his daughter from where he sits. He'd talked about it with Agnes Cassady and thinks about that young lady now, with her hurting, losing it all just the same as him. All she feels she has is the music and now that's slipping. Maybe all Oliver ever had was the music; everything else slipped off away from his grasp. And maybe all Winky wants is some music in his life, something to fill the void of a father gone for half this boy's life now.

"Hey," Oliver says to Winky, who has climbed down off the bench to play at Oliver's feet. "Hey, you tell me somethin?"

"What?"

"What *is* your name?"

He looks up at Oliver from where he kneels on the ground and his face reddens, embarrassed now to have to say it in front of this grown-up. Oliver has called him "Winky" since the first day they came across each other on that stoop and it feels now as though a secret is being imparted. "Pablo."

"Pablo? Really? Named for your daddy?"

Pablo shakes his head. "For a poet from Chile, my papi said. He wrote poetry, too."

"That right?" Oliver thinks a minute, then says, "You still wantin them piano lessons?"

Pablo nods vigorously and throws down the stick he's been using to dig in the dirt. He climbs up on the bench and slumps down once again beside his old friend.

There are places on her wrist that are tender to the touch. It's a dull pain like a bruise deep within, entwined among tendons and bone. That pain is sent up her arm to her shoulder, into her neck, before making the short trip to her brain to become one with the pain that has made a home there for the past half-dozen years. But the thin brown fingers are gentle on her arm and her hand, and she gives herself over completely to Dr. Mundra massaging her wrist—in the exact spot where a priestess had scratched her years before and from where the ache seems to emanate—and works her hand in a circular motion as he talks with her. "How has your stay been in New York?" he says. It has nothing to do with medicine, does not hint toward the test results from her MRI that she knows are within the manila folder by his side. He has been focused on her since he entered the examining room, looking into her eyes first only with his own before taking the light from his coat pocket and shining it into her pupils to see her mind and, she felt, her soul.

It's a light she's become familiar with. The church preaches that a light is saving, that when you die there will be a great light. The light of day is redeeming. Agnes's parents would often sing aloud about "skipping the light fandango." But no doctors have ever seen anything with their lights. Not anything that will help, at least. She'd first gone to New Orleans for the Tulane University School of Medicine and Medical Center and the work being done there with neurological disorders in adolescents. Her parents had taken a whole week off work, a week that was nothing like a vacation, though none of them had ever been to the city. They stayed in a hotel at the end of St. Charles, far from the Quarter and the river, and ate in the hotel room most nights or at a nearby diner that catered to transients. Agnes felt weak and tired, drained from the days of tests and answering questions. One night near the end of the week, though, her father, frustrated with the lack of answers and saddened by the pallid look of his daughter with gray circles going to black beneath her eyes, rallied his family.

"We're going out!" he said, standing in their small room with a queen bed and roll-away cot.

"Not those crappy burgers again, Daddy."

"We're going to the Quarter," he said, jumping onto the bed to the delight of the women. "We're going to eat gumbo and jambalaya, shrimp and oysters. Your mother's going to drink a beer. I'm going to drink two. And we'll hear some music, Agnes, some beautiful brass jazz like they make only down here."

And they did. And it was one of the best nights Agnes can recall, listening to the music pouring from small bars and grand rooms, taking each other's pictures in front of Preservation Hall, eating anything and everything, and watching her parents dance in the middle of a cobblestone street to a lone saxophonist. Agnes was barely eighteen and she thought she'd never see anything that made her happier if she lived to be a hundred. She didn't yet know that she wouldn't make it down but a quarter of that road.

While sitting at a table outside a café on Royal, an old friend of Agnes's walked by on the arm of a boy and left him to run up to the Cassadys' table. Terron had just moved to New Orleans to attend Loyola and was living in a nearby apartment. She invited Agnes to go out with her, but Agnes declined, saying she was there with her parents and would only be in town one more day. Agnes's parents insisted she go out with her friend—they wouldn't hear of her refusal. The need to know their daughter was having fun and laughing was as medicinal as anything a doctor could prescribe.

The two young women went back out to the Quarter, Terron's escort sent on his way, and they saw things Agnes never would have seen with her parents. They were hit on countless times by men and women sober and not-so, they ate more and drank much more, and Agnes was even persuaded to show her little titties for a few pearly beads to some lovesick sailors on leave. And through it all, both with her parents and alone with Terron, there was a nagging in her ear, a buzzing that she couldn't quite place when in a crowd. Once they moved to a quieter side street, though, she could hear the music more clearly. It was everywhere—piano, trumpet, sax, drums, bass. It reminded her of the cicadas back home during the previous summer, a sound so thick and present that she felt it could lift her off her feet and carry her into the black night. This sound, though, this music, did lift her off her feet. They were the same tunes, the same theory, as what her father played, even her piano teacher's same notes, but there was something else; it was something intangible. It was creation. She was in the cradle of music's uncivilization, walking on the same fertile ground as Buddy Bolden, Freddie Keppard, and Joe Oliver. She had the sense she might round the next corner and run directly into Louis Armstrong. She was in the birthplace and that birth was all around her, all over her. She felt more alive than she had in years.

They visited a voodoo priestess, one of the kitschy tourist traps sandwiched between a walk-up daiquiri bar and a sex-toy shop on Bourbon. They'd had enough to drink that the prospect of a palm reading was laughable, and Terron snickered at Agnes's shoulder as the wrinkled woman, dressed in scarves and mirrored sunglasses perched on the hook nose of her coffee-colored face, took Agnes's hand and looked upon it. The reflection of lines and fingers shone in duplicate from her silver bug eyes as she watched and shook her head, consulted some cards, and from a leather cup rolled an object that looked like matted string and smelled like week-old pork. She shook her head some more, grunted, and took a small piece of charcoal from a canvas bag around her neck. With it, she scratched hash marks on Agnes's thin wrist—a set of two and a set of five.

"Seven?" Agnes said. Terron tittered behind her.

"Twenty-five. You will not live to see twenty-five, sugar. I am sorry."

Terron and Agnes laughed off the prediction for the rest of the night, coming back to it as an inside joke and toasting to Agnes's relative old age. Yet Agnes scrubbed her wrist later, feeling as though she couldn't get it to come clean, and she slept fitfully that night with dreams of mirrors and her own dirty wrist invading her head.

She stayed with Terron overnight, and the next morning at breakfast, before meeting her parents at Tulane for one last round of question and answer with the doctors, Terron proposed to Agnes that she move to New Orleans. Agnes dismissed it. Then she considered it on the trolley ride to the hospital, and as the doctor there, a New Englander with a grating nasal accent, shined his penlight into her eye, something snapped. In that light she saw a glinting off brass and could hear the night's music wafting past the manicured lawn, through the automatic doors, past the nurses' station, and down the antiseptic hallways to her ears. Carried in on that music as well was the scratchy, aged voice whispering "twenty-five . . . twenty-five" in her ear. It was silly, she knew, but still . . . she should live right now. Agnes knew that her life wasn't like others' and probably wouldn't last as long; this was a fact that no doctor had told her, no doctor could tell her, nor could any voodoo witch. It was as though she were born with only a scant number of years to live and was informed of this in the womb, only to be reminded on the musical streets of New Orleans and not in the whitened rooms of any hospital.

"When do you go?" Mundra asks now in the tiny examination room of Mount Sinai, massaging her wrist again, having put his penlight back into his pocket amid pens, tongue depressors, and a small notebook. She blinks back the black spots the light leaves in her vision. He wears a salmon-colored turban today and Agnes remarks on it, saying she likes it, though she doesn't, and suggesting he get a coat to match.

"My wife would never let me out of the house in a pink coat," he says. His smile is warm; it's the same calming, caring smile she's seen on doctors' faces for years. It's something for which she's always been grateful.

"You're married?"

"Four years." He reaches for the folder.

"Kids?"

"One. A son, only six months old."

"That's nice."

The most difficult part of her decision was telling her father. She was quiet on the trip home; there were no answers from doctors packed in their scuffed and aged luggage in the back of her daddy's truck, and she waited until they were all on familiar territory to broach the subject. She also wanted to see if she still felt the same way while sitting on their porch in Tipton County and watching her mother sketch the scenery in a Moleskine notebook. She did. She had a taste of life there in New Orleans and was scared of losing her own. Though there was nothing definite in her blood labs and bone scans, nothing to read the future by any better than a Bourbon Street fortune-teller, she had a sense that she needed to capture some magic in a bottle before it was too late. An ordinary eighteen-year-old has no grasp of too late; death is an abstract, something that happens on the news and to other people, unless something has taken hold of her body to make it do things she doesn't tell it. Then death becomes tangible, somewhat breathtaking on those nights when she lies alone in bed and listens to the darkness thick with a sound that comes around only every thirteen years. *Will I hear the cicada again? Will the sky and trees and grass outside my window ever hum twice like this in my lifetime?*

She didn't take any of this to her parents. She was certain they were more scared than she, so Agnes went to her father with the one thing they shared: the music. Sitting next to him on the piano bench, listening to him improvise something soft and thoughtful, they talked about the music they'd heard on their vacation (that's what they'd all agreed to call it). His fingers were smudged with grease from the day's work and left the evidence behind on the white keys. She put her head on his shoulder and told him she wanted more than just a week of that sort of musical immersion. She told him that she wanted to live the notes and melodies and be a part of that energy. She lied and told him she felt better on the sodden streets of New Orleans than she'd felt in a long time and she knew it was because of the sounds and the history. He told her he felt it, too, and she took over on the keys, picking up on his tune while he sat beside her like a child. She told him about Terron's suggestion that she move, about plans to come home often and visits he and her mother could make. They talked, for the first time since the tremors and blackouts and pain had begun, about life. And he told her to go.

Now Mundra pulls the films from the oversized folder, and even in the overhead light of the room, before the doctor makes his move to stand and walk to the light boxes on the wall, Agnes can see them. She can see the dark spots, their shapes like continents on a map, situated within her brain like unwanted guests—like mold, like stains. She owns a thousand similes. She can't blink these spots away. He jabs the transparencies home into their clips and the sound is like a knife on bone. It's a noise she's come to loathe, one that tends to erase whatever comfort she's found in a doctor's smile. And there is her damaged skull. She wonders which continent is Dr. Mundra's.

He talks in his soothing way, pointing with a royal-blue fountain pen—*It looks heavy,* Agnes thinks to herself—and says the words, the phrases, the theories she's heard again and again and again. But he also has a hint of hope in his demeanor and appears excited by something. He opens a laptop on the examination table to show Agnes a website, one she hasn't seen, though she thought she'd seen them all. There's a study, he says, a procedure . . .

experimental . . . clinical trials . . . medication. . . . Agnes is lost in his voice, the kindness is back and it's in his eyes now as well.

And then it's gone.

Temporary results . . . paralysis . . . permanent . . . side effects . . . percentages . . . He's taken it away from her just as quickly as he gave it. He's held something in front of her like a carrot and then cut the line so it falls into the mud at her feet, filthy and inedible.

The procedure—he isn't recommending it, but neither is he ruling it out—could be done right here in the hospital. It could be done quickly and "It might . . . help," he says, "though there are worries, there are effects, and it hasn't been fully studied. It's an operation on the neck, the spinal column at the C2 and C3 vertebrae, where the nerves enter the column . . ."

She is turning around to find where she put her clothes. She's cold and hungry and has a date for breakfast she has no intention of missing.

"There could be paralysis and it could be permanent. Also, the positive effects could be temporary. They're still studying it, but it does sound promising, Agnes. Agnes? Where are you going?"

She's stood up to change into her clothes and pulled her thin, hospital gown off, standing naked in front of Dr. Mundra, who blushes. This man of science, married for four years with a newborn son, blushes in front of a thin, naked, and forward woman—a patient, a damaged person.

"Thank you, Dr. Mundra, really. I'll think on it. I'm supposed to be leaving in the next day or two, but I'll be in touch." She walks to the door and pulls at its heaviness.

"Agnes?"

"Yes, Doctor?"

"Take care."

* * * * *

She leaves the hospital and walks north along the park, trying to appreciate nothing but the beauty of the snow swirling about her feet and falling in the trees to her left. It had begun snowing the night before and hasn't stopped, and parked cars and newspaper stands wear several inches of white like an old woman's fox stole.

She'd left Oliver Pleasant alone in his apartment the previous night, having ridden uptown with him to see him safely home. When their evening had come to a close in the club, once the lights were up and the booze stopped flowing and their conversation had wound down, Oliver had rubbed his eyes with his meaty hands and said he was tired. As if on cue, Ben arrived with his overcoat. "Your car is upstairs, Ollie," he said, slipping the overcoat onto his friend's arms and over his rounded shoulders. Oliver shrugged it on and then stopped to steady himself on the table. "I'll have a waiter see you home; you're tired."

"Tired shit, I'm drunk. And tired. I'm cool, Benji baby, I'm cool."

"Ollie, please, let me send someone with you. Or wait and I'll take you myself."

"I'll get him home," Agnes offered.

"No, sugar, I'm all right, you go on. You get on back to New Orleans, hell of a lot warmer down there. Hot, as I recall, mosquitoes big as turnips . . ." He was rambling now, talking to his collar as he struggled to raise it around his jaw and button it all together.

Ben finished the buttoning for him and nodded to Agnes, who went for her own coat. She looked back to see the two men embrace and Ben slip a thick brown envelope into Oliver's coat pocket.

The cab stopped in front of a brownstone building in south Harlem just off Malcolm X Boulevard at West 115th Street. Oliver stepped out first and thanked the driver by name but didn't pay.

"You bet, Oliver. Take care," the driver said.

Agnes looked from Oliver to the driver and back. "Oh, hey, I'll get this." She dug through her coat pockets for cash.

The driver waved her off. "Have a nice night, miss."

Oliver's front room was spacious yet crammed with dusty furniture from a long-ago era. It was elegant and racked with memories; it was stacked with magazines and newspapers, and framed photos with signatures hung on every wall. The carpet was worn with traffic patterns and the glass tops of tables were yellowed from years of nicotine. The flat was well lived in. The photos—of musicians, actresses, a president, activists, icons, and legends— looked back at Agnes, welcomed her, surprised as they were to see a woman in this room after so many years. On one wall there hung hats, porkpies neatly arranged with cards in the hatbands. As Oliver dropped his coat in a chair and slumped back on a sofa, she let her eyes wander over those hats and cards that read Sinatra, Count, Lester, A. Taylor, Mingus, Monk. There were others and Agnes's head swooned, wishing her father were there to see them.

Another wall held books, a library's worth of literature with spines of gold, green, faded browns and blacks. "Where are they?" she'd asked.

"What's that, baby?"

"The missing books. Look at the shelves—some of them are empty except for the dust. Jesus, Ollie, you need to clean this place."

"The hell I need to clean for? Who's comin to visit old Ollie Pleasant these days?"

"Well, I'm here. Your kids, maybe?"

"Naw, they ain't comin by. Charlene the one took them books. Took the ones she wanted anyways, left the rest for me, I guess. For the mice."

"You got mice in here?"

"Naw, even the rats leavin Ollie be these days."

The room was warm and comfortable and Agnes liked it. There was music in that apartment; it seeped from the books and photos, and faded back into the carpet and floral wallpaper. There was no turntable on, no stereo she could find, yet she heard the melodies just as clearly as she had in the club earlier that evening, just as mysterious as what she'd experienced in New Orleans. It was the rhythm of the room, the beat of Oliver's heart, slowed now with so much time and fatigue.

Oliver had loosened his tie but didn't remove it. "Can I get you anything?" Agnes asked.

"Tea. Please."

She wandered into the small kitchen, a dingy room seemingly unused yet with a thin layer of grime on the surfaces; she found a teapot and a jar of loose herbal tea on the counter beside it.

They drank tea together and he shared more French cigarettes from a small box on an end table beside the photo of a beautiful woman. She sat next to him, feeling closer to the past than any history lesson or any Armstrong record could ever take her.

Across the room, a massive, black piano was wedged into the corner, its lid lifted just a bit, just enough for this room. It was an Imperial Bösendorfer, a wedding gift from Ira Greenberg. "Play for me," Oliver said, tilting his head back on the sofa pillows.

"Oh, no, I couldn't."

"Please."

Sitting at the piano, she brushed the fingertips of her right hand over the keys from end to end, trying to gather strength from them, trying to channel her father or, if at all possible, Oliver himself. She brought her left hand up and rested it on the keys, feeling the tremor there and willing it to stop, please, for just a few moments. *Let me have this,* she thought. *Let me play for him now, tonight.*

She played his own songs for him. Bold, she knew, but when would she ever, ever have this chance again? She played low and softly, concentrating on her left hand, both amazed and grateful that it was accommodating her. She lost herself in the music, going from one tune to another, a transfusion of music that bled from the trinkets and memories of the room, trying to infuse into Oliver's life a little of that which he'd given so much.

After fifteen minutes, or maybe it was an hour—Agnes had lost all track of time—her hand gave out in an ugly display when her knuckles crashed into the wrong notes and her arm dropped to her side. She was embarrassed and angry, but when she looked over at Oliver, he was asleep. With his head back, tie loosened, mouth agape, and a burning cigarette between his fingers, he seemed at peace. She watched him for a moment and then went over, took the cigarette from his hand and stubbed it out, covered him with an afghan, and kissed him on the cheek. "Thank you," she whispered.

She'd left Oliver's apartment for the long walk back to her hotel and had lost herself in thought as she watched the snow. It had been beautiful as it fell in the dark where she stood on the Manhattan Bridge looking at the lights of the city she'd just left, and at Brooklyn on the other side of the East River. She'd been aiming for the Brooklyn Bridge, that's the one she's always heard about, but had ended up on its sister. It was pretty enough, though, and she could see the Brooklyn Bridge from where she stood, the lights that span the cables illuminating the water and the heavy flakes appearing and disappearing into the darkness. She was suspended there between two cities, in midair like an abandoned balloon. The traffic was light, which made her feel even more alone, the cars drifting into silence behind her.

The day and hour of her death, she thinks at times, might be something she wants to speed up, something to meet head-on under her own terms. It's a bleak plan, yet it's what she'd been thinking then on the bridge when she met Frank Severs. The East River had been inky, swirling foam and glitter on its frigid whitecaps, and Agnes could only stare into it, wondering what that freezing water might feel like against her skin and in her lungs.

"Hey, I've seen you. Over at the Capasso, right?"

"Do I know you?"

"No, but I saw you at the show, Oliver Pleasant's, tonight, last night. . . ."

For a moment Agnes's head swirled like the river below her, thinking of the performance she'd just put on privately in Oliver's home. She cast her memory back into a river of liquor for any recognition of this man's face or of a club in Midtown Manhattan. Anything before her time with Oliver had ceased to exist for her. She'd only wanted to end the night alone looking at the city and wondering if this was it, wondering if her life would end beneath the surface of a frozen river after having played piano for her idol, and after having her sickness take over that recital by the end so that she finished in frustration and humiliation, even if Oliver had been asleep.

"Who the hell are you?" she said.

"Name's Frank Severs. I'm here to write a story about Pleasant. It's for a newspaper. I'm a reporter. Was a reporter, now I'm freelancing I guess. Jesus, it's cold up here."

"Where're you from?"

"Memphis."

"Shut the fuck up."

"It's true. Why? Why should I shut the fuck up?"

"Because that's where I'm from. Well, Tipton County."

"Still in my circulation area. Hey, were you at a bookstore in the Village yesterday?"

"You following me, you crazy fucker?" Her guard was up; she'd put many a bachelor party attendee and business traveler in his place in the Quarter.

"Following? No, no, the owner, Lucchesi, said I was the second Memphian he'd met that day. This is weird. Goddammit I'm drunk. What's your name?"

She softens at the mention of Lucchesi, also figuring she has nothing to lose having come to this bridge to die in the first place. "Agnes Cassady. You were at the Capasso earlier?"

"That's right."

"I think Oliver pointed you out. He pointed to someone he called a 'young man' and said he's from Memphis. You don't look so young close up."

"Thanks."

"You want a sip?" She'd stopped along the way for a half-pint of Cutty Sark and produced the bottle from deep within her coat. Frank, who had been drinking beer and bourbon with Davis McComber all evening, and wasn't sure how he ended up on the wrong side of Manhattan, nevertheless took the bottle and toasted New York with Agnes.

The whiskey warmed him, but only momentarily. "It's cold as shit out; what are you doing up here?"

"Jumping."

"Is that right?" He peered down over the railing and handed the bottle back to her. "What's stopping you?"

She pulled from the bottle before tucking it back away. "Wrong bridge. There's no poetry in jumping from the . . . what bridge is this?"

"Manhattan Bridge. I think? Don't ask me, I was heading for the clear other side of the island."

"Yeah, from the Manhattan Bridge." She peered over the railing down at the water. "You know, I bought a book from Lucchesi today, a collection of architectural blueprints and drawings, and this bridge was on the front cover. Guess I should've recognized it."

"Well, you're in no condition to go about recalling drawings. You're pretty drunk."

"You are, too. Anyway, if a person's gonna jump, it needs to be from the Brooklyn Bridge. That's why they built the goddamn thing."

"I can see that. How long have you been planning this jump?"

"Seven years, give or take."

"Getting a running start?"

She shrugged. "Waiting for the perfect moment, I guess, for the poetry in it. The music."

Frank looked up into the snowfall and at the lights on both sides of the river that reflected gold and silver in the water. "This is probably as dramatic as any time or place. I'd be happy to hold your coat, Miss Cassady, if you'd like."

"Such a gentleman. You seem in a hurry to watch somebody die tonight."

"I'm just a sucker for drama. You know, there's a good bridge back home, too. Big *M* on it. It'd be nice going down to look back up and see a letter. Dramatic."

"Been living in New Orleans."

"No bridges there?"

Agnes shrugged and drank again from the bottle. She looked back down into the water, knowing she wouldn't jump tonight. She had let the compulsion pass and agreed with herself to live another day, to feel pain again for yet another day, to lose more control for just one more goddamn day. She felt phlegm and bile rise in her throat from the decision and spit over the railing, arcing a wad of saliva far into the air. She and Frank both watched it climb, then get caught on the wind and carried away with the snow.

"You want to go somewhere, Frank? Get something to drink? Where you staying?"

He thought of Karen. He'd been thinking of Karen all night, missing her, or an idea of her anyway, and wondering where she was, who she might be with, whether or not she was thinking of him. He'd seen Agnes in the club, her white shoulders and the black dress that showed them off. No curves, but her limbs were long and he'd liked the way she moved across the room. He tried to imagine her in his bed, what it would feel like to be entwined with her, inside of her. She carried a sadness, though, that made her seem not less sexy but more vulnerable, and he could see it wasn't him she was looking for that night. Or, rather, that it could be anyone in front of her, it didn't matter who. And then he thought of Karen again. *I shouldn't have come here,* he thought to himself, not for the first time that day.

"How about a breakfast date?" he said. "I'm meeting Oliver Pleasant tomorrow at a diner uptown. If you're not floating in the East River, I'd love for you to join us."

She again considered her options and leaned on the frozen railing, hugging her shoulders. As long as she'd decided to live at least one more day, she might as well eat breakfast that day. "I'd be delighted," she said, finishing the bottle and heaving it into the air with an arc that bested her spit wad. They both watched it fall, in and out of light and into the river, and at least one of them wondered if a body, delicate yet damaged, would make much more of a splash than an empty liquor bottle. The snow and sleet burned into their faces and stung their eyes as they watched. It was the snow that Agnes blamed as she wiped the tears from her eyes.

Now, after leaving Mundra's office and walking up Fifth, she's proud of herself and her resoluteness to live whatever time she has left on her own terms. She'd seen so much of it when she was younger, the way her father's face would light up at the bravado of a doctor who thought he might be able to cure her, only to have it dashed when the study or medication didn't pan out. Sure, she's in New York for a miracle cure, for a treasure chest of procedures or pills, but so much of medicine now is habit and routine for her. Would she know what to do without the waiting rooms, forms, and bright lights in her eyes? So she listened to Mundra, absorbed what it was he could promise and what he could not, and took some literature with her. She finds that, just as she had with her mother and father, she feels bad for the doctors who seek to help her. They don't know the defeat she lives with, may not ever know it; they don't understand that she'll be dead by twenty-five, and it's nothing she can share with them; they would see it as fantasy, coming to her in fitful dreams she still has whether asleep or awake.

She feels like crying again and curses herself. People passing by are turning to look at her and she realizes she's talking out loud as she argues both sides. Mundra is offering her progress, a possible way out, and she's writing it off like it's a hoax or a promise in a fortune cookie. She takes more stock in her own death dream and in the voodoo fortune-teller who'd confirmed the notion for her. She can't think of Mundra's proposal now. She'll need to sit down with it later in the quiet when she can focus on what she might be gaining: control, painless days and nights, the hope of a life. Versus what she might be losing: She could die on the table. She could be paralyzed for good, never to play, not one note, ever again. She could lose a sense or two, her sight or, worse, hearing. With one nick of a scalpel, she could lose forever her ability to tap a key on the keyboard or to ever hear Oliver play again.

It's a heavy weight to pile on a person's shoulders, so she puts it out of her mind as best she can and stops to watch some children in the park sledding down a hill and throwing snowballs and a father and daughter building a snowman. She looks up to the sky, at the flakes rushing down to meet her, breathes in the crisp, cold air, and crosses the street to the diner.

2.

The diner is as bright and warm as it had been on Agnes's first morning in New York. Around the stained and chipped tabletop of the third booth from the back wall sits a disparate group of diners, a group of castaways adrift in their vinyl and Formica lifeboat. Trapped on this island of Manhattan is an old black man in a porkpie hat sitting beside a thin and dark-complected boy going to great pains to cut a sausage link with a butter knife. Across the table is a middle-aged man fingering his phone as he waits on a call, and next to him, a thin and pale young woman with her head resting in her open palm as she sips from a cup of coffee without taking it from her face. It is as though the steam is warming her as much as the diner's radiator heat and kitchen fires. They are four people as similar as they are unique—one at the end of his career, one lost in the middle, one who dreams of beginning, and the fourth, a child, not knowing what is ahead of him. None of them know for sure what awaits them; they're all discontent, all frightened for the future whether it be tomorrow, next year, or a decade away.

"Ain't this the hell of it," Oliver says, scraping food around his plate into one big mess of breakfast. "The morning after ain't never as glamorous, never as pretty, never sounds as good as the night before. That's the truth of whatever you find yourself in, music, novel writin, whatever; it ain't never as good after as when you're in it. Pass me that syrup."

The night before, Frank and Agnes had walked together from the bridge with her arm in his and found themselves in Little Italy beneath bare bulbs strung across a street flanked by colorful Cinzano umbrellas even in the cold of night. Frank flagged a cab for her to get back to her hotel.

"You sure you won't have a drink?" she'd asked when he'd put his hand on the door handle. She hadn't let go of him but instead pulled him closer so he could see her moist eyes in the city light and smell the whiskey on her breath.

He considered it again, however briefly, and seemed to pack a whole night's worth of pleasure into that moment before opening the car's door. He brushed his lips to her temple. "See you for breakfast, Agnes Cassady."

He walked back to his hotel. Something had passed between them on that bridge. Flirting? There may be no setting more romantic than a New York bridge in snowfall. And what man and woman don't flirt in some capacity, whether lifelong friends or sitting down for a dinner party as strangers? This, though, was a mere passing on the street, suspended over rushing water, and he knows nothing about her other than she's from his hometown and also has an interest not just in jazz but specifically in Oliver Pleasant. What are the odds of meeting that person on a bridge over the East River? She was even destined for the Brooklyn Bridge, where they might not have come across each other at all. Did that mean something? For her to be in the wrong place? Was this the fate of which Lucchesi spoke?

"Why are you here?" Agnes had asked Frank the night before on the bridge.

"I'm lost," he'd said. "And I prefer the Manhattan Bridge; it doesn't have that big-time Hollywood status. It's the underdog bridge. Besides, I can stand on this one and look at the Brooklyn Bridge."

He'd thought of Agnes as he'd walked, the sadness in her eyes, the urging in her voice as she'd invited him somewhere, anywhere. He felt as though he'd talked her off that bridge. He wasn't certain how serious she was about jumping, but if her intentions were true, he's glad she didn't go through with it. Impulsively, he called Karen. It was close to 3:00 a.m. by then and he knew she'd be angry, but he just wanted to hear her voice and to know he made the right decision not to get into that cab. He wanted to know that the decision not to find out where that ride would have ended had been his own and that it mattered. There are things Frank is missing—his wife's touch, her compassion and empathy, her welcoming smile when he arrives home at night from work. He isn't sure, though, if he only started missing them when he landed in New York, or if it's what's been missing from his life for a time. He isn't sure how long this hunger has been with him.

She didn't answer. He left a voice mail, though this morning he isn't completely sure of what he'd said, but he knows he asked her to call him. He hopes there was no anger in his voice and, if so, that it will be overlooked, understood. He'd thought of redialing but instead powered his phone off and shuffled along streets quiet with the buffer of snowfall, trying not to feel sorry for himself and thinking maybe it was time to make a change. The streetlights wore halos of light, snow clung wet to his neck and shoulders, and he thought again of Agnes, wondered again where Karen might be—and if with someone else, was she thinking of him?

At first light that morning, Frank had grabbed his phone, powered it on, and waited helplessly for the voice-mail icon. There wasn't one and so he began his day with that sick, kicked-in-the-stomach feeling of loss. He'd dressed and left the hotel, walking the entire way to the diner on sidewalks intermittently shoveled of snow. Near the park he caught sight of Agnes leaving Mount Sinai

Hospital and raised his arm, thinking to call out, but changed his mind as a cab pulled to the curb. "No, sorry, I was waving to my friend." The driver swore at him in an exotic language and pulled away. Frank stayed a block behind her for the length of the park, stopping when she did to watch children playing in the snow. He was enchanted by her warm smile, a sharp contrast to the drunk, lonely, suicidal woman he'd met on the bridge the previous night. He wondered why she had been at the hospital. Visiting a sick friend?

Entering the diner (Frank had waited outside, stamping his feet a few more minutes so they didn't enter together), she was tired all over again, her glow in the cold melting into the moist diner heat. It possibly faded from the walk, Frank thought, or maybe from whatever it was that took her to a hospital on such a fresh winter morning.

"How old are you, Winky?" Agnes asks the boy sitting across from her. She's fixated on his face, so open with wonder, since she sat down and Frank introduced them. She wasn't sure how Frank, who came in only just after her, knew the boy.

"Ten." And then, more to himself and his plate of food, "Name ain't Winky."

"It isn't?" She looks to Frank, who just shrugs, and they both look to the boy for an answer.

"This here Pablo," Oliver answers for him.

"Nice to meet you, Pablo," Agnes says. "Ten years old, so . . . fourth grade?"

"Fifth!" He sits up straighter then, jabs a fork at his plate.

"Boy, pick that meat up with your fingers," Oliver says.

"Oliver's your friend?" Agnes asks. "Where'd you two meet?"

Pablo looks up at Oliver as though he's surprised to find him there, then blinks at Agnes, who isn't sure whether it's the location and circumstance of their meeting that's causing confusion or the fact that he has a friend. "We met on the stoop."

"He lives upstairs from me, with his mama and daddy."

"Ain't my daddy."

"That's right, ain't your daddy. Wants me to teach him how to play the piano. Ain't that right, Pablo? You gonna be a concert pianist when you grown?"

"Teaching? Cool. I had a teacher when I was a girl. Her name was Ms. Gaerig. Would've much rather had Ollie as a teacher."

"Ollie!" Pablo's head tips back and he laughs, sausage bits stuck to his teeth, his lips glistening with grease.

"What do you call him?" Agnes says.

"Licoricehead."

"Pablo a racist," Oliver adds.

"I don't even know what that is," says Pablo, before adding, "Ollie."

"Why don't you teach him?" Frank says, putting his phone back in his shirt pocket. "Could be good for both of you."

"Too damn old. Too tired. I taught many a youngster when I was a younger man, but them lessons happened late at night, jam sessions after a gig when we'd all sit around and drink and smoke. That's when the young bucks'd show up, 'Pops, show me that lick' . . . 'Pops, play that tune for us slow so we can figure it.' Why he want to learn piano? Why you want to learn, Pablo?"

"Sounds good to me. Sounded real good last night—pretty, like I was in a dream."

"Last night?" Oliver says.

"Yeah, coming up through my floor. It was slow and so quiet I had to get out of bed and put my ear to the floor."

Agnes blushes and wants to remind Oliver that she played for him, maybe even remind him that she took him home, but sees it all come back to him and flash in his face with a smile. He looks over and winks at her.

"You like that, boy?" Oliver says. "It was pretty, wasn't it? It was real pretty."

This should be a happy occasion, this meeting over fried pork and eggs, a joyous meeting of like-minded souls adrift on their raft and feeling real salvation close at hand. They all have a spirit hovering above them; they've all been touched by the muse at one time in their lives or another and can sense her still there, but each has hardened in some way, whether through loss, distance, or lying too close to the real world where the muse gets skittish. The wrecks and disasters that have thrown them into this boat together have caused a cataract to form over their eyes until they can't see clearly that the muse is still there within their very souls.

They're a miserable lot, these three. All except Pablo, who's only glad to be away from home and with adults who aren't screaming at each other or at him, who aren't either lashing out or neglecting. If this is a lifeboat, he might be thinking, *let it drift away from here, let the current take me where it will; I'm ready for whatever else there is.*

* * * * *

In contrast to the welcoming environment of the diner, the facility Oliver enters now has the same glaring white light and industrial grade and color of paint as Agnes's hospitals, yet it shares none of the antiseptic smell or healing properties. There is a pungent mixture of orange-scented cleanser and feces in the air, and people stooped over, shaped like human question marks, shuffle by in worn slippers and open robes. The linoleum is green where it isn't scuffed gray, and the clocks—heavy metal IBMs protruding from the walls—are mostly stuck at different times. No matter, these people have no place to go, time having stopped for them months or years before.

It had stopped for Stanton Harris about six years earlier after a series of strokes left him temporarily incoherent and disoriented, though his motors skills were left wholly, blessedly intact. Oliver now sits across the table from Stanton, a mere shell of the man who used to play bass with him in the clubs of Harlem and on the road from coast to coast. No one would recognize the man who could at one time stand onstage and hoist by its neck, one-handed, an instrument the size of a lifeboat. No one would recognize the man who once took a knife to the thigh during a fight with two sailors on leave while Oliver and he were playing with some other cats on the south side of Chicago.

It's a memory now that Stanton Harris might not even hold. It's that weight of memory that could finally crush him in his weakened state with his brittle bones. Oliver watches his old friend as Stanton studies the checkerboard, trying to figure out his next move. Oliver wonders if he's forgotten about the game, but he knows the man's mind is still sharp despite what the doctors say—as sharp as a tool can stay in such dull surroundings.

This is where Oliver doesn't want to end up. This is what scares Oliver almost more than death itself. It's what prompted him to call Charlene and ask for a place to live, for help. It's why he's agreed to move a thousand miles away to a city he last remembers for its Jim Crow laws and the murder of a civil rights leader. Oliver doesn't want to die so slowly, surrounded by people paid a minimum wage to barely give a damn whether someone in their charge has eaten or been cleaned.

"You gonna move or sit there all day, young man?" Oliver is only two years older than Stanton and never lets him forget he's his elder.

"I'm thinking, goddammit, I'm thinking."

"Thought you'd fallen asleep on me."

"I'd as soon stay awake than fall asleep on your ugly ass. There. Your move, old-timer."

Oliver has been making this trip up to Morris Heights—next to the Bronx Zoo and Botanical Garden, where he and Francesca used to take the kids when he'd roll back into town—once a month or so for the past two years, ever since he learned Stanton had been sent to the retirement home by his only son, who lives in a duplex with five kids on Long Island. Oliver is pretty sure he's the only one who visits Stanton. So far he's put off telling him that he's moving away.

"You go by Minton's on the way up?" Stanton knows that Oliver's bus passes through the heart of Harlem on his way to the nursing home, and he always asks about clubs where they played together. He asks if Oliver had seen a mutual friend of theirs, long dead, as he passed through. Oliver explains each time, with the impatience of an old man, that everything—every goddamn thing—is changed.

"Boy, Minton's been closed for fifty years."

"Minton's closed? I'll be goddamned. That's a shame. Now, look at this old girl here; she sweet on me." A pear-shaped nurse, light-skinned with a map of freckles and raised moles across her cheeks and the bridge of her nose, walks by pushing a cart with one hand. She wears bright purple scrubs and is thumb-typing on her phone with her free hand. "Hey, sweetheart, you gonna stick me now?"

"I'll be back, Stanton. You on my list. Don't you go nowhere!"

"I ain't leavin you." Then, to Oliver, "She give me my diabetes medicine. I think she likes it."

"Lucky, I guess. I got to stick myself."

"So what you doin up here, Ollie? You just here two weeks ago. I know it ain't the ambiance. They ain't spruced the place up in never. Not even any music in these halls. You believe that? There should be music all up and down these hallways to cheer a motherfucker up."

"You got it in your room?"

"Yeah, old son of a bitch I share it with grumbles, but I don't give a good goddamn. He can grumble himself into the grave, I got to hear my boys play."

"Who you listenin to these days?"

"All of 'em. Mingus this morning."

"Ol' Cholly."

"Mingus!" Stanton shouts out at the checkerboard so the pair playing at the next table over jumps at the sound. Oliver laughs with Stanton.

The two old men sit in silence for a time, watching the board like it might get up and walk out on its own two checkered feet, each in his own thought. They rarely, at this age, think of the future. It might not be that afternoon, it might not be the next day, it might not even be in a week, but their time on this earth is limited. If they think in seasons, this might be their last. If they think in holidays, they might not live to see another wreath on the door. So they don't think about it, or they try not to.

"Respect!" Stanton shouts after a time, and the pair at the next table jumps again.

Oliver doesn't. He's come to expect these outbursts during their time together. It's something old black musicians feel they have a right to shout, something they're sure is now a common denominator just as the music, women, and drugs once were. The invective this afternoon is fired with a good amount of vitriol, and not a little spit clings now to Stanton's bottom lip and glistens on his side of the checkerboard like droplets of anger.

Oliver hands him a handkerchief. "Wipe your lip, Stanton. Respect for what?" Though he knows it's coming, and he knows how long it will last, Oliver humors his friend. It's a right his old sideman has earned.

"For us. For the colored man and musician. They took our music from us, Ollie; they took it and sold it out over radio and picture shows and television. Ofay bought our clubs and paid us shit. Shit, Ollie, that's what we worked all them years for. We made that music, that *jazz*." This last word is filled with as much rancor and spittle as "respect" had been. Stanton falls into the line of disenfranchised who don't care for the name, a description given to the services sold in old-world New Orleans cathouses. The music started there, music played for men laying their seed and for a few coins to drown out the sound and keep the girls happy. But the white men needed to name it if they were going to sell it, and "jazz"—or, "jass"—just seemed to roll off the tongue.

"It's why we ain't got nothin, not shit," Stanton continues. "Why I'm here in a old-folks home for coloreds. It ain't changed; it's segregation, it's racism, it's Jim Crow moved into a new century. Shit. I ain't want their money anyway, but I do want some respect, respect for what we—colored men—gave to the world."

By now the people at the other tables are watching and listening to Stanton. Oliver is sure they've heard it before, maybe the last time Oliver was there or when Stanton cries out in his sleep. Whether or not they remember his last outburst, he can't be sure. Oliver figures there must be speeches like this one made on a regular basis—angry retired bus drivers, cooks, maids, deliverymen, foremen, and street sweepers. They just want to talk, but more, they want to be heard. And respected. *That ain't much to ask,* Oliver thinks.

Silence falls again over their game and Stanton's head nods, exhausted from his tirade and drawing up the past. This is expected as well, and Oliver looks up to the clock mounted on the green cinder-block wall. Three twelve it reads, though who can be sure? He takes the time to consider his friend, his grayed face and patches of white stubble where the nurses had trouble shaving, or didn't care enough to attend to. Stanton's nose is wide and flat and runs just a little, his head gleams in the fluorescent lighting, and his ears are enormous. Oliver has trouble remembering what this withered elf looked like back in the day, back when they were young men full of brass and piss who would eat an early dinner of steak and fries before playing and drinking all night long, scooping up women along the way like they

were so many wildflowers before calling it a night and trudg-
ing back uptown or down into subways full of the pressed suits
and creased newspapers of men going to work. The man sitting
across from him now doesn't even have a hint of that young man,
and Oliver misses him. He wonders if anyone recognizes Oliver's
younger self, either. Probably not.

"What you doin up here, Ollie?" Stanton has looked up from
his brief nap, unaware that he'd even had one.

Oliver leans back and mops beneath his hat brim with a handkerchief. "Stanton." He lets out a long sigh. "Brother Stanton.
Afraid I'm leavin these parts."

"Leavin, huh? Where you goin to? LA? Gonna cut a record?
Make a movie?" He chuckles halfheartedly at his own joke.

"Naw, shit. Headin south to Memphis, stay with my sister and
baby niece."

"Memphis? No shit?"

"No shit, brother."

"You remember that time in Memphis when them crackers
stopped us to ask what we had in the case? You remember? You
was carryin my case and that one old cop says, 'What you got in
that case, boy?' Remember that?"

Oliver laughs at the memory. "Yeah, yeah, I remember that."

"And you says, 'I'm a piano player, suh.'" Stanton laughs, bar-
ing the five teeth he has left in his mouth—four are yellow and
decayed and the fifth is wrapped in gold, his gums run purple to
black. But he laughs at his tale and doesn't care what he looks like.
He laughs for all of their times together and for the end itself.

Oliver laughs as well, but with a pang in his gut, a growing
sense of apprehension at moving to the South. That instance was
funny and even the cops had laughed as they told the musicians
to "get their nigger asses off my street," but there was plenty that
wasn't funny. The very fact that he has to move so far from his
home isn't funny and neither is his friend finishing a life of music

and travel and swinging times in a concrete government-assisted facility that stinks like the bathrooms at Yankee Stadium.

"Hey, you get to leave here ever?" Oliver says.

"Can leave anytime I please, I ain't a caged animal. You see any bars on these windows?"

Oliver does, in fact, see bars on all the windows and heavy locks on all of the steel doors, but those might be to keep people of the neighborhood out rather than the residents in.

"Still play piano any?"

"Sure, got one in the cafeteria. Need tuning, but she still plays. Ain't got no bass, breaks my heart, not that my arthritis would let me play the damn thing anyways. Why?"

"If I set you up with teachin lessons, you think you could get there once a week? Maybe twice? Make a little scratch for yourself, get out and take some fresh air."

"Lessons? Who?"

"Boy I know. I can't teach him, I got to leave, but he wantin to learn somethin fierce. He lives in the apartment above me. His daddy went down in the towers."

"That right? Huh. Lessons you say. Yeah, man, yeah, I'll do it. You tell that boy I'll start up week after next. Can't go next week, got my dialysis and I ain't never know on what day."

That settled, the men make a couple more moves on the checkerboard and Stanton asks about Oliver's recent shows. He wishes aloud that he could've gone to one, but they won't let him out after dark, not to travel the length of Manhattan. Oliver says he understands and wishes Stanton could've come, too. Oliver tells him who all has stopped by, lies and tells his old friend that they all asked after him. Before long the nurse comes back down the hall, still pecking at her phone.

"Hey, baby!" Stanton shouts at her again. "You comin for me?"

"Here I come, Stanton, keep your pants on."

"Come on, baby, and put it in me!"

* * * * *

Charlene has her father's depth of skin color but her mother's long Mediterranean nose and green eyes. She is, quite simply, striking, though it takes some time in her presence to realize this. Her features aren't conventional, not by any stretch. Frank, sitting at the kitchen table and watching her prepare tea and pour it into two delicate cups, is put in mind not of a typical Park Slope wife and mother but of Madame Fairbanks in a New Orleans he's never even known.

"What is it, exactly, that you want with me, Mr. Severs?" she says, placing a cup in front of him and taking the seat opposite for herself.

"Please, call me Frank. I'm from Memphis, and I'm writing a story on your father and his retirement. I was hoping to get some memories of growing up with him as a father."

"I'm not sure how much growing up I did with Oliver. You may want to record the memories of bus drivers or club owners on the other coast."

"He wasn't around much, I take it?"

"Have you spoken with Oliver yet?"

"Oh, yes ma'am. I've talked with him at length and been to the past two nights of shows. Probably go again tonight."

"Well then, you've just spent as much time with him as I did collectively as a child."

The tension in the room is carried upward on steam from the tea, and despite the heat, Frank sips at it just for something to do. He looks around the well-appointed kitchen with modern appliances, granite, and exposed brick rising from the oven. The hallway he'd entered was gleaming hardwood and he can see it continues into the living area just off the kitchen. "This is a great house. Have you lived here long?"

"We've lived in Park Slope for twenty years. This was our first house and we've spent all of those twenty years restoring it to what it is now."

"You and your husband?"

"And our son, Cedric."

"Any chance you'll stop in to hear your father before his five-night stand is over?"

"I've heard Oliver play."

There are children outside in the snow—Frank can hear their calls and laughter in the awkward silences that punctuate his conversation with Charlene. What he notices, what's been nagging at him since he entered the home but he just couldn't place, is that there is no music. It may be the one place he's visited in New York that hasn't had some sort of music in the background. He suddenly wishes he was out there with those children, wishes he were anywhere else but in Charlene's kitchen in this too-quiet home. Sensing she won't open up, Frank decides there's nothing to lose and pushes the issue.

"Mrs. Wilson, Oliver is about to give up his life in New York, the place he's called home for more than sixty years, to move to Memphis with a sister he hasn't seen in decades and a niece he's never met in person. He's broke and doesn't want to die alone. Can I ask why you can't, or won't, help him in this hour? What is it that happened between you two that you can't even cross the river to go hear him play one last time?"

The anger that flashes in those ancestral Italian eyes makes Frank wish he'd kept his mouth shut. Once again he slurps the scalding tea and feels the steam on his skin. Charlene's upper lip stiffens and he prepares himself to be thrown out of her beautiful home, to be put out with those children building snowmen and throwing snowballs. But then her features soften and he sees some of Oliver's playfulness come into her eyes.

"What's your favorite Oliver Pleasant tune, Frank?"

He has to think about that, but offers "Blues for Chesca." He loves the song, but he also thinks it might win some favor with Francesca's daughter.

"That's a lovely song. Would you like to know what my favorite is?"

"Please." This is the kind of detail that works so well in stories.

"My favorite Oliver Pleasant song is 'Twinkle, Twinkle, Little Star.' Have you ever heard him play 'Twinkle, Twinkle, Little Star'?"

"Well . . . no ma'am."

"Do you want to know why my favorite song of his is 'Twinkle, Twinkle, Little Star'?"

Frank nods, feeling like a chastened boy in trouble with his mother.

"Because he only played it for me. Only me. He didn't record it; he didn't open a show with it or fit it into a set list. No one in California or Texas or Paris or Memphis, Tennessee, has heard his rendition of 'Twinkle, Twinkle, Little Star' on piano because it is a song that he played for me while I sat on the bench beside him on those nights when he was home. Those very few nights. And on all those nights when Pops wasn't home, I would step outside our house and look up to those stars and think that he was seeing them, too. He taught me that song, and to this day it's the only tune I know how to play on piano."

Frank wishes again for music, or any distraction at all to come crashing into the room. Charlene's lip that had revealed such anger only moments earlier now trembles and she stands to retrieve the carafe of hot water, glancing out a window over the sink at the children outside before bringing it back to the table. Neither cup is low enough to need a refill.

"Has he told you about Hamlet Giraud?"

"His friend the trombonist? Well, in passing, in stories of the road and gigs."

"Sure, sure he did. Did he mention how Hamlet died?" Here, the sadness that had trembled her lip fills her eyes as well, those piercing emeralds going to pools of green in an instant.

"He died in a car accident, didn't he? Here in New York?"

"He did. He died in a car accident while scuttling my father's mistress away from our house. Away from my mother's home, Mr. Severs."

In all the research he's done on Oliver that had led to information on Hamlet Giraud, he hasn't read that story anywhere. There are accounts of Giraud dying young in an early morning wreck on the FDR, and rumors that he was with an unidentified woman—a woman not his wife.

"Who was she?" Frank's reporter instincts have taken over and he assumes the crass, blunt questioning reserved for victims' families.

"Her name was Marie Broussard, from Paris. I attended Hamlet's funeral. I was eight at the time and I wondered then why we were there. We weren't churchgoing people and it was the middle of the week. My mother wore black and my father cried. I'd never seen him cry before then. He played piano and a choir sang. My mother, through it all, stared straight ahead, not even turning to look at my father, who sobbed like a child as he played that slow funeral dirge. Once I put it all together, sometime as a young woman perhaps, if not later that day, I wondered at my mother's attendance there at all. The circumstances surrounding the day, that week, make me realize just how strong my mother was." She looks at Frank, the piercing green back again and driving through his brain. "And, Mr. Severs, just how weak Oliver could be."

Frank is numb, yet his spine and scalp tingle at the same time. This story is one that's been speculated on by music historians and pop-culture fanatics for years.

"I've kept it inside all this time. I don't know why. To protect Oliver? To honor the memory of my mother? Who's to say? But I know Hamlet's children; we grew up together. I still see them and the knowledge of it, that it wasn't their father's mistress in that car, but *my* father's, is something I feel I'm wearing pinned to the front of my coat every time they're near. They know it, I'm sure of it. I can sense it every time I run across Johnny Giraud in the subway or his sister, Maddie, in the market. Their crowd knew, musicians know, but *musicians*"—this last word has been spat out—"protect their own. Well, I'm no musician and I ain't here to protect nobody no more. You dig?"

She wipes her eyes and jumps up from the table to pour her tepid tea into the sink. She refills her cup with steaming water and places the discarded tea bag back into the cup.

"This story, Mrs. Wilson . . ."

"You do with it what you will, Frank Severs. I know why you're here. I understand what it is you do and I'm telling you that I'm tired of it all. I'm too old now to keep secrets and it's been too many years of hiding and hating. I told you the story; it's yours now."

"I need to ask you one other thing, if I could."

"What else do I have? I've given it all, Mr. Severs, every drop."

Frank shakes his head slowly. "I don't mean any disrespect here, Mrs. Wilson. Christ, I never thought things would become so apparent and that the noise could be so loud, considering everybody's intent to keep so quiet."

"What are you getting at, Mr. Severs?"

"You know about Martin Lucchesi, the bookseller in Greenwich Village? You know about him and your mother, don't you?"

When Frank had arrived, Charlene kept him waiting in a paneled study just inside the front door. He'd let his reporter's eyes—working again and intensely investigative and curious—fall over the decorations, the knickknacks, and the family photos. The Wilsons collect African art and there were tribal masks, small carved idols of female shapes ripe with maternity, and photos of the Serengeti on every wall. He worked his way to the bookshelves and saw contemporary titles and a large selection of African American literature—Langston Hughes, Richard Wright, Toni Morrison, Alex Haley, Alice Walker, and Zora Neale Hurston, first editions all. Among them were older-looking volumes, the ghost of dust lining the shelves around the spines. He reached up and pulled one down on a hunch and there it was, on the inside cover, a printed "ML" with straight lines made with India ink and the wide nib of a fountain pen. It was bold, not only in its structure but also in the way it flew in the face of a marriage and with the full knowledge of both sides of the story as Frank now knew them. And then, in the back, was Francesca's scripted, feminine "FP." It was thin and lovely, almost sad, yet with a curl to the handwriting that evoked fun and a certain playfulness.

He took down another volume and found the same. Another, and there they were as well. Charlene knows, he'd realized. She's known for at least as long as her mother has been dead, but how long before that, Frank wondered.

Charlene stands from the table again and walks to the window, and Frank allows the silence to permeate the room, welcomes it this time. She buries her face in her hands and her shoulders shake and quiver with sobbing. He's sorry all of this came up, but something in him won't let the inequality rest. He can't stand to see Oliver's side of the scales tip so far with guilt and regret.

"You know?" she finally says.

"Yes ma'am. I spoke with Lucchesi yesterday."

"And he told you."

"He told me he loved your mother very much and that your mother was very lonely. They both were. But it was understood she wouldn't leave your father, or you and your brothers. Mrs. Wilson, I'm not saying this to defend any of Ollie's actions. He did what he did and that's for you and your family to work through. But your mother took comfort elsewhere and I'm just trying to understand how one is better than the other. If it is at all. Your mother was lonely, but your father is lonely now as well. He misses Francesca, and he misses you."

Charlene doesn't move from the window, but Frank feels that whatever anger she might have felt has lessened, has seeped through the chinked caulking around the century-old window and brick and cooled in the snow on the sill there. He stands and thanks Charlene for her time and for the tea. She doesn't speak but only stares out at the children playing in the street. On his way out, a glance into a sunlit room opposite the study where he'd waited before shows him an old phonograph and a wall of shelves, like Francesca's wall of books, and Charlene's now, but filled with record albums. There is a comfortable sitting chair that looks from the window out to the street, where children play. The only other piece of furniture in that room is an antique upright piano that might have, at one time, been covered with handmade quilts and flour sacks, and rolled in place across a floor covered in sawdust.

* * * * *

Agnes and Frank sit at Oliver's table and can sense the envy of this seating arrangement coming from the other patrons. Those patrons may even recognize the bottle of Campari that awaits him, or the blue pack of Gitanes and cut-glass ashtray. The couple could also feel the bitterness emanating from the hostess station as Ben bypassed Marcie to show them to this table. They talk about their day, though both hold back, not wanting to reveal their real destinations or purposes. Instead, the talk is a desultory tour of easily recognizable landmarks and sites. It's idle talk without the telling.

For Agnes, however, it is mostly true. She's spent the day alone in this city of millions, walking through the park, window-shopping, dipping into subway stations, not to board a train but to listen to the street musicians. Passing again alongside Mount Sinai, she'd spotted a tall man in a turban and rushed to catch up, but found it wasn't Dr. Mundra. She wasn't sure what she would have said, but he was on her mind. He and his offer of respite, or complete failure. The prospect of being healed, even if it's a short while, is almost too much hope to place on such fragile shoulders. It is easier, she thought as she walked the avenues, to consider the previous night and the option of leaping into the black water of the East River. That is final; that's a decision made on her own terms.

It's an odd juxtaposition, she'd thought, as she took a moment to look at the massive lion guardians of the public library, to consider the peace and beauty of playing piano alone for Oliver Pleasant in his home and the very real possibility of falling to her death only an hour later. One should almost preclude the other. Almost. There was that nasty spill at the end of her playing, though. All control abandoning her and her body reacting to whatever the broken nerves had commanded. And that's the crux of it all, that's the push she might need while leaning over the rail of the wrong bridge.

Frank, meanwhile, had stood outside Charlene's home to watch the kids there running and shouting with a wild abandon that throws all concern for decorum and, in some cases, safety out of the window. Playing in the snow is a happiness lost with adulthood for most people, and Frank misses it. He misses Karen, too, and had optimistically imagined her playing in the snow with their child. There was a bench nearby and he sat with his notebook to fill in the notes he'd taken at the kitchen table. It was cold, but he ignored it, focusing instead on what Charlene had said, wondering where it had all gone wrong within that family and wondering as well why she was too stubborn to put it all aside. Oliver has kept a table for his children these nights and wants desperately for them to show.

Midafternoon sun fell on his bench and it was pleasant sitting in Park Slope with kids playing nearby and nowhere to be until later that night. He took his phone out in hopes that he'd missed a call from Karen. He hadn't, so he called her.

"How are you feeling?" It was the first thing he asked after the greetings.

"Better. I guess my body is getting used to it all."

"Maybe that's a good sign." He couldn't explain this burst of optimism, whether it had awakened after visiting the depths of despair on a bridge at midnight or hearing the secrets of an estranged family. Or perhaps it was the sun on a frigid winter day in Brooklyn. Frank looked around, hoping that maybe Paul Auster would walk past.

"Where are you?"

"Park Slope, Brooklyn. I came by to talk to Charlene Wilson, Oliver's daughter."

"How was it?" There was sincerity in Karen's voice.

"Interesting. It's a sad situation—the family is torn apart, though she lives so close by. It's nothing new, though; the rift was born a long time ago when Charlene was a little girl."

"That's a shame."

"It really is. I wish they'd reconnect, family should be closer. It's too important."

Karen told him she'd taken a sick day and was still in bed; it had turned colder in Memphis and she couldn't face another gray day beyond their house. She was comfortable, she said, alternately reading and watching television. She was glad he called and he was, too. She wished he were there—again, sincerely—and he did, too. Desperately.

He thinks of the phone call now and imagines Karen at home in bed as Oliver plays "All of Me." He'd wanted to leave Brooklyn as soon as the phone call had ended and catch a cab to the airport to get him home, but he knew that was impractical. Another two days and he'd be there with Karen to face whatever may come next in regards to career, his writing, and their lives together.

"Where she at? I know she's out there, been here every night so far. There she is. Come on up here, Miss Cassady." Oliver scans the crowd and finally points to his own table. The crowd turns to see who he's talking about, to learn who this "Cassady" might be. They collectively don't recognize her.

Frank is confused as he's drawn from his daydream and glances at Agnes, who is just as confused. When Oliver's words finally register, she shakes her head and tries to wave him off. But now everyone is staring at her; squinting eyes and wrinkled faces turn, smiling and toasting with cocktails, urging her onto the bandstand. She turns to Frank.

"Jump," he says, and winks.

And she does.

Gazing down from the stage onto the room and people there is vastly different from anything she's used to. Talent shows in Tipton County certainly didn't carry the drama of Ben's club. The bars in New Orleans are raucous and tourists, within an arm's length of the bandstand, pay only cursory attention to what happens up there. There were nights when Agnes cussed them from the micro- phone and suggested the dive's owner simply put in a goddamned jukebox for all the attention the band was being paid. At Landon's parties, of course, she was meant to be backdrop, the liquor and young bodies circulating at the forefront. But here, with Oliver leaning back on a bar stool provided by Andrew Sexton and beside the piano with a microphone in hand, and looking around at this crowd that has come for only one person, she is truly terrified.

Placing her hand on his shoulder, she whispers to him, "Ollie, please, I can't. My hand, I'll fuck this up."

"Baby, you just play it like you did last night, ain't no differ- ence. Look at me and play it for me. Just to me. 'Night and Day,'" he calls to the band, and they take Agnes's lead.

At first she looks only at Oliver, draws upon his strength and musicianship, and the notes come easy. It's as though she's in

218

Landon's parlor again and she half expects the audience to begin changing clothes. But there's also comfort and nostalgia, and she feels as though she might be in her parents' house and her father is, if not on the bench beside her, then in the room, whether in person or as memory.

She closes her eyes and feels the warmth of the spotlight on her, lets it sink in that she's playing piano in a New York nightclub with a band backing her and an audience of jazz lovers watching. It's all she's ever wanted and it pushes everything else to the side and out of sight. Gone are the thoughts of Mundra and his pink turban, a bridge of cold steel, the passing beds of men, and along with it all goes the pain, the trembling, the fear.

Just let me stay here, right here, she thinks. *Forever.*

When she hears Oliver, she opens her eyes. He's singing, low and with the distinct phrasing of Billie Holiday. She doesn't think she's ever heard him sing on any recordings and the timbre of it— low and grumbling with years of French tobacco—is lovely. She looks again to the people and they are happy with it all.

She's so grateful to Oliver for this that she could cry, but she doesn't have time. The song ends and Oliver calls out Monk's "Blue Sphere." It is technically more difficult, and she's never played it with a band, but she manages. The music holds her up and even seems to suspend her left arm and hand, to keep it on track and in control. There are no lyrics, but Oliver stands at one point and spins, teetering from side to side. "Monk's dance!" he laughs, and the crowd laughs with him at his impression of the eccentric pianist. It's obvious that Oliver is having fun and the mood is light, and this helps to put Agnes at ease. She plays the long fills, from one end of the keyboard to the other, and Oliver jumps back as though impressed, looks back at the band, and shouts, "You cats diggin this?" The band hollers back, "Jump, Miss Agnes! Swing!" All she's ever wanted.

When that song winds down, Oliver calls another Monk tune and the band takes its cue and backs down. It's solo Agnes now and she feels Oliver is saying something to her by choosing the song "Everything Happens to Me." It's how they all feel—she, Oliver, and Frank. *It's how we all feel, every one of us,* she thinks as she takes a trip down through the keys. *All the world's shit is dumped only on each of us and it's up to us to figure out how to crawl through it.* Oliver wipes his brow and watches her hands as she plays and the place goes to a hush.

She doesn't want it to end, but neither does she wish to push her luck and lose control. Oliver leads the ovation and introduces her again to the audience: "Miss Agnes Cassady from Memphis, Tennessee, by way of New Orleans—my hometowns! Now, you step down off my stage, this is my show. Can't have you cuttin me like that on my retirements." The crowd is polite and the applause lasts through her embracing Oliver and her walk back to the table, where Frank is standing and clapping. She drops into the booth, exhausted, as Ben hands her a fresh drink.

"Well played, Miss Cassady," he says.

Andrew comes from across the room to stoop and kiss her on the cheek. "I had no idea," he says, and it's clear how little idea he has about many things. The puppyish love that she'd seen in his eyes has turned into adoration and he watches her the rest of the night from wherever he is in the club.

The last of Oliver's set is a blur with people, strangers, stopping by to congratulate her and fawn over her performance. Davis McComber comes by and Frank spells her name for him as he writes in his notebook. She's in the spotlight again and has forgotten, for the time being, her troubles and discomforts. This is all happening to her.

* * * * *

"We going to hear your grandson's band tonight, Ollie?" Agnes says, bouncing from adrenaline and ready to share it with the city.

"Grandson?" Frank asks.

"My grandson came by other night, came here to tell me he a bandleader. Wants me to come by and hear him and his boys tonight," Oliver explains. The band has quit and he's taken his first Campari and second cigarette. He's tired but has been effusive with his praise for Agnes and she's soaked it in the way he's inhaled his Gitanes. She is equally effusive with her appreciation and shock at having been called to the piano, and having done as well as she did.

"Jazz?" Frank says.

"Hip-hop. Call themselves Storyville. You believe that shit? Hip-hop. Storyville. What he know about Storyville? Tell me, 'Come on, Pops, you gotta hear us; it's your music, Pops, it's good!' What he know about my music?"

"You should go hear him. We all should."

"Come on," Agnes says. "Let's go, Ollie, it'll be fun." Some of her youthfulness shows through and she vibrates from her own performance, doesn't want the energy to stop coursing through her veins. She thinks that perhaps it's offsetting the pain and tremors, or at least burying them for a time. Either way, she welcomes the relief.

Oliver rolls his eyes at his two new friends and taps the rim of his empty glass with a fat index finger. Frank refills it.

"Where's he playing? A club?"

"I don't know, said it's over on Third. Storyville. The hell kind of name for a band is that?"

"Davis!" Frank calls out to Davis McComber, who's nearby trying to chat up Marcie—who in turn is making eye contact with an elderly, silver-haired man as he slips his date's wrap over her shoulders. "McComber! You know a hip-hop group called Storyville? Where they playing?"

"Storyville? Yeah, I know them. Why?"

"That's Oliver's grandson."

"Get the hell out. Your grandson is in Storyville?"

Oliver looks more and more embarrassed by the whole subject and leaves the discussion up to the younger people.

"We're taking Ollie over there," Agnes says.

"Oh shit, I gotta see this. Come on, follow me." Before the others can finish their drinks and have their coats brought to them, Davis is upstairs. When they join him, he hurries them with frenzied shouting over the noise of traffic. "Let's go," he says. "We'll walk, it's not far." Davis leads the group like a husky pulling a sled. They struggle to keep up, moving at Oliver's pace. Davis, impatient as always, has a half-block lead at any given time.

Davis turns the corner on Third Avenue and they lose sight of him for a minute, until they catch up to see him standing beneath a marquee, the light shining down on his wide-brimmed fedora, peacoat, skinny black jeans, and calf-length leather boots. The creamy light reflects off the snow and creates an aura around Davis as though he's an apparition, as though he's standing on hallowed ground.

And he is.

"The Blue Note?" Oliver says, looking up at the building, one of his own cathedrals. "Cedric playing the Blue Note?"

"Yep," Davis answers.

"I'll be," the old man says to himself. "The Note."

Inside, the lights are dim and a heavy bass thumps from unseen speakers all around them. Frank and Agnes look at each other behind Oliver's back, wondering what they've brought him to. Davis is already across the room, saying hello to one group before moving on to the next; he has somehow procured a beer in the brief time they've been inside.

Oliver's eyes are wide. Looking into the crowd of this holy room is like looking into the past. There are faces and bodies moving, drinking, laughter everywhere. Oliver understands it, this energy. Davis does, too, his mind able to envelop all music as a single being that doesn't discriminate based on age. He sees music as one big five-gallon bucket of notes and melodies. He can tell you how American popular music has progressed from Negro spirituals to blues to rag to swing to bop to the rock and roll of Elvis Presley to the Velvet Underground to Elvis Costello to REM to Pearl Jam and Lady Gaga. But he won't. He doesn't see one form of music ever going out of style to make way for another; there's room for everyone and it all lives in Davis's head. His assumption, the precious naïveté of a music devotee, is that everyone feels the same way. He writes about music the same way that Pollock splattered and coated a canvas in paint. One paragraph on Nina Simone will flow seamlessly into another on Madonna. His world has no shadows; it's the simple world of constant, shining light.

But there is no denying that the electricity in this room is different than in the Capasso before Oliver's show. It's static and it raises the hair on Agnes's arms. Oliver pulls the handkerchief from his pocket to wipe his brow and cheeks as his eyes scan the room as though looking for old friends. Sonny Rollins, the white-haired colossus, had stopped in to pay his respects to Oliver earlier that night, but it isn't such a face he looks for now. There will be no old-timers, save for Oliver. He's looking for Charlene, hoping that, while she may not come to see her old, broken-down father play, maybe she'll make the trip from Brooklyn to Manhattan to see her son.

Frank brings them all drinks and they take their seats as the lights are dimmed and the music along with them. A drummer comes from behind the blue curtain and claims his seat, starting in with a four-four rhythm that further hushes the crowd. Agnes is distracted by Oliver, wondering what he thinks and whether he'll stay for the show or leave during the first number. A horn section—saxophone, trumpet, and trombone—comes onstage and blows in unison. They aren't the well-dressed musicians of Ollie's group; instead they're wearing sagging blue jeans and T-shirts or hoodies (one has his hood up so the trombone appears to grow from the dark cave of his face) and sneakers. The group fills the stage the way Ollie's had, one by one, the instruments blending in together like a family, slowly building up in time to something that might be great. A percussionist comes aboard followed by the DJ, who steps up on a riser and dons his headphones, tilting them on his head and over an ear the way Sinatra might have worn his pork-pie. The DJ is focused and at work, and it's the only instrument, if instrument is the right word, that Oliver doesn't recognize. The jockey picks up a vinyl record, looks at both sides, gently blows unseen dust from one side, and places it on a turntable. When he gives it a push, a piano fills the air. It's immediately recognized by Oliver and Agnes. Davis, too, knows the tune. It's one of Oliver's: it's "A Night Under Diamonds" from 1952, and the grin on Oliver's face lets Agnes know it's the original, not a cover. The piano line has been extracted and plays in a loop. Mingus and Roach had played on that session, and on this stage, and the stand-up bassist is bearded like Mingus—heavy, too. The drummer keeps good time, and Oliver nods his approval.

By the time Cedric hits the stage, the group at the table is laughing and nodding together, with Frank and Agnes taking as much delight in Oliver's mood as Oliver is in hearing his piano played back to him in this setting. But it's the sight of Cedric that fills Oliver with pride. He's wearing a smart suit with a light green porkpie worn low over his eyes and sunglasses. Even with such a costume shielding his face, Frank can see hints of his mother and Oliver in his features, and he wonders if his eyes are the same shade of green as Charlene's. Cedric holds a microphone, the cord looped over his hand, and struts around the stage rapping something Oliver can't understand. The old man knows poetry, appreciates the meter, yet isn't quite sure what Cedric is getting at. But the showmanship he appreciates, and though the musicianship of his backup players is questionable, the passion and the energy are there. Cedric carries himself like a man yet acts like a boy, jumping from side to side onstage, into and out of the red light that floods the players and bathes the music. Rings on his fingers catch the white spotlight, and all that Oliver sees and hears glitters.

The crowd loves it, too. Eats it up the way Oliver remembers crowds in the 1950s and '60s calling for his own music. That never changes. The music might, despite what Davis McComber thinks in his hi-fi mind, but the people's enjoyment and fervor for it never will, whether it be jazz, rock and roll, or hip-hop. This new thing, though, this fusion of the past and the now, is like looking down into the eyes of a newborn child, one whose nose and mouth favor your own but whose understanding of the world around him and the possibilities that lie there are light-years ahead of what you've grown to know.

The people are up and swaying, and Frank and Agnes join them on the floor. Oliver watches these two young people move together, their bodies lithe—Agnes's maybe more so than Frank's in her crushed velvet dress, a dark green against her alabaster skin—and he takes great pleasure in their laughing together. Frank leans into her to say something in her ear and she throws her head back and laughs. Seeing Agnes happy and letting go does Oliver good. That girl is too damn young for so much weight on her thin white shoulders; pain, real and imagined, is for later in life, long after a life has been lived and money and love and most of the fans have wasted away or fled. *At her age?* Oliver has been thinking. *Shit, girl should have the world on a string.*

The sax takes a solo and it's a wild ride that puts any doubt about that particular boy's musicianship to rest. Oliver wonders where he's come from—not from school. He's rising and squeaking in a way that would have made Bird proud. But maybe it's the liquor in Oliver's ear—that, and the hour. Cedric points, directing the crowd to his saxophonist, taking pride in what he can do.

That's good, that's good, respect what it is those around you and with you can do; they got your back. Through it all, Oliver's piano fills the voids and rolls the crowd along. Agnes and Frank bend and fold together, closer now, crowded in with the other sweating bodies so eager for more.

The mass of arms and legs feeds off of what's happening onstage, and those onstage take their cues from the people. It's just like Harlem 1938, Oliver thinks, except the faces tonight are white and black, not just black, but the same feeling is here, the power is everywhere. He's transported back; it's something he hears in his ears, sees with his eyes, and knows in his heart. He is completely overwhelmed and thankful to his grandson. And it's what he's thinking as the music winds down, and as the people gasp for air and return to their tables for a sip at their drinks.

"That's for my pops," Cedric calls out, shielding his eyes from the glare of the lights. "Where he at? I saw him. There he is, my pops, everybody, Oliver Pleasant, best damn piano player in New York City. Give it up. Let's all give it up for Pops Pleasant!"

The crowd applauds, looking around, but no one knows where he's pointing or of whom he's speaking. Agnes knows and she squeezes Oliver's hand. Frank slaps his shoulder and Oliver lifts his hat to wipe his brow again. It's a night of firsts, a night when those who never expected it are being recognized and praised by audiences they never might have known.

Davis McComber, leaning on the bar across the room, scratches furiously in his notebook.

* * * * *

Frank stands in Oliver's kitchen with Agnes while she prepares his tea. He notices it's the same brand and flavor he'd had in Charlene's kitchen that morning. Watching Agnes in the small space between the sink and stove, waiting for the water to boil, Frank feels as though he's been given a glimpse into an earlier time in this home, the way these rooms must have lived and breathed back when there was a whole family living here. From all the stories he's heard, he can picture Francesca in this kitchen, telling her daughter to get the cups down for tea, chasing after her twin boys as they scamper back and forth from kitchen to living room. She'd tell them to quiet down, not to disturb their father, who would be leaving soon for work, or for the road. She'd have a glimmer in her eye as she thought of the unfinished novel on her bedside table, the one she would finish later that evening, and about the bookstore she'd visit in the morning to pick out new novels for the week. She'd have coffee at the café next door to that shop, and she would have company.

"Take this in to Ollie if he's still awake. If he's not, don't wake him, just let him sleep," Agnes orders, and Frank feels like a child himself, careful not to spill the tea on the carpet.

Entering the living room, the sight of the bookshelves jars Frank and he nearly does spill the tea. The empty spaces on the shelves are like slots in a puzzle, and Frank has seen the pieces that fit into those slots. A part of him wants to tell Oliver all about it, to let him know that Francesca wasn't so lonely all those years, let him know that while he was in Paris with Marie Broussard or in a hotel room in Memphis with someone whose name he can't remember now, or possibly never knew, that Francesca was having coffee with, talking for hours with, and making love to a man that would make all the pain and loneliness disappear for a time. But the night has had enough emotion, enough surprises, and Frank lets the old man be, keeping the story to himself.

They sit in the presence of Oliver's piano and memories, listening to the awkward shouting from the apartment above. In the room—a small, mid-twentieth-century museum of jazz and popular culture—the smell of herbal tea and Oliver's cigarette smoke permeates the air. They are all exhausted and grateful, it seems, for what silence the room allows.

They had left during the show—reluctantly, for Frank and Agnes, who were beginning to set off that spark that two new lovers might make. Not that such a relationship is in their future, not as far as Frank is concerned, but that spark, he has to admit, feels good. The crowd had been thick when they left and they'd had to weave through, making way for Oliver to get to the door. He'd grown tired and weak during the show, yet enthralled with his grandson on the stage.

The thing that has been lost over the years is passion, missing from Frank's work, his marriage, his very existence. It's that thing he found in college at a small, smoky bar, surrounded by friends and Karen, alongside a set of tracks that sped away to some diminished point in the future. And it's that thing regained in New York City over a matter of hours, through the course of days. He sees it in Agnes and saw it briefly sated this evening, that need and want that make her very limbs twitch with anticipation. And it's there, in the old soul of Oliver, who has lived in a state of creation since the earliest days. He even saw it in little Pablo, a boy who wants nothing more than to be an adult, yet in a state of suspended childhood. And did he not witness, only that afternoon, while standing on the precipice of a grave holding more than two thousand souls, the spirits of men and women who would never know a life complete? Do we not owe it to those gone, to those still with us, to ourselves, to live to the fullest of our capabilities? To the extent of our passion?

Frank has gone back in his mind, again and again since arriving in New York, to that little office alongside the unfinished nursery, back to stories untold, and he has felt a guilt like a pinching in his heart for those pages. He's felt, as well, a void for Karen and what it is they've tried to accomplish. A guilt, too, over his thoughts about Agnes and his wonder at what her body might feel like even as his loving and comfortable phone call from earlier that afternoon still buzzes in his ear. But it all goes back to the passion, to a muse as explained by Oliver and his life on the road, to his Parisian mistress, and to the devotion, still, that he feels for Francesca.

(INTERLUDE NO. 4)

THE MYSTERIOUS DEATH OF

HAMLET GIRAUD AND JANE DOE

by Davis McComber
davismccomber.com

In 1966, forty-four-year-old jazz trombonist Hamlet Giraud was driving north on the FDR, presumably heading for Harlem. It was a wet spring night, not raining, but the thunderstorm that had passed earlier that evening left the road slick and dangerous. The danger would prove very real as his car, a '62 Plymouth Fury traveling at a high rate of speed, crossed the median and hit an oncoming delivery truck. Dead were Giraud and his passenger. The driver of the truck, fifty-two-year-old Max Shropshire, a Brooklynite heading home to his wife and five children after a long day of dry goods deliveries, escaped with a broken femur, wrist, and clavicle and a concussion.

A police report from that night stated, "Dead: Mr. Hamlet Gerad [sic], Negro male, 44. Dead: Jane Doe, Caucasian, age unknown . . . at a probable high rate of speed, the driver [Giraud] crossed the median and struck an oncoming vehicle . . . strong odor of alcohol from wreckage . . ."

Little else is known regarding the wreck and Giraud's death. The woman in the car was not his wife, who was at home with their two children in the Bronx at the time. Giraud had recently returned from Europe with the Oliver Pleasant Trio, a tour that, by all accounts, was a success.

The jazz writer Jackson LeDuc was with Pleasant in a Greenwich Village jazz club when he received word of Giraud's death. LeDuc wrote in his 1971 memoir, *An Angel on a Train*, "Oliver was drinking gin pretty hard that night and we were sitting at a corner table listening to the band. A gig he'd been playing earlier had ended in a brawl and he'd left before the set had finished and happened in to where I was. He seemed distraught and even more so when Little Jimmy Scott came over and said, 'You hear about Brother Giraud?' Oliver said he hadn't, neither had I, and then Jimmy told us that Hamlet had died in a car wreck not an hour earlier. It was a shock to both of us, to all of us in the club. Oliver looked like he'd lost a family member. He took a drink straight from the gin bottle and asked a question I never did understand. He said, 'What about the girl?' Jimmy hadn't mentioned a girl, but then he said they were both dead. I've never seen a man so upset. . . ."

Giraud's passenger, "Jane Doe," has heretofore been unknown, a mystery both in legal circles and jazz circles, and of trivial interest to pop-culture enthusiasts for decades.

Unknown until now.

Marie Broussard of Paris, France, had come to New York to visit a friend—a lover—and her life would end here as well.

Bassist Stanton Harris, eighty-three, is retired and living in the Bronx View Convalescent Center. He fills in the gaps of the night: "I was there. We was playin Fig's, halfway through the second set and it was good. We was on fire that night, hard to believe it was so long ago, when this white woman comes in the club like a hurricane and makes straight for the bandstand, straight for Ollie on piano. From where I was standin, I could see the front door clearly and I liked to keep an eye on all the pretty ladies that came in. And this lady was the prettiest, but she had somethin on her mind; she was in a bad way with drink or drugs or somethin. Anyway, she come straight toward Ollie and he don't see her because he's full into whatever melody we was playin. But we all see her, all of us up on the stand, and it was Hamlet that jumped off the stand to stop her. I believe she aimed to do Ollie some harm, but everything came to a stop and this woman was screamin about Oliver this and Oliver that in an accent. She was talkin about Harlem and Paris and mamas and I don't know what. The whole club was watchin like it was a part of the show. Anyway, they got her into a corner someplace to calm her down, and then Hamlet left with her. They put her in Hamlet's car and I never saw her again, which is fine by me. That broad was in a bad way."

Marie Broussard was the longtime mistress of Oliver Pleasant and the two lived as husband and wife when Pleasant was working in Europe, as he frequently was in the 1950s and '60s. Broussard's mother, her only known relative, had been in bad health and had recently passed away. Broussard was a freelance photographer working in the fashion industry and when she failed to arrive in Italy for an assignment, the designer inquired and eventually filed a missing-person report in Paris that reads, in part, "Marie Broussard, 32 years old . . . photographer . . . mother recently passed . . . address uncertain" and a handwritten note on the file obtained via e-mail makes note: "known drug user, in frequent company with American jazz musicians." The file was left dormant and closed, unsolved, sometime later.

But why was she in New York? Had she ever been before? By all accounts she was here for Oliver Pleasant, and the most striking account has come to light recently to once again focus attention on this dark trail. Charlene Pleasant Wilson, the forty-eight-year-old daughter of Oliver Pleasant, said in her Park Slope home recently that Marie Broussard came to her parents' home the night she died in the wreck with Hamlet Giraud.

"She was half out of her mind and my mother, worried for her children, wouldn't let her past the threshold," Wilson explained. "My brothers were in bed, but I came out of my room when I heard the commotion. Miss Broussard was drunk and demanding to see Daddy, said she'd been with him all this time in Paris but her mother had died and she was alone now. She said she wanted him for good. I can still see her in the doorway—it was storming then and lightning flashes lit her silhouette and her frantic, angry face. My mother finally had enough and I watched from behind as she squared her shoulders and got full in front of Broussard and said, 'I don't know who you are or what it is you think you're owed, but it is not in this house. This is the home of me and my children, and you will leave its doorway now. My husband—*my* husband—is working at a club in Greenwich Village, and if you feel you are owed something by that man, then you take your business to him.' I'd never heard my mother speak like that and I don't know that I'd ever been as proud of her as I was then. But then I got in trouble for being out of bed when I laughed as she followed that speech with, 'You dig?'"

The Pleasants have remained silent on the reason why Marie Broussard was in the car that night with Hamlet Giraud until recently, and have left the Giraud family to bear the pain and wonder for all these years at his dying in a car with an unknown woman. The Giraud children refused to speak on the matter, as did Oliver Pleasant, who has retired and moved to Memphis, Tennessee.

Charlene Wilson, however, carries the weight of the decision by her parents not to speak out. It's a weight that, she's ashamed to say, "has become easier to bear over time, but no less wrong for having done so."

It's a mystery answered, but a tragedy still.

Special thanks to freelance reporter Frank Severs (Memphis) for his help with this story.

NIGHT FIVE

1.

Oliver greets Pablo on the stoop the next morning with a stack of record albums.

"What're these?" the boy says.

"Records. Shit you don't know could fill up this street."

"Ain't got a record player."

"Boy, I got to carry everything to you? You young—come up and get it."

Pablo has never stepped foot inside Oliver's apartment. It's laid out the same as his own, but more lived in. Where Pablo's floors are wood, warped and stained in places from the neglect of a woman still too heartbroken and tired to keep up and a man that uses the place as a rest stop, Oliver's floors have lush carpet and furnishings everywhere. The sofa in the apartment upstairs features a secondhand decor with edges gouged and frayed. There are very few pictures, one or two of the boy's father, who had worked in the kitchen of the restaurant at the top of one of the towers, and a few of Pablo as a bald-headed baby. But nothing like this. His eyes take in black and white faces that look like they go back to the beginning of time. He recognizes some from his history textbook at school.

"Go on, you can touch it. Ain't gonna bite you."

Pablo had been standing at the edge of the great expanse of piano, all black and gleaming. He eases up onto the bench and picks one key to depress. The tone that comes out fills the room and makes his scalp tingle.

"A," Oliver says.

"Hmm?"

"That's an A. A good one, too—you'll make a fine musicianer."

"You gonna teach me, Ollie?"

Oliver sits on the bench beside him and the wood of it groans beneath his weight. Pablo fears it might crash to the floor, but he sees that Oliver pays it no attention. Oliver sighs as he had with Stanton. "Can't. I'm gonna be leavin soon, son."

"Leavin? Where to? Vacation?"

"Naw. Naw, no vacation, it's for keeps. Goin down south to a place called Memphis. You heard of Memphis?"

Pablo shakes his head.

"Well, it's there, and it's far as hell from here so I can't cart all this shit with me. Want you to have some of it, startin with them records. I can't teach you, but I'm gonna make sure you taught, you hear me? You keep that music with you.

"Pablo, you remember how I talked to that man at the diner about why somebody might start to playin music? How I started and why? You recall that?"

"No." Pablo is upset but can't explain it. He's become used to loss in his young life, has known people to go, so why would this man, this relative stranger, talking about leaving upset him like this? He can't explain it and doesn't yet know the key ingredient of loss in the recipe of music. It was a lesson learned by Oliver in New Orleans seventy years earlier after he left Leona Thibodeaux behind on the docks of that city. Pablo wipes away a tear with the back of his hand.

"Well, I did, and I been thinkin it's because it must have filled somethin up inside me, somethin I needed but didn't even know I needed at the time. It's the only way I can explain it. Like when you sittin around watchin your television or whatever and you want to eat a pear just out of nowhere. That's your body tellin you that you *need* that pear. You like pears?"

"No."

"Now, you remember when I told you about church? When we's in the park, you remember?"

"Yeah, I remember that. You said your preacher cussed you."

"That's right. That was at my mama's church when I was a boy your age. In New York and out on the road I found a different kind of church, but I'm gonna tell you a secret now. You listenin?"

In a near whisper, his voice thick with saliva, Pablo answers, "I'm listenin, Ollie."

"Church inside you. All the time it's inside you and it can be whatever it is makes you whole. It can be love, it can be hurt, it can be laughter, music, maybe even some poetry. For me, church is that sweet swing, boy, that soft, soft music. And maybe it is for you, too, I don't know. But I do know that you heard it night fore last. You say you heard it and what did you do? You got down out of bed and got on your knees, ain't that right? You got on your knees and put your ear to the floor just to get closer to it. I'm gonna tell you somethin else now. Your daddy? He's in there, too." Oliver puts his thick, sausage-like finger to Pablo's chest. "And I know if you fill up your insides with whatever it is makes you whole, and maybe it's music, then your daddy will have somethin to know you by."

Oliver plays a soft song, "God Bless the Child," for Pablo, who sits and watches those massive hands move over the smoke-stained keys. It's the first time he's seen Oliver play. He finishes with another song, one for a little boy. "You know that one, don't you?"

Pablo nods. "Twinkle, Twinkle, Little Star."

"That's right, son. That's right."

Oliver sends the boy back upstairs with an armload of jazz records, a head full of thoughts, and a portable phonograph he carries by the handle like a lunch box. At the top of the stairs, Pablo looks back and nods. "Thanks, Ollie."

Oliver nods back at his protégé.

* * * * *

In Oliver's apartment the previous night, Agnes had taken his shoes off and loosened his tie, having again taken the burning cigarette from his fingers, and then walked him to his bedroom down a long, narrow hallway with walls covered in picture frames. She eased him back onto his bed and then took a moment to look around and gain perspective on where and how an icon spends his sleeping hours. It looked like any senior citizen's bedroom anywhere, an environment decorated in rumpled clothes, a small television with rabbit ears on a nearby cane-back chair pulled from the kitchen, a night table with its surface filled to capacity with pill bottles, a clock, wadded tissues, and a lamp. On a table on the opposite side of the bed, though, Agnes saw only a lamp, a silver hairbrush, a picture of three young children playing in the snow, and a Bible. It looked as though it had been left untouched since the day Francesca died. There was profound sadness in this tableau, an unoccupied side of a marital bed being the loneliest desert in the world, she thought. She had the sudden urge to crawl into that side of the bed and give her own loneliness a home, to slide in beneath the sheets and occupy it just for a few hours, just so it could know again the warmth of flesh and dreams on its pillow.

She was pulled from her fantasy by Oliver, eyes open, watching her. "Charlene? That you?"

"It's me, Ollie, it's Agnes. Agnes Cassady. Frank and I were just leaving; you get some sleep."

"Agnes. How you? You sounded good tonight, sweetheart, real good. I want you to have something. There, on that bureau there, by the mirror, take that hat there."

"The brown one? Here?"

"Yeah, that's it. That's for you."

"Whose was this one, Ollie?"

He closed his eyes again to sleep. "That one's mine."

She bent and kissed him on the cheek, and whispered, "Thank you."

* * * * *

After she said goodbye to Frank and left Oliver's place, Agnes had gone straight to Andrew's. When he opened the door, she realized he wasn't alone. There was a wariness in his eyes as though the past might be standing on the dark and smelly landing to his apartment instead of a still-glowing Agnes Cassady. She glimpsed someone behind him, rising from the mattress on the floor. It was the bartender from Ben's, the tall and graceful black woman with the Afro and earrings. She still wore the earrings, but nothing else. Agnes was momentarily caught off guard when the woman stopped and turned full to the door as though daring Agnes to enter. It wasn't that she'd expected Andrew to be alone; she hadn't really thought about it. It was the grace and elegance of this nude woman—her skin shining, purple nipples pointing outward, and jaw set firmly—in the midst of Andrew's filth and disorganization that stirred something in her. Not a jealousy over Andrew, but an envy for having such a perfect body with so much self-control.

"Hey, Sexton," Agnes said, "you were supposed to meet me at Tommy's an hour ago for that tattoo. He said we could use his office. The fuck?"

"What? Oh yeah, right, the tattoo. Shit, I forgot. . . ."

The bartender had gone to the bathroom, the only other place she could go, and came out almost immediately fully dressed. She looked just as elegant in clothes, and she made a point to kiss Andrew heavily on the mouth before leaving.

"I'll call you," Andrew said halfheartedly after her as she disappeared into the shadows of the stairwell. Then, to Agnes, "Hey, look, I'm sorry about that."

"Shut up, Andrew." She entered his apartment and flung her coat onto a small wooden chair. She left an oversized, brown porkpie on her head and kissed him just as his last guest had. "Did you see me tonight?"

"See you? You were amazing. I had no idea you could play like that. How did it feel?"

She kissed him again. "How did it feel? There's nothing to compare it to."

"Like a good meal, or love?" he said hopefully.

"It was like a great fuck," she whispered, slipping to her knees and taking him into her mouth, tasting the tall, graceful woman on him.

They lay in his bed afterward, not speaking. She was tired but didn't feel like closing her eyes. She didn't have long left in New York and she didn't want to spend it in darkness. Andrew breathed steadily beside her until she was sure he had fallen asleep, and then she got up to stand in his window. She put Oliver's hat back on and stood looking across the street at the brick building where it was mostly quiet and some lights glowed warmly inside apartments, and she could see movement in still a few others. Below, on the sidewalks, there was no one. New York does sleep.

She thought of New Orleans and of her apartment. She thought of Sherman—she'd told him she'd call yet hadn't. The cold coming through the single-pane glass touched her skin and it occurred to her that she missed the heat and humidity of the South. She thought of Landon Throckmorton, who had sent her to New York to visit his doctor. Or was it something more? Had the old man foreseen all of this or planned it as he had the train ride to Memphis? Had he known she'd go to hear Oliver play, that she would meet him and eventually play for him in his home and onstage in front of an audience? *Maybe Landon is fate,* she thought. *He's in control of all of this.*

She'd told Sherman that Landon was paying for the New York trip simply out of kindness, because that was the truth. She didn't know just what Landon thought of her, or what he might expect from her when she returned, but maybe Landon did know all; maybe he was a specter flying over her, then sitting on her shoulder to help guide the way just as the muse might. She'd let it happen and was curious if there might be more. Stranger things had come from New Orleans.

He hadn't touched her at all on the train ride to Memphis or back to New Orleans, perhaps out of respect, or for the circumstance of that funereal trip. It wasn't until the following New Year's Eve when she'd played at his party, one that would last until well into the morning and see groups breaking off to find bedrooms or soft indentations where the illusion of privacy might be had in that massive Victorian home, that he placed a hand on her. Exhausted from the long night, she'd fallen asleep in an upstairs bedroom, recalling only the last sip of scotch and moonlight that fell through the window. She'd awoken sometime just before dawn with a start and the feeling that she wasn't alone. She wasn't. Landon lay beside her, fully clothed in a tuxedo that contrasted against her nakedness. She's not a modest woman, but she was startled by the company. She lay on her stomach, arms crossed beneath her head, and looked at him and he smiled back. And then she felt his thin, cold fingers at the small of her back. He ran his flattened palm up her spine and over her shoulders, back down over her ass and bare backs of her thighs. He didn't ask her to turn over; there was no overt sexuality. He didn't touch himself. He seemed to get whatever it was he needed from palm on skin, and she let him. It was as though he were inspecting his porcelain or the fabric on an antique settee; perhaps he was looking for any damage. She drifted back into sleep at some point, and when she woke up, she was in the same position but with a soft afghan pulled over her, and Landon was gone.

There were other similar instances. Similar in the sense that she was only expected to lie there naked while Landon touched her. He still didn't penetrate her or undress himself, but he did request that she go to a particular bedroom, undress, and wait for him. And other times there was someone else there as well, different women or young men—eighteen- or nineteen-year-olds—and they, too, would lie naked beside Agnes. Landon would touch them in the same chaste, inquisitive way. He seemed to look at the bodies as though they were art, and indeed they were in their own ways, the boys hairless and smooth and the girls like Agnes herself, with a lack of curves and her angular hip bones and shoulder blades—androgynous. They must have appeared delicate side by side, like fine china or most lifelike sculptures. Several times Landon took photos with an old Polaroid camera; Agnes never asked what became of those photos.

Agnes isn't sure Landon Throckmorton is capable of feeling guilt, living as he does on the edges of society, within a world he's created for himself and peopled with those who look the other way from his eccentricities. But she feels they have a connection and that this connection is why he arranged for her to go home and escorted her there. And she feels he took advantage of that by touching her body, yet she feels some culpability, as though perhaps she crossed a line by accepting what he would offer for those nights of lying still while he became familiar with her. She shrugged it off. It is whatever it is and all part of the experience of being Agnes Cassady for as long as that being exists.

She turned from the windows and lay back down beside Andrew, closing her eyes and drifting to sleep.

* * * * *

"You talk to your wife?"

"Yeah, yesterday, that's why I was late to your show. I wanted to talk to you, too, beforehand, but time got away from me trying to rush back."

Frank and Oliver are back at the diner. It's the morning of his last show and Oliver assumed he'd be eating alone after sending Pablo upstairs to listen to records. Frank has shown up, though, and Oliver is grateful for the company.

"Rush back? Where'd you go to call her?"

"I was in Brooklyn. That's what I wanted to talk to you about, but your show had already started and then with the excitement of Agnes playing and Cedric's show, I just never did get around to it."

"Brooklyn? What you doin there?"

"I went to see Charlene."

"My Charlene?" He stops salting his food, the shaker held in midair. "What for?"

"I wanted to ask her a few questions for the story, and to get to know someone you're close to."

"Guess you found out how close we are." He puts the shaker on the table and slides it, crashing it into a bottle of ketchup and mustard. "Talkin to me is one damn thing; I don't know how I feel about you snoopin around, though."

"Oliver, I wasn't snooping." Frank pushes the food on his plate around with a fork. "I just went to talk to her."

"What she tell you?"

Frank gets uncomfortable and is growing testy; he looks around for the waitress. "Where is she? This coffee is cold already."

"Answer me, boy. What Charlene have to say about her daddy? You so goddamn anxious to tell a story, tell me a story."

"You probably know, don't you?"

"Why don't you go on and tell me anyway?" Oliver says. Then, more to himself, "Can't believe you just run off and talk to my Charlene. Not even bother to come to me with it first."

Frank sighs and loses more of his patience. He's spent the past few days in a disorienting haze away from Memphis and his home, and Karen. Hell, if he is honest with himself, he's been in this haze since leaving work and without the comfortable, familiar grid pattern of the newsroom with its familiar voices and focus on tasks to right him. And now he's taking it out on Oliver. He wants to stop, but he can't help himself; the anger feels good, the vitriol is cathartic. "She talked about your time away, how lonely Francesca was, and how much your kids missed you. But that's not news to you, is it? What would you expect, that you'd win father of the year?"

"I don't expect nothin but maybe just a little respect for a old man who spent so much of his time and gave so much of his life to music."

"Respect? From Charlene? Come on, Ollie, it was all for shits and fucking giggles. It's only music." He knows it's wrong even as it leaves his spittle-covered lips—Charlene wouldn't even agree with such a statement. Frank has a lifetime of uncertainty built up within him—with his writing and his marriage, and the family they've tried to start, now with unemployment—and he knows that music has given Oliver the only certainty the old man has ever known. And now Frank, petty and envious, is trying to take that from him.

Oliver begins to drink his coffee but stops and sets the mug down on the table harder than he means, the saucer beneath it clattering. "Only music? What you say? Who told you that, 'only music'? Charlene say that? Let me tell you about 'only music,' son. Let me tell you about ridin that bus from New York to Chicago down through Missouri and Tennessee and Ken-*tucky* in the mid-dle of a summer tryin to get to New Orleans, the one safe place we know of in the South, but then our goddamn bus driver gettin lost in Alabama. Nineteen fifty. You know what it is for a bunch a sweaty Negroes to get lost in the backwater of Alabama in 1950?" He's staring into Frank's eyes now, and Frank thinks he sees a hint of an Oliver Pleasant in his twenties all full of hellfire and yearning.

Frank feels small and tries to look away, but he can't.

"No, 'course you don't. And you know what for? For to take that music to the people. The one goddamn thing them people had, the one thing they could call their own. They couldn't get their fingers into it, no, but then again, neither could the white man. So they held on to that music, that 'only music.' And no, I know Charlene didn't say nothin about 'only music,' neither. You know how I know? I know 'cause Charlene remembers what it's like to be told you can't eat here and you can't piss there. She knows what it means to be second class and she knows that what we was doin was takin a first-class music to them people as just a taste of some-thin they didn't think they could have. Just like at my Hillbillie's on them nights. It's a taste of freedom. Even my children know what that taste like. You know what it means to have your children get a taste for that so late in life, Frank? Hmm? Frank, you know about children, or you just think you know about *my* children? *My* life? What you know about it all? About bein a father and havin to travel from place to place to support a family. You think that shit's easy? You think it's all one big party?"

Frank finds it difficult to swallow. He finds it even more diffi-cult to speak, but manages to choke out a sentence. "No, Oliver, I wouldn't know anything about it. We can't have kids." It's the first time he's phrased it in such a way to Oliver. He gulps down his cold coffee and feels it churn in his gut. "But I'll tell you this, if I did have any, I'd be with them right now."

"Instead of up here in New York? Your wife up here with you, Frank?"

Frank slices into his eggs, but he only manages to move them around even more without taking a bite, his appetite having suddenly vanished. The days have been stressful away from Karen and not knowing where they stand or where she's slept, and what his future holds.

"She told me about Hamlet, too." He's not sure why he says it, but, again, he can't help himself. "That sounded like a real party, Oliver, a fine time. Why was Marie Broussard with Hamlet that night and not you? Why was she even here and not in Paris where you kept her? Marie Broussard part of your freedom ride, Ollie?"

The waitress comes by with coffee, but she turns before reaching their booth to avoid the storm blowing there.

"Hamlet, huh? You ask her about that? Got all up in my business, didn't you, boy? The hell gives you the right to go askin my family questions about me? Who the fuck you think you are comin from down south to put your nose where it don't belong? What the hell you think you'd get?" Oliver's appetite is undiminished and he pushes a forkful of pancakes into his mouth.

"You know what I got from Charlene, Ollie? What a selfish prick you could be. When I asked her why she wouldn't help you out, why she was sending you a thousand miles away to live, she talked about hurt and grown-up anger, but she should have just said, 'Because my daddy is a selfish prick.' Would have made my day a lot shorter."

They both sit and stew in their anger and this surprise argument. Neither leaves, both too stubborn, but Frank hasn't finished. "I can't believe I felt sorry for you, all alone and broke and giving up your life, forced to move away."

"I don't need your pity. I don't need you to feel sorry for me. I been around a long time, son. I seen shit you only read about in history books, if you even paid attention to any of it. Livin this long is work and I sinned a lot, but maybe my greatest sin is pride, and my pride don't need you goin around to my kin to ask for help on my account." He stabs his index finger in the air at Frank. "You dig? My business, not yours."

"Got it."

"Good. Now go on."

Frank reaches for his wallet. "I'm paying for this."

"I don't need you to pay for shit, just go."

Frank gets up to leave and takes his time to wrap a scarf around his neck but fumbles with it, looking down at Oliver. He's angry and reluctant to leave it this way. He waits a beat, then two, but Oliver won't even look at him, so he turns to go. At the door, though, he turns to come back and stops halfway. By now, the other customers in the diner are paying attention to the scene.

"One more thing. I came up here to see you, just to see you. Agnes came to see you, and a club full of strangers have paid to see you and listen to you play for the past four nights. You aren't alone; you've got a world of people who are willing to help if you'll only ask. Pride? Pride isn't your greatest sin, old man—a lack of faith in the people around you is your sin. The people still here, Oliver, not Duke, not Dizzy, not Coltrane or Monk." He turns and hands the waitress a wad of cash, and says back to Oliver, "I got this," before storming out the door.

Frank walks blindly down crowded sidewalks, brushing against people without turning to offer a southerner's apology. He loses his scarf somewhere around Sixty-Fifth but doesn't even notice, he's still so hot with rage. He turns into the park on a whim. Without a grid pattern and iconic buildings to orient himself, he loses his way. The scenery of trees dusted with white powder and joggers whizzing by slowly begins to relax him and the anger leaves, the void now filled with regret.

By the time he's traversed most of the park, he's already ashamed of himself. He'd never meant to lash out at Oliver that way. He's taken out his anger with his own situation on this old man who already feels alone, spewing his bottled-up rage at an unsuspecting friend instead of at the newspaper's publisher or Karen when he'd felt it. He'll make it up to Oliver somehow, he knows he will.

How the hell do I get out of here? He sees light glinting off a flurry of cars and heads for a break in the trees, an exit that dumps him out at Columbus Circle. He turns left, unsure of where to go, but thinking he might just find his hotel and lie down until it's time for Oliver to play one last time.

* * * * *

Agnes sits and watches New York glide past her as though it's slipping through her fingers. She'll miss it. The cab she's in will stop at Mount Sinai and wait while she runs in to leave a note written on hotel stationery for Dr. Mundra. She'd written it with the same finality of a suicide note. Possibly with the same outcome, but this isn't the first suicide note she's written. While writing it, she sat at the small desk in her room, her left hand laid out before her and trembling, fingers twitching out of control, and she didn't work to stop it or hide it as she might have normally. Instead, she let it lead her way.

Doctor, thank you for all you've done. I've decided to return to New Orleans and live out what time I have left the best that I can, if I can. Take care of your wife and little boy. Treasure them. —A. Cassady

In the backseat of the cab, she wears a man's porkpie pulled down over her ears and touches her wrist at the spot where Mundra had only a day before massaged it. She wishes that she could have the pressure of such soothing fingers on her daily. The spot is raised now and tender, not only from the usual nerve pain but also from the markings left by Andrew. She'd woken him before first light, when she'd risen up from the dream of a wrinkled, brown face with mirrored eyes telling her she was going to die. Finding herself in Andrew's arms, she'd felt unexpectedly safe.

"Andrew, wake up," she'd said, shaking him. "Come on, get up."

"What? What is it?"

"I want you to tattoo me."

"What are you talking about?"

"Come on, get up. It has to be now."

Sitting in the small wooden chair where she'd thrown her coat and Oliver's hat only hours before, she showed Andrew the spot on her wrist and explained what she wanted there. "Hash marks. Two and five, right here." She hadn't explained why, and he hadn't asked. He took his tools from an old cigar box at her feet and prepared the black ink and motorized needle. He took her hand in his to hold it still, and as he worked, she told him she was leaving. She told him she needed to be back in New Orleans, to play regularly somewhere, anywhere—that she had felt so at home at the piano onstage with Oliver, but she knew it wasn't the New York crowd that made her feel that way. She knew it was the piano itself.

"I can go with you," he said, intent on his work and not looking up into her eyes because he knew he would lose all focus if he did.

"Don't be silly, Andrew, your home is here."

At that, he looked around his apartment and laughed. "Not much of a home. I can wait tables and ink anyplace."

"Might as well do it here."

"I can make a home for us. Take care of you."

"With what? We going to make a tent out of your *Star Wars* shower curtain?"

He looked into her eyes then and flipped the switch on his rig. The sudden silence was deafening. "I'm not exactly what you see."

"No? Are you a superhero? Do you twist that thumb ring of yours and turn into somebody else?"

"I turned into somebody else to become this. My parents don't like who I am."

Andrew's ambiguity was beginning to piss her off; she wasn't in the mood for games. "Who the hell are you?"

"I'm rich. Richer than you'll ever be. Or, I could be. My folks are wealthy, my whole family is."

"Why aren't you?" She looked around the room. "I mean, why live like this?"

"Because they don't want me to be who I am. They want me to be who they are. I want to be an artist." He looked again into her eyes. "I am an artist."

"It's that important to you? Living in squalor to follow your dream?"

He shrugged. "It's the only thing, isn't it? Isn't being a pianist the most important thing to you? Isn't it why you're talking about rushing back to New Orleans now?"

It was her turn to shrug and she hugged her bare shoulder, feeling more naked than ever now as she looked again out the window.

"Take me with you, Agnes Cassady."

She put her good hand on the top of his head and ran long, delicate fingers through his thick hair. "I have to go," she whispered.

In the cab today, the black marks look striking against her white skin and the blue veins of her wrist. The scars are raised and red, but that will fade. Everything, she thinks, fades. She looks up from her reverie of the night before and her silent goodbye to the city of New York in time to see Frank rushing along the sidewalk and turning into the park, his scarf flying off unnoticed and into traffic. She considers having the driver stop so she can catch him, wrap his scarf around him against the cold, and tell him goodbye. Maybe she'll even ask him to escort her to the airport or all the way to New Orleans. But she doesn't want company. For the first time in a long time, Agnes only wants to be alone.

* * * * *

Oliver is impressed with the movers' progress. He'd planned to stick around when they came to the door after Pablo had disappeared at the top of the stairs, but he quickly grew restless watching these strangers pack his life into cardboard boxes. Most of those boxes would be sealed up in a warehouse on Staten Island. Why? He didn't have any idea—it was a service the moving company offered. He knows he'll probably never see most of it again. They have Benji's name and number, and, acting under power of attorney, he can deal with it all "once I'm in the ground," Oliver has said. Some of it will be sent to Memphis, but he doesn't want to impose too much on his niece, and besides, he'd insisted, "I don't need a whole hell of a lot anyway." Some foundation or other for jazz over at Lincoln Center is interested in much of the memorabilia, but Oliver has left that up to Benji as well, the ugliness of business being his forte.

He's tired, too tired to care much anymore, and that row with Frank has taken the wind out of him. All Oliver wants is a nap before his show. He finds the foreman, a withered ogre who may be older than Oliver himself but with the wiry muscles and stooped shoulders of a life's work spent on trucks and beneath furniture. Oliver left it all in this man's hands because he is a fan—he knew who Oliver was before they introduced themselves and even rattled off a discography in case Oliver wasn't sure himself who he was. "I'm tired as shit, man, I got to get some rest. You handle this?"

"You go on and lie down, Pops. We'll wait to get the bedroom. My boys'll pack that up while you gone later—you playin tonight, right?"

"Yeah. Hey, you want to go? I'll put you on the list, probably ain't nobody else showin up anyways."

"Yes sir, that'd be fine. That'd be just fine. Hey, where you want that piano to go? Only thing in here ain't got a note on it."

Oliver walks to the piano and places his palms on the closed lid, rubs his hands over it as though smoothing a sheet over a lover. He finds a pen and, on a yellow sheet of paper the movers use to keep track of what goes where, he writes: "Upstairs, Apt. 2D." He bends at the waist, his palms still in place, and touches his lips to the cold wood. "Goodbye, old friend," he whispers.

* * * * *

As he enters the lobby of his hotel, Frank is greeted by a warmth that cheers him and then a sight that brings his heart up into his throat. There in the sitting lounge, beside the blue-white vapors of a fake fireplace, sits Karen. He hesitates, scared that it's a mirage, that the cold of the park has pervaded his brain and left him confused. But it is her and she beckons to him. They hold each other for what feels like years. All those years where there might have been distance, or coolness, are warmed and brought back to life in this embrace.

"What are you doing here?"

She shrugs. "I missed you."

"I missed you."

Upstairs in his room, they don't speak. The shock and elation of having her near has left Frank silent, and the only sound is the hushed whisper of fabric as it falls to the floor. First her coat, then his, then her blouse and his shirt, and so on until they stand naked in front of each other with the light of the city falling on their skin. He looks at her as though for the first time and she drinks it in, recalling the passion they first felt for each other. Without speaking, they each reminisce about a little bar along the railroad tracks, a grassy hill in springtime when the whole university, the whole world, and their life together, was spread out before them. They remember walking through that first tiny apartment together, laughing over the secondhand furniture and the way the metal-frame bed rattled and squeaked beneath them. A two-story, century-old house appears before them and they look up at its possibilities staring back, daring them to make what they will of it and to fill it with laughter and soul.

Now, there in a hotel room in New York City, Frank and Karen take that dare again, together. They kiss and taste and love and laugh again until the bright white of memory gives way to the star-filled sky of hopes and dreams. There in a hotel room in New York City, this couple makes love and learns to love all over again.

Later, she asks about Oliver's show, mentions the time, and suggests he get ready so he doesn't miss it.

"I'm not going," he says.

"Why not?"

He doesn't tell her about the argument at Junior's. He'll explain it all later once he understands it better himself, and he doesn't want to ruin what they have just then. "Everything I need is right here. I've missed you so much, Karen, not just this week but for too long."

"Frank. I'm right here; I love you."

They order room service, sparing no expense for steaks and desserts. The money will work itself out, she says, this accountant whose adherence to the bottom line has never wavered. She has faith in him and knows he'll find work, that something will come along.

He watches her move around the room, happy to have her there. She goes to the restroom to wash up and then the window to take in the view. "What's this?" There are scraps of paper with illegible handwriting, as though hastily written, scattered on the table.

"Notes for a novel."

"What's it about?" she says, going to the door for the room service.

"A bookstore clerk who falls in love with the wife of a jazz musician."

"Sounds romantic."

They eat and drink and make love again.

At midnight, he rises and stands in the window, surprised at the moonlight and how it can compete with the false lights of the city. Karen sleeps the way she always does, the way she has for the seventeen years he has slept beside her, on her back with one arm thrown over her head. He watches her for a minute, drinks in her body. He knows this isn't the end, that their life isn't a novel to be neatly wrapped up in a cozy, romantic hotel room. There will be things to work on, issues to deal with in a very real, probably painful way. But this is a start and that's all he's hoped for—a first sentence on a blank page. Karen seems willing to work with him, and that, alone, means more than anything.

He looks back to the city. He wonders how Oliver's show was, wishes the best for the old man, and thinks that maybe, hope-fully, their paths will cross again one day. Perhaps in New York, or maybe at home in Memphis.

* * * * *

From the piano he can see that his new friends are not there. His eyes scan the crowd, see the same type of expectant faces he's seen every night, every year for his seventy years at the piano bench, but he doesn't see Frank Severs or Agnes Cassady anywhere. His reserved booth is empty, the bottle of Campari standing vigil over that desert of white.

What he eventually sees, though, through smoke and the rheumy eyes of age, fills him with such happiness and emotion that he has trouble finishing the song he's been playing. He can feel his face flush and, at the same time, his hands falter for a split second, half a note, and Oliver, for the first time all week, misses a chord change. No one in the audience notices. The rest of the band does, but they forgive him this misstep without even a glance. He wouldn't have noticed their looks anyway; he is lost in a stare at the center table, the one he's asked Benji to hold all week. Being shown to that table by Marcie are his two sons, his grandson, Cedric, and Charlene with her husband. He thinks maybe he's imagining things, that maybe his tired eyes are failing him. He thinks perhaps he died back in his apartment in his sleep while the movers packed up his life. Maybe they packed his old, dead body into that piano and shipped it off to go stale in a warehouse on Staten Island. Maybe heaven is a club in the basement of a New York City hotel where he can play piano night and day for his family.

He tips his head—gleaming under the lights for the first time in as long as he can remember without his trademark porkpie—and his sons clap, Cedric lets out the whoop of a seventeen-year-old boy, and Charlene smiles. *That smile,* Oliver thinks, *is the smile of Francesca.* Tears blur his eyes and he turns them back on his hands to guide the fills and melodies that impress everyone in the room.

"Baby girl," he says as he comes to his daughter from the stage, holding his arms wide and enfolding her as though she were six years old again and not a grown woman standing beside a husband and teenage son.

"Daddy."

He takes the time to go around the table and hug his sons, his son-in-law, and Cedric. He whispers in his grandson's ear, "Hell of a show last night, son. You got it in you. You got it, baby."

And then it's back to Charlene because the mere sight of her has let him know that everything will be okay and that, whether he ends up in Brooklyn, Manhattan, or Memphis, he has his family, still and always.

"You sound good up there, Daddy. How are you feeling?"

"Oh, Charlene, I can't complain. Feels good when I'm at the piano, don't even notice the arthritis or diabetes or nothin. Just music."

"Music always had that way with you, didn't it?"

"It did. Yes ma'am, and it still does."

Oliver has champagne sent over for the table and Ben stops by to greet this further extension of his family, one whose patriarch, in some ways, was his own father, Ira. Oliver and his children talk, catch up, comment on the crowd and on his retirement. Charlene keeps a distance, but it's melting into softness. She doesn't mention Frank Severs's visit, or how she'd spent the rest of the day in her music parlor alternately crying for her family and angry at the intrusion. She doesn't tell Oliver that she almost came to the show the night before, that she's put on a dress and shoes every night this week with the intention of taking a cab across the Manhattan Bridge to hear him, but that it took a stranger from the South to jog her priorities, and her brothers to promise to come into town so they could present this united front of Pleasants. She's been thinking so much about her father these past weeks leading up to his final shows as he'd called her and left messages asking her to come. She'd sat listening to his albums and had, once or twice, pulled one of those old books of her mother's from the shelf just to hold it while she did so. She wanted to feel the weight of it, the weight of memory on her soul.

Charlene has known about her mother and Lucchesi since she was barely a teenager, since one morning when she'd suddenly become ill and had to stay home from school. Her mother had errands to run and was unable, or unwilling, to suspend them for a sick child. So Charlene was bundled up and they took a bus to Greenwich Village, where her mother poked in and out of shops before turning into a bookstore where Charlene had never been. Francesca browsed, taking books from their places to flip through them. She put most back but kept a few. As Charlene pretended to read a Nancy Drew mystery, she watched her mother at the counter asking the clerk, a bearded man with a sparkling smile, some questions. He answered and she laughed, tipping her head back lightly and touching him on his sleeve. He winked and smiled even wider.

There was something between the two that Charlene, even at a young age, could sense. It would be years before she put a name to it, before she herself would know the touch of a man, the feeling of love in laughter. She also noticed that the clerk rang her mother up for her purchase but put another book on the stack before placing them all in a bag. Later that evening, Charlene took that book from the shelf where Francesca had placed it and opened it to find "ML" written in the corner. She thought nothing of it until a few weeks later when she was looking through her mother's books and saw the same letters in the same spot on another book. She kept looking to find more of the same, and her curiosity led her to the "FP" in her mother's handwriting in the back of those books.

Charlene would notice, too, as she grew into a woman, her mother's light mood when she would return from shopping trips, always with new books, and her eagerness to go out on these errands when Oliver was out of town. Charlene found she looked forward to those days, to her mother's easy happiness that replaced the loneliness the house had come to know in her father's absence.

And it wasn't until recently—Charlene grown into a woman with her own child, her own husband, her own feelings of sadness and loss that all adults come to know—that she has seen her parents as people, as a man and a woman with their own needs and regrets independent of children and family. She's come to understand her mother's infidelity, not in relation to Oliver's but on its own. Her parents were flawed, but their flaws shouldn't detract from their love for her or her brothers, or even their love for each other.

After her talk with Frank, she'd sat in that room with music playing and a book of her mother's on her lap and missed them both, missed them together as husband and wife, father and mother. And then she'd gone into her room and put that dress on for an evening in Manhattan.

The audience mingles and drinks, taking cursory notice of the party in the center of the room, a group of people who appear to have no interest in anyone or anything around them. They are insular, this family, caught within the vacuum of lost time and the urge to make it all up.

Oliver lingers. He doesn't drink or smoke, but considers his children as adults and the similarities in speech and comportment between them and their parents. He doesn't even think about returning to the show, but the band has taken the stage, tuning and noodling on their instruments, and Ben hovers, happy for this reunion in his club but also considering his paying guests.

During the second set, Oliver calls his sons onstage. It doesn't require much to convince them—they are showmen born of a showman, and have come straight from the airport, their instruments close at hand. As they take the stage to applause, Oliver introduces Rodney and Will, heckling them lightly about their chops the way musicians do. His sons understand this fraternity; they were baptized into it as babies under the watchful eyes of Dizzy, Coltrane, Bird, and Hawkins. The band steps back for them, fists bumping, hands shaking, and when Rodney lifts up his trumpet and Will his trombone, Oliver calls out a Basie piece that's all speed and fire to test his sons. They give it right back. They've been on the road now for nearly twenty years and Oliver realizes quickly he won't trip them up this evening. The now-seven-piece band is loud and raucous, louder than previous nights, and Ben looks around wondering if it will overwhelm this elderly crowd, but they all swing along with it, realizing what they're witnessing. Davis McComber, at the bar with his composition book and beer, realizes it, too.

Oliver doesn't allow time to breathe but goes into the next—a Lester Young tune—without even calling it out. It's like water cutting through rock, just as smooth and sharp as he'd want with his own traveling band.

He laments then that he and his boys have never worked together professionally. There were nights in their apartment when Oliver would encourage his boys to bring out their instruments and he'd put Charlene on the bench with him to take the high notes while he took the low. These are memories he cherishes, all the stuff of photo albums and lore, nights when McCoy Tyner or Hamlet might stop by and be given an impromptu show. But there was never any recording, no traveling, not even a five-night stand of shows with his family for Ben's club or one of the dozens smaller in the Village and Harlem.

He wonders if Charlene still plays. She does, but not so that she'll take the stage with Oliver Pleasant. She's nowhere near the level of her father, or of Agnes Cassady, whom Oliver wishes he could have introduced to his people. He looks around the club again—no Agnes, no Frank. But here they are, his kids.

The last number is not called out. Oliver lets the final notes fade on Prez's tune and waits for all to go quiet before he picks out a melancholy few notes with his left hand. The melody, the sadness, is immediately recognizable and the three Pleasants ease into "Blues for Chesca," the tune Oliver wrote for his wife in 1966, shortly after the death of his best friend, Hamlet Giraud. The rest of the band fills in, but keeps a respectful distance. Charlene leans over to Cedric and whispers in his ear. He nods and she wipes a tear from her eye. The audience, the real devotees, bow their heads as though an invocation has begun in church.

Heart is poured into this final song and a soul circles the room from bandstand to the front of the club and back, and it envelopes the congregation in its meaning. The song fades out as it began, into the ether and heavenward, and a standing ovation goes out to the two younger men as they exit the stage. Oliver beams with pride and takes the show back for himself with some old-fashioned Dixieland jazz.

As the show winds down, the band departs on this last night as they'd come in the first night and each night since. One by one, they lay their instrument down as if at the feet of a deity. It's the end of the night, the end of the last week, and the end of an era. No one is ready to see Oliver go, least of all Oliver himself. The saxophonist leaves, bowing to Oliver. He's followed by the trumpet, who kisses the tips of his fingers and touches the piano. The rhythm section stays with him for a few extended minutes, winding down the music in an improvised salutation. The bassist lays his big lady down, removes a handkerchief from his pocket, and wipes his eyes, this massive thumper soft inside. The drummer's beat drops lower, then lower, and then fades out altogether. He rises and places his sticks on top of the piano before exiting. The musicians have been shed like a comfortable, expensive suit, and Oliver is truly sad to see the music go, knowing he will never don such refinement again.

Only Oliver remains. The house lights are dropped even lower and a lone spotlight picks up his hands, these hands that have given music for seven decades. He hasn't thought of this moment. As a boy in a rough-hewn restaurant with a sawdust-covered floor, playing piano for uninhibited black folks to dance by, he never thought of this moment. As an adolescent at the elbow of Marcus Longstreet in New Orleans, or rolling in the beds of Madame Fontaine with his first lover, he never thought of this moment. In his first nights in New York, married on one of those small stages to the love of his life, on a steamer heading to Europe, or in a small Parisian flat with his mistress, he never thought of this moment. Yet here it is. And when it comes time, he merely lets the final note fade, takes that last one for himself, and then pulls the lid closed over the keys. The crowd is hushed in a reverent silence as Oliver rises. He finds it easier than he could have ever expected to leave that stage because there, at a table in the center of all of these unfamiliar faces that have come to hear him play, waiting on him, is his family.

CODA

Highway 51 cuts through the Delta heading north from Mississippi and into Tennessee, where it jogs and jives through Memphis until it cuts through the heart of that city, past a king's castle, the children's hospital, and neighborhoods thick with oak trees and magnolias. It snakes past broken-down cars and rusted-out buildings, factories long since dormant, and pawnshops doing a brisk business. Beyond the city's limit, the asphalt tears into fertile land filled with cotton, soybean, and kudzu. It's a road that's been traveled by slaves and freedmen, carried Jim Crow's laws and dusty promises of a better life. And, through it all, it has brought the music and musicians beating that pavement for bigger audiences and sweeter sounds.

In view of a corrugated-metal shack gone to rust and a wood-sided barn there lies a small cemetery plot off to one side of the highway with the smell of the river in the distance. On this day it's as though water is everywhere, standing in nearby furrows plowed for seed and collecting in the sky overhead. A solitary bird soars and dips into the clouds and over the alluvial plains. It's a gray day and even the clouds carry with them a sadness. A band stands near a freshly dug hole, idle and waiting for their cue. It's a true New Orleans marching band brought here to play as if for royalty, for one of their own. The players hold their horns and drum, rocking back and forth on brogans as black and scuffed as their own faces, as the preacher says his final words of heaven and peace, of better places while maybe just touching on damnation and repentance. Near the grave, the men will wait until a single white rose is thrown onto the casket and the first shovelful of dirt is laid on top, followed by another and another, until what's left is a grave lying beside another that still looks all too fresh. When it's all said and done, there will be two white markers side by side like keys on a piano: father and daughter.

And only then will the leader call out and the band will strike up "West End Blues," with the trumpet sending that soul up to heaven.

"Hell of a thing," Frank says. "She was so young, so much talent and promise."

"Tragic is what it is," Oliver says, shuffling along with a walking stick now, holding on to his niece's arm when he feels unsteady. "Men write about tragedy. Shakespeare and them, but this here, this is tragic. Shame."

They walk from the cemetery in silence, though Oliver hums lightly under his breath along with the tune's melody. The big bird overhead has moved on to a field alive with whatever it searches for this morning.

"You ever find out what happened in the end?"

Oliver shakes his bowed head. "Don't know for sure. Didn't ask, neither. Reasons ain't never brought nobody back."

Frank and Oliver have been meeting every so often for lunch at Rachel's Diner, Frank having replaced Stanton Harris as Oliver's reason to get out of the house. The argument the men had in New York has never been mentioned again, both choosing to leave it for Lucy, the waitress, to toss into her bus tub that day with that morning's dirty plates and mugs. Oliver has settled into his niece's home and he and his sister spend evenings on the porch looking out at the river and reminiscing about childhood, Hillbillie, and all the good times and bad. It's not such a bad life now. Quiet is what it is, but he still feels the need to get out and see a city, stretch his legs for an afternoon.

Frank still writes. He's begun a blog to tell stories of his seventeen years as a reporter, and he's taken on some construction work with Rachel's cousins to fill in the gaps of freelancing. He's also agreed to renovate Hank the photographer's broken-down duplex for him, more because he's tired of Hank's complaining and whining than for any money offered, and because he has the urge to see a thing completed.

Once the casket is lowered and the people pay their last respects, the group walks from the cemetery for a bit up Highway 51 so that traffic has to go around or stop altogether, the drivers having never seen anything like a true New Orleans–style funeral. Men and women in black walk and sway with the music and their emotions. Handkerchiefs, bright white in the gray day, dab their eyes and flutter in the wind like tethered souls. Agnes's mother leans on her sister's shoulder, her own lacy handkerchief hanging listlessly at her side.

"Where'd all this come from?"

"New Orleans," Oliver says. "That man there, the old one in the sharp suit? He bought out a whole train car and brought all these cats up. All of 'em, even that white boy there on baritone sax. Boy ain't had a dry eye all day. That one there, too, you recognize him from Benji's? He ain't a player, but he been down there with Agnes and that old man brought him up, too. They all stayin at the Peabody, playin a gig up on the rooftop tonight."

"How do you know all this? You a reporter now?"

"Hell no, don't nobody need reporters no more," Oliver teases. "That young man on trombone. His daddy was a sideman up in Chicago and New York. I been knowin him for years."

Frank shakes his head in wonder at the network of musicians, even those nearly a century old, playing music even older than that. Music, in all of its variations and venues, is the world's oldest social network.

The procession carries them to a farmhouse up the road where Oliver will sit in the family room at an old upright piano with a well-worn porkpie hat at rest on top and play slow songs for those assembled as they drink coffee and iced tea and eat casserole and potato salad off paper plates. They shake their heads in grief and loss, and with curiosity over the chicken salad recipe. Later, once the crowd has thinned, the music will grow naturally faster, and horns and drum and whiskey will fill in the music's rests. The melancholy will be pushed into the corner with a fat calico cat unaware of the reasons behind the day. A rug will be rolled away and men and women, cousins, aunts, friends, and neighbors will move to the sound of Oliver Pleasant like no one has in more than a year. Like no one ever will again.

Frank will sit on the porch with Agnes's mother and listen to stories she tells about Agnes as a little girl with her father. He'll offer his handkerchief to wipe her eyes and then ask her to keep it, and he'll tell her how nice it is out in the country, how peaceful. "No cicadas this year," she'll say, and smile. "When it's their time, you can't hear anything for the calling. But now it's just silence."

Indeed, for miles around, all the way from that house back down to the small cemetery, all that can be heard is the music.

* * * * *

The next morning he rises early, as has become his habit. It's the quietest time of the day now and he sits at the desk in his small office on the second floor of the house where sun streams through the window, the cloud cover of the previous day having blown away in the night. On the wall above him is a framed story from *DownBeat* magazine about Oliver Pleasant's retirement and return to Memphis, written by Frank Severs, freelance reporter. He's had other work since then, and makes ends meet with his various projects, but the mornings are reserved for his novel.

He's lost in his thoughts, banging on an old college typewriter as though it were a piano. The story moves along and he doesn't hear Karen enter. She comes up behind him and he stops once she's near. He puts his arm around her waist and pulls her closer.

"How's it coming?" she asks.

"Good," he says. "Really good, like it's coming up from within, where it's been all along." He leans over to kiss the fuzzy top of his daughter's head, held in the crook of Karen's arm. He breathes in deep that smell of life.

ACKNOWLEDGMENTS

I would like to thank all of those who have been there through the years to help push me along in my writing in general, and this book in particular, especially Stacey Greenberg, Andria K. Brown, David Wesley Williams, Elizabeth Alley, Katherine Alley Borden, and my mother, Elaine Fachini May.

My large and boisterous family instilled a love of storytelling in me as I sat listening to their own stories and our family's folklore. I hope to pass it on to my children, who amaze me with their intellect and curiosity every day.

A big thank-you to Jodi Warshaw, with Amazon Publishing, who pulled this manuscript from a slush pile, unbeknownst to me, and made a dream come true with one simple e-mail. Amara Holstein read that manuscript with true diligence and edited with affection.

Finally, to the creative community of Memphis—the writers, musicians, painters, sculptors, and photographers—your art and dedication are a true inspiration; be sure that the world at large is as impressed by what you do as I am.